Crush

I hope you
enjoy this tale!

Joye

Also by Joye Emmens
She's Gone A Novel

Crush

A Tale *of* Two Vineyards

Joye Emmens

ISBN: 9780990687634 (paperback)
ISBN: 9780990687641 (epub)

Library of Congress Control Number: TXu002136813

Heart Rock Press, Ventura, CA

for David, my love

Let the beauty of what you love be what you do.

Rumi

Chapter One

Professor Clark, my graduate adviser, walked to the podium. The guest speaker followed. With his lean build, he glided across the stage. He stood tall and relaxed in a white linen long-sleeved shirt and blue jeans. While the professor introduced him, he scanned the audience, and his eyes landed on me in the front row. I sat up straight and wished I'd worn something more flattering than jeans and a T-shirt. Mom always told me never leave the house without looking your best. His brown eyes met mine before he took the podium.

So, this was Lucien Laroche. I was to be his ambassador for the weekend. Professor Clark had asked me to take Lucien to consult with two wineries near Santa Barbara. Since I was going to my nana's vineyard in the valley already, it worked out perfectly.

"Biodynamic agriculture springs from a spiritual worldview called anthroposophy," Lucien Laroche stated. His French accent had me. "A biodynamic farm is a living system. A self-sustaining ecosystem that is responsible for creating and maintaining its health without any outside or unnatural additions. Each farm has its own unique characteristics."

I followed his every move. His presence held my attention. My undivided attention.

"The celestial bodies transmit forces to the earth that affect the four elements, earth, fire, air, and water, which in turn affect the four parts of the plant, the roots, the flowers, the leaves, and the fruit. Thus, the biodynamic calendar regulates planting, pruning, and harvesting."

He went on to describe the European origins of the biodynamic movement and the adoption of the practice at numerous farms and wineries in France.

When Lucien's talk ended and the smattering of applause died down, Professor Clark invited the audience to stay after with questions. I had a lot of questions.

The room cleared out. I was the only one who went to the stage. Professor Clark and the Frenchman stood talking.

"Olivia," Professor Clark said, "this is Lucien Laroche. Lucien, this is Olivia, your guide for the weekend. And congratulations, Olivia!" He turned to Lucien. "This last class culminates Olivia's master's degree."

"Almost. I still need to find a research internship. I've canvased all the certified biodynamic wineries in California, with no luck. I had hoped to intern at one near the central coast so I can be close to my grandmother's vineyard."

"That's a tall order. You may have to go to Oregon, but I'll make some inquires. Now, my apologies to you both, but I must run to another class. Olivia, can you take Lucien to his next appointment?"

The professor shook Lucien's hand and strode away.

I looked at Lucien, not knowing where to start. He put out his hand. "Call me Luke."

"It's nice to meet you, Luke." I liked the way his name rolled off my tongue. I shook his hand and smiled.

"The pleasure is all mine. Your grandmother has a vineyard?"

I nodded. "Clos de l'Harmonie."

"Why don't you intern there?"

"It's not certified yet. I applied for the conversion from organic to biodynamic in January, when my grandfather was still alive. We should have approval by next January."

"Are your parents involved with the vineyard?" Luke asked.

"No. They live in Santa Barbara, thirty minutes away, but they have no interest in farming. They're into sailing. My mom couldn't wait to get out of the valley and away from the farm. She's going to sell it when my grandmother passes away. But me, I love the farm and the vineyard. I've spent every summer there since I was five. They had to drag me back to school in the fall every year."

"I've heard Santa Barbara is beautiful," Luke said.

"Yes, but probably not as beautiful as France," I said.

His smile disarmed me. I was off-balance, and I'd forgotten the questions I wanted to ask. Tonight, I'd write them out to ask him on the drive. We'd have five hours in the car tomorrow to talk about biodynamics.

We walked out into the bright May sunshine. Luke looked up his next appointment on his phone. We both leaned in and squinted at the screen to read the location. Our heads were close. His hand stroked his five-o'clock shadow even though it was only eleven a.m.

I stepped back and found my voice. "Professor Lee's office is on the other side of campus."

We started walking, weaving our way through throngs of students.

"What are your plans after you graduate?" Luke asked.

"After I complete my internship I'm going to manage my grandparents' vineyard and winery," I said.

"By yourself?"

"I'll bring in seasonal workers to help prune and harvest."

Luke raised his eyebrows. Why did everyone think I couldn't manage this? Luke followed me up the stone steps and into the building that housed Professor Lee's office. I stopped outside his office door.

"Here you are. I'll pick you up at eight a.m. tomorrow. Which hotel?" I asked.

"I'm staying with Professor Clark, actually. He and his wife are planning a wine pairing dinner. The age-old French versus California duel. But I have a surprise for him, the latest vintage from my winery."

The glint in his eye made me smile. "I'll pick you up at Professor Clark's house then. I know where he lives—I've been to a few wine tastings there myself over the years." I did my best to walk away nonchalantly. I glanced back and called, "See you in the morning!"

"Thank you, Olivia," Luke said as he watched me walk away.

He made my name sound exotic with his accent. Was I really going to spend three days with this handsome Frenchman? Maybe he'd even give Nana's vineyard a once over and advise me.

Chapter Two

*L*ucien stood outside Professor Clark's house, appearing fresh in a long-sleeved blue shirt, jeans, and dark sunglasses. His wavy long dark hair ruffled in the morning breeze. I parked and opened the back door of my blue MINI Cooper.

"Bonjour, Olivia." Luke laid his small suitcase on the back seat and then carefully placed a six-pack wine carrier on the floor. The car was already filled with my boxes. I wasn't returning to the University of California at Davis.

"Good morning, Luke." He exuded so much charisma it was hard to stand so close to him. We got into the car, and I headed for the freeway. "How did the wine pairing go?" I asked.

His wide smile said it all. "No contest. Biodynamic wines are magic. My wines mirror the unique richness and beauty of my family's land."

He stared at me, and I flushed. Today I had dressed in a skirt, an embroidered blouse, and strappy sandals. My hair fell long over my shoulders. I felt glamorous in my oversize sunglasses. Mom would approve, almost—but I could never truly live up to her standards, and frankly, I didn't want to. Some of her snooty country club rules were extremely trivial.

"Nice car," Luke said.

"A present from my dad when I got my undergraduate degree. My mom is still mad I switched from premedical to viticulture and enology. She considers wine making a hobby. I need to prove to her that it's a noble profession. And I will." I was talking too much and too fast.

"Noble indeed. Are you always this passionate about wine?" Luke asked.

I smiled and kept my eyes on the road. "Pretty much. I want to make my papa and nana proud."

"But your grandfather is no longer living," Luke said.

"Oh, but he is. He's a star in heaven keeping an eye on me." I smiled. "That's what he told me during his last days."

Luke chuckled. "I like you, Olivia. You have something in you, a little spark."

I blushed and kept my eyes on the road. The way he pronounced *little* made me smile internally. I reached in my leather bag for my notebook and handed it to him, my hand unsteady. "I wrote down some questions for you on the flagged page."

Luke took the notebook and flipped through to the questions. I felt his eyes on me. "You're serious about this, aren't you?"

I nodded. For once, I wasn't going to mind the five-hour drive.

I loosened up. Luke was easy to talk to as long as I kept my eyes on the road. His whole presence was distracting. I was drawn to him. We talked all the way south. After cutting over to Highway 101, we stopped for a quick lunch. The scenery softened as we neared the Santa Ynez Valley. Oak trees dotted the landscape, and green grasses waved in the breeze. I breathed deep. This was home.

"Do I get to see your grandmother's vineyard?" Luke asked.

"Yes, if you're not too busy."

"I'm not busy. I have no plans today. And I came all this way to see California vineyards."

"You'd be welcome to stay over at the farm. We can cancel your hotel. There's a guest room always made up." It was my brother's room when he visited, but he never came around anymore, and now he was serving a yearlong jail term.

"Will your grandmother mind?"

"Not at all."

"I'd like that. Hotels are lonely."

"It's decided then. We'll stop and get groceries for dinner."

Chapter Three

I turned up the long drive past the faded Clos de l'Harmonie sign. The two-story wooden farmhouse sat back on the property on a small hill overlooking the vineyard and tasting room. We passed the orchard with fruit trees draped in pink and white blossoms. I parked, and we got out. I took a deep breath. "I love it here," I said. Luke stood, taking it all in. From his expression, he wasn't sharing my enthusiasm.

"Who tends the vineyard?" Luke asked.

"I do the bio applications, but another vintner contracted for the vine maintenance and harvest after my grandfather died. But only for this year, since I was away at school."

"Olivia, a vineyard needs full-time care."

The comment stung, and I sucked in my breath. But he was right. The vineyard was in a sad state. "I try and get down as much as possible. Once I finish my internship, I'll devote all my time here."

I gathered the groceries I'd bought for a simple dinner of pasta, salad, and bread. "Let's go see my nana." We strolled toward the house. My papa's 1957 rusty red Chevrolet pickup rested in the carport next to an aging tractor and the four-wheel quad. The barn, once a covered horse arena, stood forlorn, listing slightly toward the hill. It housed the wine-making operation and tasting room. Some biodynamic preparations hung from an oak tree, curing for the summer. The gourd-like pouches swayed in the breeze. Chickens wandered through a large gap in the dilapidated fence separating my nana's property from her neighbor's.

I knocked lightly on the door. "Nana? It's me, Olivia." She was expecting me. I opened the door. "Nana?"

"In the kitchen," she called.

I looked back at Luke and motioned him into the living room. It never changed. The dark plank flooring shone, and the couch and chairs were arranged comfortably for conversation. Books and magazines lay on the coffee table. This always felt like home to me. Mom and Dad's place in Santa Barbara was modern with glass tables and white couches. I could never truly relax there.

In the kitchen, Nana was rolling out a piecrust. She glanced up and stopped. Luke towered behind me. "Oh, hello, Olivia didn't tell me she was bringing a friend."

"This is Lucien. Lucien, this is Nana, or Stella, I guess, to you." I heard the fluster in my voice.

"It's a pleasure to meet you, Lucien." She held up her flour-coated palms and smiled.

"The pleasure is all mine, Stella. But please call me Luke."

"And please call me Nana if you are a friend of Olivia's."

"Luke has a biodynamic winery in France, and I'm his ambassador, so to speak, for the university this weekend."

"Lucky me," Luke added with a smile.

I was the lucky one. I exchanged a side glance with Nana. We seemed to share the thought.

"We brought groceries to cook for dinner, and I offered Luke the guest room. I didn't think you'd mind."

"Not at all. I look forward to hearing about biodynamic wine making. It's Olivia's passion, but I don't quite understand it. All those spiritual remedies. Her mother thinks it's voodoo."

Luke caught my eye and we both laughed.

I gave Luke a quick tour of the house and showed him the guest room. Luke had calls to make to confirm tomorrow's appointments, and he needed to call France. Did he have a girlfriend there? I tried to envision her. A sophisticated, beautiful young French woman like I'd seen in the movies. They didn't even try to be beautiful, they just were.

I went back down to the kitchen to start the pasta sauce. Despite the disrepair on the outside, the inside of the house was impeccable. Mom sent her housekeeper up once a month to clean the floors and windows. The housekeeper and Nana enjoyed working together and talking. Nana always made her lunch when they finished, and they shared a glass of wine on the front porch. Mom's only connection to her childhood home was sending her housekeeper. That was her loss.

Nana put her pie in the oven.

"I'm making my old standby, pasta," I said.

She smiled and gave me a proper hug. "I'm glad you're home."

Nana got out the canned tomatoes from last year's garden and fresh garlic. Together we set to work. I chopped fresh mushrooms, garlic, a bell pepper, and an onion and sautéed them, adding the jar of tomatoes then letting the sauce simmer. Nana grated fresh parmesan for the bread.

"I need a research internship to finish my degree, Nana. I'm hoping for something nearby, so I can help you here. But there aren't many biodynamic vineyards in the area. It's tough to get certified, and then it's a real commitment to maintain it."

Nana contemplated me with kindness in her eyes. "You'll find something fitting."

I gave her a hug. "Thanks for your support, Nana. You understand. Mom thinks I've thrown my life away 'to the vines.' But I'm going to get Harmonie back into shape and prove I can be successful."

"I believe in you," Nana said.

After dinner we retired to the porch. We sat and rocked, watching the sun highlight then fade into the rolling hills.

"I let the garden go this year, and the goats and sheep are pretty much on their own in the big corral," Nana said. "I can't do it all anymore."

"Your orchard and berries are thriving," Luke said. "I took a walk around earlier."

"That's Olivia's doing. Any spare time away from school, she is here, working. You're a godsend to me, Olivia."

"I wish I was closer to help with the animals," I said. "I'm going to fix the chicken fence in the morning. They're wandering over to the Haywards'."

"Old man Hayward passed away last month," Nana said.

"Oh, I'm sorry to hear that. He was always so kind to me as a girl. But his son used to tease me. And not in a kind way, either. What's going to happen to the property?"

"I don't know. His son inherited it. He just moved in with his teenage daughter. There seems to be a lot of activity over there lately."

From our seats, we watched a truck come slowly up the long driveway. The Valley Oaks Winery logo adorned its doors. A man wearing a cowboy hat and boots got out, carrying a bottle of wine. He made his way up the front steps. I recognized Tom, the vintner who had the contract to care for and harvest Clos de l'Harmonie's grapes this year.

"Evening, Stella. I didn't know you'd have company."

"Evening, Tom. You know my granddaughter, Olivia."

"Of course." He winked at me and tipped his hat.

"Hi Tom," I said. I didn't like the way he managed the grapes, but it was the deal Nana had set up when Papa died. Thankfully, it was only for this year's harvest. Tom set the bottle on the table and stared at Luke.

"Tom, this is Lucien, a winemaker from France. Lucien, this is Tom, owner of Valley Oaks Winery," I said.

Luke stood and offered his hand. "It's my pleasure to meet you."

Tom shook his hand hesitantly. "Evening." After an awkward pause, Tom asked, "Care to taste our new vintage? This is from the small lot of grapes I bought from you two years ago."

"What a treat," Nana said.

"I must say, the grapes have lost their magic," Tom said.

"Lost their magic? Our vintage is still aging in the barrel and it's excellent," I said.

I went into the house to get a corkscrew and glasses. Luke followed me in. "Friendly fellow, that Tom," he said.

I laughed. "It's a small world here, and there's a lot of competition."

"The entire wine world is small. We should share and work together." He reached for some of the glasses and we carried them out to the porch together.

Nana smiled and reached for the bottle. The artistic label glinted. "I love tasting a new vintage," she said. "Hmm. Fifty percent Merlot, forty-seven percent Cabernet Franc, and three percent Malbec. I'll drink to that."

Everyone laughed, and the tension eased. Tom opened the bottle and poured us each a glass. Almost in unison, we swirled the wine and took a sip. It tasted young with berry, cocoa, earth, and spice and an abrupt finish.

"What brings a Frenchman to our valley?" Tom asked. "Still trying to find out our secrets?"

Luke squinted, absorbing the insult. "I'm consulting with some wineries in the valley, and I gave a lecture at UC Davis. I fly home Sunday."

Luke and I exchanged a glance. I was giving him a ride to the airport. My heart sank. Sunday would be here far too soon.

"How many acres do you cultivate in France?" Tom asked.

"Fifty acres in Mourvèdre, fifty in Syrah, twenty-five in Sauvignon Blanc, twenty-five in Cabernet Sauvignon, ten in Grenache, and ten in Cinsault." Luke took another sip and held the glass up to the porch light.

Tom raised his eyebrows in surprise. Not only was Tom's vineyard small, his vines struggled, and he had to source grapes from others. We all took another sip, and the conversation died.

After some time, Tom cleared his throat. "So, Stella, I'm still interested in buying your place. I have a new offer to make. You can stay here in your home as long as you like. What do you say?"

"Ha! I thought you said the vines had lost their magic?" Nana said.

"It will take an incredible amount of work and chemicals to turn this vineyard around," Tom said.

"We have never used chemicals on our farm, and I don't intend to now. The answer is no," Nana said.

Luke swirled his wine and took another sip. "I'd leave out the Malbec. It undermines the Merlot."

"I agree," I said. And something else. "Did you add yeast?"

"Yes, of course," Tom said.

I shook my head. "Those grapes do not need additional yeast. You killed the natural flavor."

Tom made his departure shortly after, mumbling something about Frenchmen under his breath.

"That's the fifth time he's been here this month. At least he brought wine," Nana said.

"He ruined your grapes by adding yeast," Luke said.

"Nana, don't sell," I said.

"Of course I won't sell," Nana said. "Olivia, would you please bring us out some pie?"

I went into the house. Luke started to follow. "No, Luke, please stay out here with me," Nana said. "I'm starved for company and not for the likes of Tom."

Luke laughed. "*Oui, Madame.*"

On a tray, I brought out three slices of peach pie topped with Nana's homemade whipped cream and a Clos de l'Harmonie bottle of wine. Dessert on the porch was my favorite thing. In the summer, I'd sit out here in the twilight with my grandparents enjoying whatever Nana and I had concocted for dessert. Even fresh berries and cream were savored until the last bite.

I poured out Tom's wine and refreshed our glasses with a pour from our cellar.

"Luke," Nana said, "tell me about your family and your life in France."

"My life revolves around wine. From sunup to sundown, as you must know. Our vineyard has been in my family for five generations. We always ran a sustainable operation, but I convinced my parents to convert it to a biodynamic vineyard and winery."

"That sounds familiar," Nana said.

"A number of wineries in Europe have converted to bio farming."

Luke paused and took a bite of pie. His eyes widened. "Delicious. These peaches are from heaven!"

"What we can't eat or sell during the season, we flash freeze and use all year," I said.

"Where do you live?" Nana continued her questioning.

"In Bandol, on the estate with my parents, two sisters, and one brother-in-law. There are three houses set apart and a guesthouse. Everyone works at either the vineyard, winery, or tasting room. I like all three." Luke took another bite.

It sounded idyllic. A family operation.

"Do you have a girlfriend?" Nana asked.

I flinched. Leave it to Nana to get more information out of him over a piece of pie than I had on a five-and-a-half-hour car ride.

"No." He shook his head, and the waves in his hair moved in rhythm.

"Really?" Nana said.

"Really. I'm almost thirty, and I'm getting a lot of pressure from my mother to marry."

He shook his head again. I longed to touch his hair.

"Don't you want to?" Nana asked.

"Yes, yes, but being a winemaker is a different kind of life. I haven't met the right woman yet. The women I've met think the vineyard is fun to visit for a weekend but can't wait to get back to Paris or Nice or Lyon and get on with their careers."

He sounded sad or lonely. We sat in contemplation, eating the pie.

"I'm going to turn in," Nana announced, standing.

Luke rose and gathered the plates. "Me too. Tomorrow is a full day, right, Olivia?"

I smiled up at him.

"Thank you both for a beautiful evening." He drank the last of his wine. "Your Clos de l'Harmonie grapes are unique. *Au bon terroir.* Unlike any I have tasted."

"Good night, Luke, good night, Nana. I'm going to stay out here a little longer." I listened to the murmur of their voices as they went into the kitchen. I tried to picture the farm from an outsider's eyes. Everything needed repair. I knew I had a filter on because of my memories. Mom would sell the vineyard when Nana passed away. On many occasions, I'd overheard her talking excitedly to Dad of plans to buy a second home in a ski town or Hawaii. Her plans kept changing, but I tuned them out. For now, I'd enjoy Clos de l'Harmonie, and the vines would be mine again after Tom's harvest.

Chapter Four

I awakened early to feed the chickens and repair the fence. I cut a piece of chicken wire and wove it into the gap.

The sound of someone clearing their throat startled me. A man stood behind me, his hands stuck in his brown Carhartt jeans pockets. He wore a blue LA Dodgers cap.

"Morning," I said. Mr. Hayward's son? I hadn't seen him since I was a kid. "What happened to the fence?"

"I was teaching my teenage daughter how to drive the truck. She got something mixed up and barreled into the fence."

"Is she okay?"

"Just fine."

I stood up. "I'm Olivia, Stella's granddaughter."

"I remember you as a little tomboy. You turned into a real beauty. I'm Leroy Hayward. Do you remember me?"

Of course I remembered him. He used to tease me until I cried. "Yes. Sorry to hear about your dad."

He adjusted his ball cap. "Yeah. Well, my daughter and I have moved in."

I surveyed his property. Rusty farm equipment lay abandoned, and the barn sagged and needed paint.

"What are you planning to do here?" I asked.

"I'm exploring my options. There's a lot I can do. I'll keep raising the longhorns for now though."

I nodded. "Good luck," I said.

Leroy spit a wad of chewing tobacco, turned, and walked toward his barn. My stomach heaved. I hurried to finish the fence.

I found Nana and Luke in the kitchen, drinking coffee. I set down the eggs and poured a cup. Luke smiled at me. His shirtsleeves were rolled up, and I noticed a worn leather band on his left wrist. I smiled back yet had a hard time meeting his eyes. "I'm going up to shower and get ready," I said.

"I'll make omelets when you come down," Luke said.

"I love a man who can cook," Nana commented.

I drove the MINI Cooper along Alisos Canyon Road toward Los Alamos, the first of our two stops. The sprawling vineyards and gently rolling hills made for a scenic ride. I explained to Luke that the region had six American Viticulture Areas (AVAs) planted mostly in Burgundy, Rhône, and Bordeaux grape varieties. "Our AVAs are not like yours. Ours are delineated by geographic region, not by grape varietals. In the northern region, the cool marine influence allows Burgundy varietals like Pinot Noir and Chardonnay to thrive. In the southern region, with warmer nights, cooler days, less fog, and sandy soil with limestone, Bordeaux and Rhône varieties reign."

Luke nodded. "Have you been to those regions in France?"

I glanced over, shook my head, and looked back to the narrow road. "No, but it's a dream I have."

"Coming to California and touring this region has been a dream of mine. And now I'm here with the best tour guide. I couldn't have dreamed you up."

I met his eyes and smiled. "Thank you."

I pulled into the Figueroa Winery driveway and parked near the entrance to the tasting room. Two brown Labs slowly got to their feet. Luke grabbed one of the bottles he'd brought from his winery, a 2012 Syrah.

Henry, the owner, greeted us in the tasting room. I'd known him for years.

He gave us a tour of the vineyard, compost piles, and gardens, and we ended the tour back in the tasting room. Excited about getting his operation certified as a biodynamic farm, Henry asked Luke question after question. Henry had applied to the Demeter Association for certification and was now waiting on the final approval inspection, which would be in September. He was understandably nervous. I was too. Clos de l'Harmonie's certification inspection was scheduled for January. I hoped to learn something from Henry's inspection.

"Let's do a taste test," Luke suggested, motioning to the bottle he'd brought. "It's a fruit day, and according to the lunar calendar, fruit days are the most auspicious days to drink wine."

Henry brought out his 2012 Syrah and opened both bottles.

We took a sip of Henry's Syrah. It was lighter in color.

"Pepper and black cherry," I said.

We tasted Luke's Syrah.

"Boysenberry and spice," Henry said. "It's so distinct. Like I'm standing in your vineyard in France."

Luke smiled. "We don't use cultured yeast or sulfites, so the terroir is preserved and protected. While sulfites are allowed as an additive, we don't use them," he said. "Grapes contain all of the antioxidants and phytonutrients needed to age gracefully in a bottle."

"And this is a graceful wine. Cheers," I said.

Henry and Luke lifted their glasses and took sips. After more discussion, we bade Henry farewell and drove on through the sun-drenched rolling hills to the next winery appointment.

The vintner at Alta Vista Winery led us on a similar tour, and Luke answered countless questions. He described how precise observation of natural phenomena and knowledge of the spirit are integrated in wine making.

I struggled to keep my eyes off Luke and engage with the vintner. But Luke energized me, and I was falling for him—which was ridiculous. He lived in France, and I doubted I'd ever be as sophisticated as the women there. I thought of my past boyfriends. Like clockwork, at about the three-month mark, I'd realize the relationship lacked something and that I wasn't in love. And then I'd move on.

In the car, after we'd said goodbye to the Alta Vista vintner, Luke declared he was famished. "I'll buy you lunch. Let's go to the best restaurant around here," he said.

"Hmm… how about we stop at my friend Violet's café, get some sandwiches, and drive to the coast? There is a perfect picnic spot at the beach. It's about twenty minutes. You should see the Pacific Ocean before you leave tomorrow."

"You're full of surprises. I'd like that."

Chapter Five

*N*ana was asleep in her chair on the porch when we drove up. "Now there's a good idea," Luke said.

I laughed. "Why don't you go rest? I'll see you at dinnertime."

"I can rest on the plane tomorrow. We have things to talk about," Luke said.

I considered him. His face was so serious. I tried to think of any loose ends we needed to discuss. Transportation to the airport?

"I wish I didn't have to leave so soon," he said, reaching for my hand.

His hand was rough with calluses but warm. My hand disappeared beneath his. His brown eyes searched mine. Was he feeling what I had been trying to suppress? He put his hand behind my head, leaned in, and gently kissed me. He tasted of boysenberry and spice. Like France, I imagined. I closed my eyes and melted into him. Never had I felt like this. It reached my whole core. He pulled back to study me. "Olivia," he said slowly and bent to kiss me again.

After dinner, Luke and I sat on the porch. Nana had insisted on cleaning up since I had cooked.

"I have a plan," Luke said. "Will you hear me out?"

I nodded. Was he planning another trip to California?

"Come to France and do your research internship at our vineyard. We have a small guest cottage you could stay in. There's not much of a kitchen, but my family eats the main meals together, anyway."

My mind swirled. Go to France and work with Luke?

"Olivia, I know it sounds crazy and sudden, and it's not like me, but I've fallen for you, and I think you for me. I'm twenty-nine and I know what I want in a woman—I just never thought I'd find you. I feel the stars have finally aligned."

I was at a loss for words. At twenty-five, I didn't need to ask anyone's permission. Why was I hesitating?

He stroked my hand. "Say yes."

I nodded. "Yes, I'll come," I said. He leaned in for a kiss.

The screen door squeaked, and we both pulled away. Nana eased into her chair. Her arthritis slowed her down these days, and she looked older in the porch light. How could I leave her? But I wouldn't be gone long. I'd complete my internship and see how things went with Luke.

Luke took my hand and cleared his throat. "Nana, I've invited Olivia to come to France and complete her internship at our winery. Do we have your blessing?"

He was such a gentleman. I squeezed his hand.

"You are your own woman, Olivia. You don't need my blessing," Nana said.

I gulped. She sounded so sad.

"But since you asked, yes, of course you two have my blessing. You're in good hands with Luke, Olivia. I can see that."

I got up and gave her a hug. "Thank you. That means a lot to me, Nana. I won't be gone long."

Luke rose. "This calls for a toast." He went into the house to get a bottle of his wine.

"Olivia," Nana said, "he's a good man, and I can tell from his eyes he'll be good to you. You'll be good for each other. But my advice is, before he leaves tomorrow, introduce him to your folks. Your mother is going to worry about you going off to France with someone you've only known for a couple of days. I think if she meets Luke, she'll be less concerned."

I sank into my chair and rocked. Nana was right. I had to deal with

Mom. Dad would approve and think of it as an adventure mixed with romance. He'd always been supportive of my aspiration to be a winemaker. He'd come up to Clos de l'Harmonie many times to help my grandparents and me bottle wine.

But Mom had a different vision for my future. She wanted me to become a doctor. I'd tried to pursue that goal in my first year of college, but I didn't have the passion for it. I wanted to be a doctor of the vines, participate in the spiritual evolution of the earth and make the best damn wine. I was such a disappointment to her.

Luke returned with three glasses and an opened bottle of his wine, this time a Grenache. He poured the wine and stood tall. "A toast to Nana, Olivia, and Clos de l'Harmonie."

"To France, Luke, and Olivia," Nana replied. "May your futures be bright."

I basked in the goodwill and my swell of feeling for Luke. I stared up at the stars and raised my glass to my grandfather.

"I love a full-bodied wine," Nana said. "This is magnificent."

"Luke," I said. "Is there another bottle left?"

"But of course!" he said.

"Good. We're going to need it tomorrow. You're meeting my parents."

Nana let out a giggle of sorts and took another sip.

Chapter Six

In the morning, Nana came out to the porch to send us off. We hugged. "Good luck with your mom," she whispered. "I want to hear all about it."

"See you tonight," I said.

Luke stepped forward. "I'll see you again," he said. "I'll take care of Olivia. So will my family. We are all very close." They embraced.

Nana said something to him I couldn't hear. Then she sat down in her rocker and watched us drive off. She appeared tired, or sad, or lonely.

We drove down Highway 101. The landscape on the left was ranchland, undeveloped and wild. On the right, the ocean stretched deep blue to the horizon. My favorite part of the coast. It never failed to rekindle my spirit.

"Are those oil wells?" Luke asked. He pointed to the oil-production platforms offshore.

"Oh, don't get me going. Oil production on this pristine coastline. We've had more than one oil spill, and there are leaks all the time. People around here don't want them, but they're on federal land. The government leases tracts to oil companies."

"What do you mean with the expression 'Don't get me going'?"

I smiled. "I mean don't get me started. Uh, no, I mean I could talk on and on about how dangerous they are to the environment. They are ticking time bombs. We don't have the technology to stop or clean up oil spills."

He raised an eyebrow. "I want to get you going."

I laughed.

We were meeting my parents at the harbor on Dad's sailboat. He spent

Saturdays sailing and Sundays tinkering with the boat. Mom would join him later for cocktails and to read or chat with others on the dock who had a similar Sunday routine. Boaters were social. It was the perfect place to introduce Luke, amid all the harbor distractions.

Last night when I had called my parents to let them know we were coming, I had debated whether to tell them about France and Luke or spring it on them at the boat. But Mom didn't like surprises. She was a planner.

Dad had answered the phone. I had told him about the internship, and he was intrigued by the "opportunity," as he'd called it. "I'll let Mom know," he'd said. "You bring the wine, and we'll bring a picnic." Classic Dad. He went with the flow, and he supported my dreams.

Nervous about Mom, I glanced at Luke. He sat so calm and cool in his white linen shirt and dark cotton pants. He placed a hand on my thigh and applied a little pressure.

I forced myself to keep my eyes on the highway. His touch distracting, I bit my lip to concentrate.

"We'll get some time alone before my flight, yes?" Luke asked.

I nodded.

"Good."

At the entrance to the dock I entered the code into the keypad and swung open the heavy gate. Luke followed me down the ramp with the wine. Toward the end of the dock, on the left, Dad's sailboat, a thirty-eight-foot Salona, glistened in a slip. Mom sat in a deck chair, reading a book. She wore a coral tank top, white shorts, and expensive sunglasses. Her blonde hair, a shade lighter than mine, was styled smartly.

Luke and I stood in front of the boat steps. "We're here!" I called.

Mom jumped up and waved. Dad set down his polishing cloth and walked over and reached out a hand. I took it, smiling. It was good to see them.

Luke followed me on board. We gathered on the stern. "Mom and

Dad, this is Lucien Laroche, a prominent winemaker from France. Lucien, I'm pleased to introduce my mother, Eve, and my father, Theo."

Luke took Mom's hand and kissed it lightly. "Pleased to meet you."

Mom blushed. Luke extended his hand to Dad. "It's a pleasure to meet Olivia's father." They shook hands, and Luke handed Dad the wine. "What a beautiful yacht, and this setting…" Luke took in the view of the mountains, the houses dotting the hills, and the harbor. "It's stunning." He turned to smile at me. "Thank you for inviting me."

I wanted to reach out and touch him. I wanted to put my arms around this man.

Dad broke the spell. "Let's have a glass of wine, shall we?"

I moved to the outdoor lounge area and took a seat. Mom followed. "We have to catch up," she said.

"Yes, I have lots to tell you."

We both watched Dad open the wine and set out glasses. He looked good. Fit and trim in his crisp khaki shorts and Tommy Bahama shirt. His sandy hair a bit grayer than I remembered. It had been a few months since I'd seen them.

Luke described the varietal and vintage, and he and Dad were quickly deep into wine talk. I turned to Mom. "You know how I have to do a research internship for eight weeks at a biodynamic winery? Well, I haven't found a winery in California that has the time to take me on, but Luke invited me to come to his winery and vineyard. It's a family-run biodynamic operation in France."

Mom raised her eyebrows. "And it's for eight weeks?"

"Yes, or until I finish my research. But the plan is eight weeks. And then I'll have my master's degree."

"In wine." Mom shook her head.

"It's more than wine, Mom. You know that. There were only eight students in my graduating class."

"There's a reason for that. With your smarts and science background you could have become a doctor."

"Let's not go around and around again. We've been doing that for years. You should be happy. I've found my passion. I'm carrying on your parents' profession. I'll make you proud someday. It just doesn't happen overnight in the wine world." I always got so worked up around Mom. It drained me. I had worked and gotten loans to pay for school after I changed my major. But she still wouldn't let up. I met Luke's eyes and attempted a weak smile. "What do you think about France? Nana is supportive."

Mom let out a big sigh. "It's fine, honey. Perhaps we can come visit you while you're there. I'm so preoccupied with Jameson. I don't understand why he doesn't want me to visit him in jail."

"He's embarrassed to be there, even though he protected that woman and stopped her assault."

"The judge didn't think so," Mom said.

"Mom, if the woman hadn't fled after he freed her from that guy, she could have testified. He got a bad break."

I got up and gave her a hug. My older brother was her favorite. She'd had big plans for him, and he had disappointed her. We both had.

Dad and Luke joined us with wine.

"Try this, Eve." Dad handed us a glass of wine, deep cherry in color. "It's Lucien's bio wine, a Mourvèdre and it's amazing."

I took a taste and savored it. "You've been holding out on me," I said to Luke.

Luke raised his glass with a twinkle in his eye.

Mom took a sip. "It's really quite good."

We sat back and enjoyed the view. The gentle lap of the water and clang of the ropes hitting the masts soothed me. I slept on the boat alone sometimes when I visited from school.

Luke cleared his throat. "I've invited Olivia to complete her research internship at my family vineyard. I hope you both approve."

I straightened. He was not one to brush things under the rug, I was coming to realize. He was direct and to the point. I liked that.

"It's up to Olivia. I think it's an exciting opportunity, especially after tasting this," Dad said as he lifted his glass in the air.

"She'll do what she wants. She always has," Mom said.

And that was that. Dad got out the picnic, and we sat on the deck, enjoying the sun, nibbling on cheese and fruit.

"Lucien," Mom said.

Oh no, now she was going to grill him.

"Please call me Luke."

"I just finished decorating a home on the hillside. The design turned out exquisite. You'd be perfect in a photo shoot out on the deck. Exactly as you are now. You'd be stunning. You're a natural."

I put my head in my hands and shook my head. "Jesus, Mom, he's a winemaker, not a model."

"Real people are better than models. And Olivia, you're a natural beauty, you could be in it too. Oh, what a magnificent piece it would be," Mom said.

"I'd love to, Eve, but I'm flying back to France this afternoon," Luke said.

He probably would have done it, too.

We fell into small talk for a while. I checked the time on my phone.

"We'd better go." I stood up. "I have to get Luke to the airport. I'm going back to Nana's tonight. I'll let you know my travel plans. And Mom, Jameson will be out soon."

"You have to leave?" Dad asked. "What time is his flight?"

"It's at six o'clock, but he has to pick up some things. Uh, you know, gifts for his family," I said.

"Ah, yes, good idea," Mom said.

Luke handed Dad his cell phone. "Will you take our photo?"

Dad snapped a few pictures of us with the mountain backdrop and handed the phone back. "Thank you," Luke said and shook Dad's hand goodbye.

We walked back along the dock. "Gifts for my family? It's actually a good idea," Luke said.

I laughed. "I had to get out of there. I was embarrassed about Mom's photo shoot idea! By the way, I do know a perfect store for gifts."

"Your mom was fine. She's a businesswoman. Always thinking about her projects. I'm the same way."

We walked up State Street to a shop run by local artisans. Luke picked out gifts for his two sisters and his mother. I asked for them to be gift wrapped. The thick hand-dyed wrapping paper tied with twine and a sprig of lavender tucked in sideways was almost as nice as the gifts.

At the airport, we checked Luke's bag and sat on a bench. The airport was so small it only took minutes to get through security. Instead of feeling happy or excited, my heart grew heavy. I didn't want him to leave.

He put his arm around my shoulder. "Promise you're coming?"

I nodded. I couldn't find my voice.

"And not just for the internship?"

I smiled and nodded again.

Luke hugged me. "I'm so happy. When will you come?"

"I need two weeks. There are a few things I need to do at Nana's."

"Only a few?" We laughed. "Message me every day. I'll call you when I get home." Luke unclasped his leather bracelet and wrapped it twice around my left wrist. "Think of me." He lifted my face and kissed me hard, hungrily. We sat back in a glow and held each other's eyes. "You know, I almost didn't come on this trip. Always trust your instincts."

I hugged him and heard his boarding announcement on the loud-speakers. He hugged me harder. Tears formed. I tried not to cry. Why tears, when I was so happy?

Chapter Seven

*O*n the drive back to the valley, I tried to remember every detail of Lucien Laroche so they would stay with me forever. His wide smile, his hands, his eyes, and his kiss. Everything was happening so fast. Too fast? I made a mental list of what I needed to do: plane ticket, practice French, letter to brother, call Cody, my friend and classmate, to ask him to check on Nana and the farm, change to an international phone plan, goodbye dinner with parents, research topic to Professor Clark. I smiled. I wish I could see the professor's face when he read my email about where I was going.

I had two weeks at the farm with Nana. I should meet Leroy's daughter. Perhaps she could feed the chickens and collect the eggs. Was she the farm type? Nana would need help until I returned. The farm was too much for her. Panic speared me. There was so much to do. I would need to map out my research project before I left so I could get right to work when I arrived. I touched Luke's leather band. Well, not right to work.

I pulled into Nana's drive. I found her in the living room watching a singing talent show on TV. I sat near her in one of the comfortable armchairs.

Nana turned the sound down. "Is he off?"

"Yes, he's off," I said.

"How did it go with your mom?"

"Fine. She didn't really care. She's worried about Jameson, though."

Nana nodded. "We all are. But he'll get out soon."

I told Nana about Mom's photo shoot idea. She shook her head and laughed.

"When do you leave for France?"

"In about two weeks. I'll get my ticket tomorrow."

"That's good." She turned up the sound. "I like this contestant. I hope he goes on to win."

I closed my eyes to listen and fell asleep. I awoke sometime later to my phone vibrating in my lap. Nana had gone to bed, and the TV was off. A text from Luke. "Got to Los Angeles. Boarding my plane to Marseille. I miss you." He attached a picture of the two of us from the boat. I was so happy he'd thought to take it. I responded "Miss you too. XO." Was *XO* universal?

I woke early and made coffee. On my laptop I searched for the best airline connection and price to Marseille and booked a one-way ticket.

On the porch I sipped my coffee and called Cody. What exactly did I want him to do? Cody had graduated in my class. He was searching for work in a more traditional vineyard as a production manager, up north or anywhere. His girlfriend would graduate in a year as a veterinarian.

"Ah, you miss me already," Cody said, panting.

"Are you okay? You're out of breath."

"I'm out for my morning run. But I'll walk and talk. What's up?"

"I found an internship," I said.

"Wow, what happened between today and last Thursday?"

"A lot. I'm going to France."

"What? Ah… with the biodynamic Frenchman, I surmise."

"Yes. I leave in two weeks."

"So, what's your research premise? Biodynamic wines won't give you a hangover?"

"Ha ha. Listen, I'll be gone for two months, and I wanted to ask you a favor."

"Wait, do I detect a love interest?"

I smiled into the phone and twisted Luke's leather band. "Yes, it's crazy. I'm crazy."

"I'm not going to deny that. Good for you, Olivia, good for you. So, what favor can I do?"

"If you can, would you come down once a month or so and check on the place? Mend the chicken fence or whatever is rattling in the wind. Tom is harvesting the grapes, and Nana has a hired hand to check on the livestock. I'm going to find someone to look after the orchard and the berries."

"Sure, I love Harmonie and your nana. Maybe she'll bake me a pie."

"Of course she will. You can stay in the guest room. Bring your girlfriend if she wants a getaway. I can ask my dad to take you sailing."

"Now you're talking. But a pie would be plenty of payment. Maybe I'll find a job down there."

"Thanks, Cody. Get back to your run, and I'll call you before I leave. Good luck with your job search."

I breathed a sigh of relief and took a drink of coffee. Cody was a good guy. He wanted to grow grapes and leave wine making to others. He'd find his way. And Nana liked him. He'd driven down with me in the past on long weekends and school breaks and we had worked on the farm. He'd spent a month here one summer, and my grandfather loved the help. I knew he'd find a job soon with his knowledge and dedication.

My next call was to an orchardist my grandfather had used occasionally. I needed him to tend the orchard and deliver fruit to Violet's Café while I was away.

Nana came out with coffee in her favorite rooster mug. Her wavy hair had been brushed, and her cheeks shone rosy and soft. She appeared refreshed and beautiful in the morning light. "You're awfully busy out here," she said.

"Let's go into town today. I'll take you out to lunch at Violet's Café. I want to catch up with her."

"I'd like that. I have a few things to do in town myself," Nana said.

I told her Cody would stop by once in a while to check on the farm and stay the night. "Cody said he'll call or text you ahead of time, so the pie will be ready."

She smiled and rocked. "I like that young man. And I get lonely without Papa."

The next morning, I walked to the Haywards' through the gate in the fence my grandfather had built. He and Mr. Hayward had always shared equipment or lent a hand to help each other. At the back of the property a tractor was parked next to a fresh earth excavation.

I pulled the rope and rang the bell by the screen door. Leroy came to the door, unshaven, in a tank top and Carhartt jeans. "What do you want?"

I stepped back. "Is your daughter here?"

"No, she's at her mom's until this afternoon."

"Oh, well I wanted to meet her and ask her a favor."

"Well, she's not here. Anything else?"

"I'm going to be gone for two months or so, and I thought she might help with the chickens. She can have most of the eggs."

"Humph."

"And if you see anything off at my grandmother's, will you call my mom?" I handed him a piece of paper with Mom's number. "Nana's getting older."

"We all are. Didn't they teach you that in college?"

He was always mean, but it seemed worse now after he served in the war.

"What are you doing out back?" I said.

"None of your business. It's exploratory."

I raised my eyebrows. "Oh, I see. Well, goodbye, Leroy. Have a nice day."

Did he have PTSD? Or nerve gas sickness? I walked away.

"I'll send Hailey over when she gets back," he said.

I turned around and waved. I couldn't get out of there fast enough.

The two weeks flew by as I worked in the vineyard, orchard, and cellar. I downloaded an audio file of French lessons onto my phone and listened to them while I worked. I must have looked crazy talking to myself all day, but no one was around except Nana. I met Hailey, and she was enthusiastic about caring for the chickens over the summer and more excited about graduating early from high school in January. She came over often, happy to have female companionship next door. She and Nana got along fine.

Mom insisted on buying me new clothes for France, so I took Nana to Santa Barbara for the day. I let Mom buy me a few things but nothing fancy. Dad cooked a celebratory graduation and send-off dinner for me. It was nice. I wished Jameson had been there.

Luke and I had been messaging, and I had given him updates. I told him I was nervous about coming, and the day before I left he sent me a beautiful note that warmed me.

Olivia,

When I received the invitation to speak at UC Davis and meet with other vintners I was flattered, but it was a busy time at the winery. It's always a busy time, and I almost didn't come. But to visit California's wine country has been a dream of mine. At my talk, I saw you in the front row, relaxed and listening. You were so beautiful. When Professor Clark introduced you as my "ambassador" for the weekend, it was I who was nervous. It's okay to be nervous about coming here. Nerves are good. It means you feel something.

We are meant to be together. I know this is real, Olivia. It's a once-in-a-lifetime feeling. Please get on the plane, and I will be waiting for you at the airport.

Yours,

Luke

Chapter Eight

On the plane to France I tried to remember everything Luke had told me about his family. They all lived on the vineyard property and worked together, a close-knit family. I couldn't imagine my family working together at anything. We were too diverse, except for me, Nana, and Papa. We had worked as a team.

I couldn't even remember Luke's family's names except for his little sister, Lili, who was my age. Why hadn't I written them down? Luke said they were curious about me and asked a lot of questions he couldn't answer, like who was my favorite football team? Which meant soccer, of course. I didn't follow soccer in the US, much less internationally.

Luke said it was normal to be nervous and to just be myself. What if his mother had a local girl she wanted him to marry? I put on my headphones, turned on my French lessons, and closed my eyes, twirling Luke's leather band on my wrist. I needed to relax and try to sleep.

Finally, the pilot announced the descent to Marseille. Out the window the clear turquoise sea sparkled. Boats dotted the water in small coves and harbors. Red-tile rooftops were pressed together on hillsides. Cruise ships made white wakes far out in the Mediterranean Sea. A magical scene in miniature.

I retrieved my one suitcase at the baggage claim and waited in the customs line. I felt tired and slightly woozy from the thirteen-hour flight. The customs inspector scanned my passport, squinted, and asked, "What is the purpose of your trip?"

I hesitated.

"Business or pleasure?" he asked.

"Pleasure."

"Welcome to France." He stared past me to the next person in line, and I moved into the roped-off waiting area.

I saw Luke at once. His beige linen suit set off his long dark hair. He was tan from working outside. He held a sign with my name as he scanned the passengers. I made my way toward him, waved, and caught his eye. His face lit up with a bright smile, and I couldn't stop smiling either.

We embraced for a long moment, neither wanting to let go. Finally, we pulled away to gaze at each other.

"The sign is a nice touch," I said.

He touched my hair. "You're more beautiful than I remembered," he said.

"I'm a little crumpled from the trip. But you're very handsome in your suit."

"*Ma mère*, my mother, taught me picking up people at the airport is an honor, an important duty, and one must dress for the occasion."

"*Ta mère est très intelligente.*"

"You've been learning French?"

"*Oui.*" My face ached from smiling.

"Let's get your other bags and get out of here."

"This is it." I had my purse, laptop bag, and one suitcase.

His eyebrows rose in disbelief. "My younger sister takes twice as much on a weekend trip to Paris."

I laughed. "I'm efficient, I guess."

"I like that." He took my arm and suitcase and led me outside into the bright French sun.

Luke loaded my bags into a small Peugeot and held my door open. "You must be exhausted. Are you hungry?"

"Yes. I'm famished."

"Marseille is filled with fine restaurants, but it will be too busy and noisy after your flight. I'll bring you back here sometime to see the sights when we do a wine delivery. Today I'm taking you to Cassis, a small town with a harbor and good seafood."

It sounded perfect. I was tired but also energized. "Do you personally deliver wine?" I asked.

"Occasionally. I forge a relationship with our buyers. You'll come with me, and I'll show you around. I want you to see everything, including Paris this winter."

This winter? I needed to get back to Clos de l'Harmonie and get the vines in shape after Tom harvested. But I'd think about that later. I smiled at Luke. It was a good thing I'd mapped out my research project before I got here. There were going to be a lot of distractions.

Luke drove expertly along the winding road with views of aquamarine coves and pebbly beaches with narrow inlets framed by steep limestone cliffs. On the left were terraced hillsides of grapevines, immaculately manicured. I sat back and soaked in the idyllic scenery. Thirty minutes later we arrived in a quaint fishing village.

At an outdoor café across from the harbor, the waiter greeted Luke by name. Luke ordered for us, bouillabaisse and a white wine from Cassis. The waiter brought the wine and poured us each a glass.

Luke made a toast. "To us, to wine, to France."

I lifted my glass and sipped. "It's good." Light green reflections bounced off the crisp, cold wine. I checked my phone. "It's a fruit day," I said. "A good day for wine."

"You have the bio calendar on your phone?" Luke asked.

"Yes, a couple guys in my class made an app for it. I was the beta tester."

"Could you get it for me?"

I tilted my head, grinned, and took another sip. "Maybe."

Two men passed and greeted Luke. They nodded to me.

"Do you know everyone?"

"Not everyone. I do in Bandol. My family has lived there, on the same property, for five generations. Everyone knows everyone. It's a beautiful village."

He reached for my hand and squeezed it. "I want you all to myself. I don't want to take you back to the manor until we've had some time together. They're excited to meet you. My mother is planning a special dinner."

"The manor?" Now I was nervous.

"It's an old two-story stone house."

I took another sip of the crispest wine I'd ever tasted. I noted a hint of minerals and eucalyptus on the finish. "Tell me about your family, and their names again. I only remember Lili's name."

Luke rattled off names.

"Can I take notes?"

Luke laughed. "You won't need to. In two days, you'll have everyone figured out, including their personalities and their likes and dislikes. We're open and honest, and that's why we get along. Well, most of the time."

The waiter arrived with bowls of bouillabaisse and a basket of crusty French bread. My jet lag made everything seem like a dream, with the pastel-colored buildings, outdoor cafés, and shops surrounding the calm harbor, and Luke, sitting across from me.

Chapter Nine

*L*uke drove up the winding road outside the small coastal town of Bandol. The Mediterranean Sea glimmered below, and a rocky mountain range jutted up in the distance.

"That's Gros Cerveau," Luke said, pointing at the mountain.

He turned onto a gravel road between two giant cypress trees swaying in the breeze like the masts of a ship. A sign with a crest announced Domaine Laroche.

Luke reached for my hand. "We're here." We drove up the long gravel road bordered on either side by row after row of bushy, thick-trunked grapevines. The vines were planted between expertly constructed low rock walls that followed the contour lines of the terrain like an amphitheater.

"How old are these vines?" I asked.

"Eighty years."

The road curved to the left, and I caught my breath. Ahead, at the top of a rise, sat a massive two-story Provençal house. Its beige stucco, light turquoise shutters, and a red-tile roof beckoned.

"The manor is the main house and tasting room. The soul of the *domaine*," Luke said.

He drove up the hill, past the manor, toward numerous other structures.

"The big stone building is the winery and barrel storage. The other three buildings are houses."

The houses spread across the sloping hillside among trees all had the same beige stucco, tile roofs, and turquoise shutters. At the largest house, masses of flowers spilled onto the walkway from flower beds surrounding the house. Luke parked outside the smallest house, which was farthest up the hill.

I followed him past a hand-hewn wooden table with rustic chairs outside the front door. There was a perfect view of the comings and goings of Domaine Laroche and glimmering sea below. Luke entered the one-room cottage and set my suitcase on a low table. Fresh flowers sprung from a vase and scented the room. A bowl of fruit sat on the small kitchen counter next to the sink and a French press. Luke checked the small refrigerator, and found it stocked with yogurt, milk, and cheese. Out the back door a private patio with two chairs and a table afforded a view of the mountain. A refreshing breeze from the hillside flowed through the screen door.

Luke stroked my hair. "I'll leave you now. Take a two-hour nap. It'll revive you from jet lag. It will help you this evening. I'll be back at seven thirty. Dinner is at eight."

"Thank you. It's so amazing. You, this cottage, the manor. I'm looking forward to meeting your family tonight. And you're right. I am tired."

I was on the verge of slurring my words. Luke poured me a glass of water and set it by the bedside. He brushed my lips with a kiss and left out the front door. I set my phone alarm, lay on the bed, and instantly fell asleep.

I awoke to the chime of my alarm. I'm here. I'm really here. I unpacked some clothes and toiletries and headed for the shower. A basket filled with small bottles of lavender-scented shampoo, conditioner, and body lotion sat on the counter. Someone had thought of everything. Luke's mom?

I combed out my hair and dressed in a black skirt and white cotton blouse embroidered with a delicate pale-blue paisley pattern. It was a warm evening, and I slipped on black sandals.

I put on dangling earrings and Luke's leather band. A knock sounded. "Olivia?" Luke said.

I opened the front door, and he stepped back, surprised.

"Is this okay?" I asked, motioning to my outfit.

"More than okay. I thought you'd still be sleeping. You look beautiful. Are you nervous?"

I nodded.

"I was nervous before I met your parents. But I ended up enjoying myself."

"I feel ignorant. I don't even speak French!"

"Everyone speaks English to varying degrees. We do a lot of business in English. It's the universal language of the world."

Relieved, I smiled.

"So, we can go down at eight o'clock or go now and you can meet them as they trickle in. I warned them not to scare you off."

"Let's go now," I said, terrified of meeting them all at once and being on display.

We walked down the driveway to the manor. Luke led me through the back door, and we entered a large kitchen with numerous counters, hanging pots, and dishware stacked on open shelves. An attractive woman with stylishly cut short dark hair and gold earrings stood at an old gas stove. Surprised to see us, she said something to Luke in a playful, scolding tone. She wore an above-the-knee blue dress with a white linen apron.

Luke smiled and responded in French. Too fast for me to understand. He switched to English. "Mother, I'd like you to meet Olivia. Olivia, this is my mother, Marguerite."

I stepped forward. She wiped her hands on her apron.

"*Bonsoir, Madame.* It's a pleasure to meet you," I said. I bungled the cheek kisses by starting on the right side, and our heads collided.

"Luke should have brought you in by the front door, but he tells me you are to be treated as family, not as a guest. I will honor his request. Welcome to Domaine Laroche." She forced a smile at Luke as if to say, There, was I pleasant enough?

"Come," Luke said. "Let's find Angelica."

"Thank you," I said and followed Luke out of the kitchen and into a massive dining room. A young woman with long dark wavy hair, wearing slacks and a beige silk sleeveless blouse, moved about, setting the table. She stopped and stared.

"Angelica, this is Olivia."

"I'm pleased to meet you," I said.

"*Oui.* Same." Angelica skimmed my cheeks with a kiss. "*Parlez-vous Français?*"

"I'm learning," I said.

"Are you tired from your trip?" she asked.

"A little," I said.

Angelica stared at the leather band on my wrist and then looked at Luke. She returned to setting the table. Luke winked at me and led me into a large living room with tall ceilings, an enormous fireplace, dark wood antique furniture, and a large couch covered in red velvet now faded to pale pink.

Through the living room, adjacent to the entry's double front doors, a staircase led up to the second floor. A smaller side room with French doors overlooked a patio and large rectangular stone swimming pool.

"Wow, everything is so beautiful. And old."

"The house was built in 1835."

A handsome man strode into the room. He had short hair with a little gray on the sides—an older version of Luke.

"*Mon père.*" Luke smiled. "Olivia, this is my father, Bernard."

"*Bonsoir, monsieur*, it's a pleasure to meet Lucien's father."

"*Bonsoir*, Olivia. You are more beautiful than the picture Luke showed us." He brushed both my cheeks with a kiss.

I blushed. "Your home is lovely."

"Ah, but you are here for the grapes. Far more interesting than old furniture." He smiled at me.

The dance of heels clicked on the tile floor behind me. A young woman burst into the room. "*Bonsoir*, Papa. *Bonsoir*, Lucien. Olivia?"

I nodded.

"I'm Lili." She kissed me on both cheeks not once but alternately three times on each side. A pleasant rose scent wafted from her. "I am so happy to meet someone from California. I want to go there someday. Hollywood! Beverly Hills! Rodeo Drive! Luke said Santa Barbara was gorgeous."

I opened my mouth to respond, but she talked nonstop. She wore a tight black skirt, silk top, three-inch-high heels, and a shimmering gold necklace with colorful stones.

"Your cottage?" Lili asked. "Is everything okay? If you need anything, just let me know."

I laughed. "Everything is perfect. Thank you. The flowers are beautiful."

Lili beamed. "I cut them from Angelica's garden, below your cottage. I cut bouquets for the tasting room every morning. Luke said we are the same age? Twenty-five, yes? I should take you to Paris for a weekend. Shopping!"

"Hold up, Lili. Our busy season is here," Luke said. "Paris is for winter. Besides, I've already promised Olivia I would take her there."

Lili squeezed Luke's arm. "He makes us work nonstop. But you'll like Paris. It's extremely romantic."

We walked back into the dining room. Angelica had lit candles. I wanted to sneak a photo to send to Mom, but there would be plenty of time.

A man was seated at a small desk in the corner of the room, writing in a notebook. Luke led me over. The man stood. "I'm Phillipe, Angelica's husband. And you must be Olivia." He brushed my cheeks with his lips.

I smiled. "It's my pleasure. You're the agricultural engineer?"

"*Oui.*"

"I'd like to spend a day with you sometime and learn about your methods."

"Luke can show you everything about Domaine Laroche," Phillipe said.

"Oh, okay," I said.

Angelica and Marguerite entered with steaming platters and set them on the table. Bernard walked around the table and poured a dark red wine. Luke pulled out a chair for me, and I sat down. Thankfully, he sat next to me. Lili brought out baskets of bread, her clattering heels on the shiny tile marking her entry. When everyone was seated, Bernard raised his glass. "Welcome, Olivia! *Santé!*"

Everyone raised their glasses. "*Santé!*"

Across from me, Marguerite and Angelica exchanged a side glance.

Angelica drank water. Did that mean she didn't want to toast me? I took a sip. Dark fruits and earthy tones with a smooth finish. I wanted to read the wine label.

Marguerite passed around a tureen of soup, and we ladled it into our bowls. I waited to let others start, but everyone sat still, watching me. Luke leaned over and whispered, "Our guests start the meal."

"Oh," I whispered, "I thought I wasn't a guest." Luke grinned as I dipped my spoon into the steaming mushroom soup. Everyone followed suit.

When we'd finished the soup, Angelica cleared the bowls and spoons. Marguerite removed the cover from a platter of sautéed veal in a rich tomato-vegetable sauce. Luke served me and then himself and passed the platter. I paid close attention to the protocol.

Once everyone was served, I took a bite. "Delicious!" I said. "And so is the wine. Is this your vintage?"

Luke caught his mother's eye and smiled, and I noted the forced smile back from her.

"*Oui*, Domaine Laroche, ninety-five percent Mourvèdre," Bernard said. "Mourvèdre vines are the pride of Bandol. Tell us about your grandparents' vineyard, Olivia."

I took a sip of the Mourvèdre. "My grandparents bought the property in 1967, and in 1973 planted thirty-five acres, or fourteen hectares, in Syrah, Grenache, Sauvignon Blanc, Cabernet Sauvignon, Cabernet Franc, and Pinot Noir. It's named Clos de l'Harmonie. It's an organic vineyard with an orchard and berries, and next year, I hope, it will be certified as biodynamic."

Luke added, "I tasted the peaches in her nana's pie." He kissed his knuckles and extended his hand in a small gesture.

"The wine-making facility and tasting room are in a big barn," I continued.

"In a barn?" Angelica asked, squinting.

"It's converted. Remodeled. There are no animals in it. It's clean. In California, tasting rooms are often in old buildings or old barns on the property. Although they wouldn't be considered old by you with all this history here." I waved my hand around. Stop talking. I was making a fool of myself for our little vineyard. But nerves kept me talking. "At Clos de l'Harmonie, it is all about the wine. I can show you pictures. It's nothing as grand as this though."

I got nostalgic thinking about it. But Clos de l'Harmonie had gone downhill fast since my grandfather died. I shouldn't even be here. I should be with Nana turning Clos de l'Harmonie around. Once I finished my research paper, I'd be back there. My eyes were wet.

"Let Olivia eat her dinner. She's had a long trip," Luke said. His foot nudged mine under the table. "We'll have lots of time to talk."

Marguerite and Angelica leaned into each other in a silent gesture I didn't understand. Lili jumped in and entertained everyone with a story about a group of Australians who had visited the tasting room earlier that day.

When we finished dinner, I rose with Angelica to help clear the dishes. "No," she waved me away. "Not tonight. You must be tired."

Tired was an understatement. Jet lag grabbed me again. Luke walked me back to the cottage. In an awkward moment at the door, he kissed me. "I'll see you in the morning. Phillipe and I have some work to do in the winery."

"Tonight?"

He nodded. "We're installing a new bottling machine. Sleep well, Olivia." And he disappeared into the night.

I lay on the bed and inhaled the lavender-scented pillow. Visions of the day passed beneath my heavy eyelids. The dinner seemed to have gone well, but Luke's family seemed wary of me. Except for Lili. I smiled, thinking about her sparkly enthusiasm.

Chapter Ten

In the morning, refreshed by sleep, I sat in front of the cottage with a cup of coffee. Down below, a hum of activity was underway. A truck eased up to the loading dock at the winery, and two men loaded cases of wine into the back. Bernard and Phillipe stood talking beside the large arched doorway.

Luke came around the corner.

"You look happy. Ready for the tour?" He kissed me on the lips. "We'll start with the Mourvèdre vines, biopreparation gardens, compost area, and winery, and finish in the tasting room. Then I need to get to work. We start the green harvest today."

"I can help."

"Don't you need to start your research project?"

"I want to get a feel for Domaine Laroche first," I said.

"Phillipe will be happy. We're behind."

Phillipe happy? He seemed so serious. It was the engineer in him, I guessed. I grabbed my notebook and walked up the road with Luke. Before us, rows and rows of vines with bright green leaves snaked across the slope, the roots disappearing into stony cobbles. The vines were short and bushy, crowned with gnarled lumps of old wood.

"Mourvèdre thrives in rocky landscapes," Luke said. "We have three thousand hours of sunshine a year here. It suits the temperamental Mourvèdre. They are slow and difficult to ripen."

"You don't stake them?"

"It's the goblet method of pruning. Years of spur pruning produce the few branches at the head, like a goblet. Because they are low, they absorb heat from the stones and continue to draw it in at night."

I gazed at the acres of vines, the rocky mountain in the distance, and the sea below. Vines and vines as far as the eye could see. Domaine Laroche terraces merged with other vineyards in an endless sea of brilliant green. The plot gave me an impression of freedom and a gentle peacefulness without any wires or stakes.

"The regulations of the Bandol Appellation require a density of at least five thousand vines per hectare. The low walls, *restanques*, are over a hundred years old. To grow vines here, one must first be a builder of walls," Luke said.

Luke came up behind me and wrapped his strong arms around me. "I'm so happy you're here," he said. He moved my hair aside and kissed my neck. I leaned back into him. He sighed. "Phillipe has us working here, in the Mourvèdre plot, for the green harvest. Come on. Lots more to see."

I followed Luke past the compost piles, one of the most important components of biodynamic farming. We walked through the row of vines to a small road and headed down the hill to the gardens. Rectangular plots were laid out on terraces. Each plot swelled with plants used in the biodynamic preparations: yarrow, chamomile, nettle, dandelion, valerian, and horsetail. I grew the same plants at Clos de l'Harmonie and used them as prescribed. These terraces, well maintained and healthy, were impressive and quite beautiful with the sea in the distance. My plots had become overgrown with weeds while I was at school.

We came upon Angelica kneeling before the valerian, weeding with a three-pronged hand rake, earbuds in and eyes on her task. Luke tapped her shoulder, and she started.

She smiled at him, but her smile faded when she noticed me.

"*Bonjour*," I said.

She responded and went back to weeding.

"Angelica loves to read, but there is no time, and at night she's too tired. She's listening to an audiobook. She wasn't trying to be rude."

I too loved audiobooks, especially when working outside in the vineyard. They transported me while I worked.

We entered the winery through the massive doors and went down the stairs into the underground barrel room. I breathed in the scent of wood barrels and angel's share, the small amount of wine lost to evaporation. It was cool and peaceful.

The barrels were different sizes, and some of them, the largest I'd ever seen. "How big are these barrels?" The cellar acoustics projected my whisper.

Luke laughed. "It's not a library." His laugh and voice bounced off the mysterious cellar walls. "They hold eight thousand liters. The small ones between twenty-five to fifty hectoliters."

Phillipe came around the corner. "*Bonjour*, Luke, Olivia."

"*Bonjour*, Phillipe," I said.

"Impressive," I said.

Phillipe walked to the new bottling machine and tinkered with a setting.

"Our Bandol reds stay true to the AOC—sorry, the appellation d'origine contrôlée—and are matured in barrels for at least eighteen months," Luke explained. "But we keep them in the barrel longer. The grapes are harvested by hand when they reach their optimum level of ripeness. They are destemmed, lightly crushed, and poured into vats. The temperature is controlled, and no additional yeasts are added. The grapes' natural properties set off the fermentation process, which lasts about three weeks." Luke continued on about the process of changing containers for the secondary fermentation process.

At last, Luke took me to the tasting room through the entrance from the house. Visitors parked and entered through formal double wooden doors off the parking lot. In the cavernous room about ten tasters were stationed around the large rectangular counter. Lili, engaged in a description of the wine she'd poured for a foursome, wore a stylish blue sleeveless dress cut on the bias. Her neck sparkled with small blue topaz stones cascading on a silver chain. Her earrings matched. She held everyone's attention. The tasting room embodied Old World charm, but the wine displays were chic. Just like Lili.

"Olivia!" Lili's voice sang high into the beamed ceiling. The visitors turned to see who had arrived. I was delighted by her enthusiasm until I remembered I was wearing work clothes—ragged jean shorts, T-shirt, and running shoes. Luke smiled at me and took my hand, and we sidled up to the counter. Lili pulled me toward her across the wooden counter and kissed me three times. I remained unsure of the kissing protocol. She kissed three times and others kissed only once. I didn't know quite what I was supposed to do and with whom. I'd ask her sometime when we were alone.

"*Bonjour*, Lili," Luke said. "We'd like to taste the 2005 Bandol rouge."

"*Oui*, but of course. Good choice." She went through an open door behind her and returned with a bottle, expertly opened it, and poured us a taste. Then she moved off down the counter to pour more wine for the guests.

I held my glass up to the light. Its hue was an impenetrable dark red. I swirled my glass and inhaled deeply. I took a sip and held it in my mouth and swallowed. Silky smooth and vibrant at the same time.

"Can you guess what the blend is?" Luke asked.

"Mourvèdre." I paused, swirled my glass again and inhaled its magic and sipped. "Grenache." I tasted the body and fruit.

"There's one more," Luke said.

I took another sip. Another varietal was involved, I could tell, but I couldn't identify it. "Syrah?"

"No," Luke said. "Cinsault. Close."

"The blend is superb."

Lili came back and leaned over to Luke. "I'm slammed. I need help this afternoon. I have two tours coming." She glanced at me. "Olivia?" she said.

"We're on green harvest when we leave here. Besides, Olivia's French isn't great, and she doesn't know our wines yet. Maybe in a month or two. If she wants to."

Lili frowned and went off to another customer. I felt for her. I spoke minimal French, and I didn't know their wines. But I knew I could prune the green harvest. Luke and I departed through the private door to the manor and stopped in the kitchen. Marguerite stood preparing food on the long wooden worktable.

Luke gave her a kiss on each cheek. Just one.

"*Bonjour*, Marguerite," I said.

"*Bonjour*, Olivia," she responded but did not look up.

Luke poured us both a glass of water. "Lili may need some help this afternoon," he said.

"I'll check on her," Marguerite said. "We need to hire another person for the summer. Business is good." She smiled at Luke. "I have someone in mind. I'll call her this afternoon."

"Good," Luke said. He cut two pieces of bread, then sliced hunks of cheese and handed one to me. I was starving.

Luke and I joined Phillipe and Angelica in the Mourvèdre plot. Angelica wore her earbuds. A small tractor with a crate on the back was parked between the rows. Luke handed me a bucket with a handle and pruning shears.

Phillipe hurried over. "I'll explain and show you," he said. "We conduct the green harvest on root days, which are good for pruning. Today and tomorrow until ten p.m. are root days. All our work here is timed with a biodynamic calendar. The calendar…"

Luke cut him off. "She knows the calendar. She has an app on her phone with it."

"An app?" he said, mystified. "Anyway, in the Bandol AOC we voluntarily limit our yield. We're allowed forty hectoliters per hectare, but we keep it between twenty-five and thirty hectoliters per hectare to allow the grapes to express their essence. We leave five to six bunches per vine. One vine, one bottle. So, in the green harvest we prune the excess fruit. I'll show you." He leaned into the vine and quickly snipped off small green grape bunches and dropped them in the bucket. "Okay?"

"Okay," I said.

Luke winked at me, and we started down the row. I worked quickly.

I had pruned vines and harvested grapes for as long as I could remember. We pruned side by side. Angelica continued to listen to her audiobook while she worked. Luke and I talked, and there were times of silence. Phillipe came over to inspect my work and nodded. We quickly got through two rows, then Marguerite arrived with a picnic. She unfolded two picnic blankets on the low stone wall and laid out the food. It looked heavenly.

After lunch, we resumed pruning. Luke and I quickly outpaced Phillipe and Angelica. Luke enjoyed this. I could tell from his smile when he occasionally glanced at Phillipe in the next row and back to me. We stopped at eight o'clock that evening.

Phillipe drove the tractor to the compost area to add the green harvest into the piles. We followed the tractor down the hill. Angelica trailed behind us. Luke stayed to help Phillipe, and Angelica and I walked back to our houses in silence, her earbuds in both ears.

I was beat. I showered and slipped on a sleeveless white dress and a necklace, a string of turquoise beads Nana had given me, an old Native American piece. I fingered the cool stones and thought of her.

Dinner was at nine o'clock, so I had thirty minutes to relax and think. I gathered my notebook and phone and went out to the private back patio.

I sent my parents an email. I had texted them yesterday that I'd arrived safely, but yesterday seemed long ago and a blur.

The view out back was serene. The vines went on forever and softened into pine trees beneath the craggy mountain. I put my feet up on the opposite chair and opened my notebook to my project. Vineyards treated with chemicals killed the native yeast. Could I test for this?

"Olivia…"

"*Bonsoir*," I said. "I'm out back."

Luke had showered and wore jeans and a long-sleeved white shirt. His hair was still slightly wet and combed back.

"I thought you'd be napping after all the pruning." He smiled. "You impressed Phillipe."

"He told you?"

"No, but I can read him like a brother. First, he was nervous. He checked your first two rows and later every other one. If there was anything wrong, he would have called you out and sent you on your way. We don't let just anyone into the Mourvèdre plot."

"I'm really intrigued with the Mourvèdre grape," I said. "It's grown in California but more for use in a blend."

He reached out his hands and pulled me to my feet. "I'm intrigued by you," he said.

He wrapped me in his arms and kissed me. The same volt surged though me, and I reached up and smoothed the back of his hair. He smelled like lavender with a touch of musk. We stood apart and regarded each other. His eyes searched mine, and he caressed my cheek. "I want to take it slow, Olivia. I never want this feeling to end."

I nodded. I understood.

"I want to properly court you, and not just here at *le domaine*."

I smiled and motioned to the mountain. "This is a very romantic place, you know."

"*Oui, oui*, but my family is everywhere." He checked his phone for the time. "And they are gathering now. Are you ready?"

"I need one minute."

"Ah, I know about this one minute with women. It really means fifteen or thirty."

"No, really." I put on some lipstick and came back out. Luke had taken a seat. "I'm ready."

The dining room table was set. Bernard and Phillipe sat at the end drinking a glass of wine. Three bottles were open on the table. I hoped there was a Mourvèdre blend. I wanted to study it more on the palate. Bernard jumped up to greet me and kissed both my cheeks, once. Phillipe waved a greeting.

"Please, sit down," Bernard said. He pulled out a chair.

Luke sat next to me and poured us a taste. Deep red in color.

"How was the green harvest?" Bernard asked.

"It was sad," I said.

"What do you mean?" Bernard asked.

"It was sad to prune all those Mourvèdre bunches for the compost heap. Now I know why you must plant at least five thousand vines per hectare, because you prune off most of the fruit."

The three men laughed and raised their glasses. "*Santé*," Bernard said.

"Will you be joining us tomorrow?" Phillipe asked. "It's still a root day."

"Yes," I said.

"Good," Phillipe said.

I took a small sip and savored the taste of leather and red fruit and the silky finish. Lili burst into the dining room chattering to Angelica. They carried platters of food. Lili still wore high heels. How could she wear them day and night? She sat on my other side.

"Oh my God, I love this." She touched my necklace.

"My nana gave it to me. It's an old Native American piece."

"Indians?" Lili asked.

I nodded.

"Are there still Indians in America?" Phillipe asked.

"Yes, there is a tribe in the valley I live in," I said. "In fact, that's why my papa used the word 'clos' in the winery's name. There is an old rock wall on the property built by the Chumash Indians."

Marguerite set down a covered platter. "*Lapin aux olives*," she said.

Rabbit. I'd eaten duck and pheasant but never rabbit. Marguerite sat down next to Angelica and started to pass the platters, naming the dishes, obviously proud of her cooking skills. The food smelled divine. The conversation was lively, partly in English for my benefit but often slipping into rapid French. I wanted to learn to speak fluently so I paid attention. I could understand about half of it.

"I hired someone to help Lili in the tasting room," Marguerite said. "I called Nicole Gravois, and she has agreed to come work. With a flexible schedule, of course."

"Nicole Gravois?" Angelica said and shot a glance at Luke. "I thought she lived in Paris?"

"She's staying at her grandparents' house in town. She wanted to spend the summer on the coast."

"Why would Nicole want to work here?" Phillipe asked. "She's some hot model, on the cover of *Vogue* and all that."

I caught a glance between Lili and Luke. Luke shrugged with an I-don't-know-anything-about-this look on his face.

"Hmm," Angelica murmured, as she considered her mother.

"Luke and Lili will train her on the wines," Marguerite said. "She starts tomorrow morning at nine."

Maybe I could join them and learn about the wines too. Then I could also help in the tasting room.

Chapter Eleven

I woke early the next day and dressed in shorts and a T-shirt, ready for a full day of pruning. Phillipe, worried we wouldn't finish, had requested we start at seven. I sat on the back patio drinking coffee and hoping Luke would stop by. At six forty-five, I grabbed my hat and sunscreen and walked up to the Mourvèdre plot. I sat on the old wall where we had finished the evening before and waited.

Phillipe came up the road on the small tractor, pulling an empty crate. Angelica hung onto the side, talking and laughing. I waved. She saw me and said something to Phillipe. What had she said? When they arrived, we each took a bucket and pruning shears and started pruning our respective rows. Still no sign of Luke.

Halfway down my row I heard whistling. Luke was walking toward me. "Sorry," he called, "I got stuck on the phone with a buyer."

I instantly felt better with his presence, working side by side. At nine thirty, Luke got a text. "It's Lili," he said. "I have to go train Nicole." He noted the time. "She's late," he said under his breath.

I waited for Luke to invite me and looked over the row at Phillipe. No, we had work to do here. The bio clock ticked.

"I'll be back soon," Luke said. When Phillipe and Angelica turned back to their row, Luke gave me a quick kiss.

Marguerite showed up a little after noon with lunch.

"Where is Luke?" Phillipe asked.

"Oh, he's eating with Nicole on the patio," Marguerite said.

Phillipe frowned.

I had worked fast and almost kept up with them. I looked a mess, my hair drenched with sweat under my hat. I pictured Luke and the Paris model eating lunch on the patio by the pool. A jealous flare spiraled in my chest.

Luke returned shortly after lunch. "It's about time," Phillipe said.

"She wanted to talk about everything but wine," Luke said, shaking his head.

"Come here," I said. Luke stood before me. "You have lipstick on both cheeks." He rolled his eyes, and I wiped the lipstick off with my bandana imprinted with the California state flag. At least there wasn't any red on his lips. I envisioned a pouty-lipped model perfectly attired in designer clothing. I put on more sunscreen and continued to prune.

We worked our way quickly down the row as Luke described the varietals and vintages. "The Bandol red blends must have at least fifty percent Mourvèdre to be called a Bandol wine, but some have up to one hundred percent," Luke said.

"I want to try the one hundred percent vintage," I said.

"*Oui*, you will like it. It will turn your lips red."

At dinner, keeping up with the conversation in French was exhausting, just as speaking English was for everyone else.

"Why are you so quiet, Olivia?" Lili asked.

I smiled faintly. "I'm listening."

"She worked hard today," Luke said. "We finished."

"We all work hard," Marguerite said.

"*Oui*," Bernard agreed.

"Except for Nicole," Lili said. "She was practically useless."

"She'll learn," Marguerite said.

"I have a friend in town who is back from college for the summer. He would be much better, and he knows Bandol wines," Lili said.

"Nicole is a good girl. We know her family," Marguerite said.

"Nicole said she can't wash the wineglasses because of her nails." Lili

held up her hands. They gleamed with pink polish and were carefully manicured. "I have nails, and I wash glasses."

"Give her a chance, Lili," Bernard said. I stole a glance at my hands.
They needed more pampering than I gave them. But nail polish didn't last
long when you were tending a vineyard.

I needed to go into town for a few things. I wondered if Lili would
take me, or Luke or I could take a bicycle. I thought about riding a bicycle
through the French countryside and smiled internally.

"Olivia." Luke nudged me. "Angelica asked you a question."

Around the table everyone stared at me. "I'm sorry."

"Luke said you have an older brother. What does he do?" Angelica
asked again.

I froze. I should have expected this simple question. I had to be honest
but talking about Jameson was tough. Would it put my family in a bad
light? I took a small sip of wine. "Yes, Jameson." I stalled for time, trying to
think. "He's…" I paused. "He graduated from college with an art degree."

"And now what does he do?" Angelica asked.

"He's in prison."

Marguerite's eyes grew wide, and she looked at Bernard.

"We're sorry to hear that," Angelica said.

"Why is he in prison?" Phillipe asked.

I held Phillipe's eyes. "He was in a sports bar watching a Dodgers baseball game on TV. In the back of the bar this man was assaulting a woman
who was struggling to get away from him. Jameson freed her, and she fled
the restaurant. The man got belligerent and threw a punch at Jameson,
so he defended himself." I stopped and looked around the table. "There
was some property damage to the restaurant, the man accused Jameson of
starting the fight, and he was blamed. Without the woman as his witness,
he was the one charged."

Marguerite shook her head.

Tears formed in my eyes, and I wiped them with my French-print
cloth napkin.

Lili gave me a weak smile.

Angelica and Lili got up to clear the table. I rose to help, but they waved me away.

"Not tonight," Angelica said.

Luke walked me back to the cottage, and we sat on the back patio. A rising moon loomed on the horizon. He took my hand. "You're worried about your brother, aren't you?"

I nodded. We were both silent for a moment.

"Tomorrow afternoon we're going into Bandol. We've been holed up for three days working. You must want to see the town."

I smiled. "I do, and I need a few things."

"We can stop anywhere you'd like. We have wine deliveries, a few *domaine* errands, and after, I have a surprise for you."

He was a considerate man. Did he have a bad bone in his body? I hadn't seen any flaws or weaknesses, but we all had them.

Chapter Twelve

The next morning, Luke stopped by my cottage. "You're on your own for the morning," he said. "Explore the vineyard or winery, relax, or swim in the pool. Be ready at two o'clock and bring a bathing suit." He started to whistle as he turned the corner.

I sat on the back patio, daydreaming, gazing at the vines stair stepping up to the base of the mountain. We were going swimming. I had wanted to swim in the Mediterranean since catching the first glimpse of the turquoise coves from the plane.

"Olivia!" Lili called through the screen door in the front.

I went through the cottage and opened the door. We greeted each other with three kisses. She swept through, a basket on her arm filled with soap and shampoo, fresh flowers, croissants, ground coffee, yogurt, and milk.

"*Merci*, Lili."

"I want to make you feel welcome. Eventually you can stock up from the pantry. I'll show you next week where everything is."

She moved like a whirlwind, changing the flowers, putting the coffee into the canister, leaving new soap in the bathroom. "So, what are your plans today?"

I studied her dress. Perfection, a sleeveless coral shift high above the knee, with black flats. She noticed me peering at them. "I know. I can't walk in heels up these primitive roads. They get ruined."

"Luke and I are going into town at two o'clock to run errands, but I'm free until then."

"Good, you both need some free time together, out of here."

"I love it here."

"*Oui*, so do I, but I love to go to town. Come to the tasting room later. I may need some help."

"What about Nicole?"

Lili rolled her eyes and dashed out the door. The faintest trace of rose perfume lingered in the air.

I took my notebook out to the patio with coffee and a croissant. The flaky pastry melted in my mouth. The French knew how to eat. And drink. I opened my notebook to focus on my research project. But I had more questions than answers. Drawn to the winery, I took my notebook and headed to the cellar.

I passed Angelica weeding the flower beds, earbuds in, in a world of her own.

The big wooden door to the winery stood partway open. An old bell with a rope was mounted outside for visitors to ring when picking up wine or delivering supplies. I slipped through the opening. The smell of aging wine was always comforting. The scent reminded me of Clos de l'Harmonie and the countless hours spent in the calm and quiet cellar room monitoring the progress of the wine. Downstairs I found Phillipe three rows back, a glass pipette in his hand and his notebook open.

"*Bonjour*," I said.

I had startled him. "Ah, Olivia. *Bonjour.*" He eyed my notebook. "Are you doing your research?"

I wouldn't let his tone bother me. I was a temporary intern to him, an outsider. "Almost. I'm working on my premise."

"Ah, yes. Here, tell me what you think of this." He handed me a glass and dipped his pipette, which winemakers call a wine thief, into the barrel opening and gave me a splash of a deep red wine. He nodded to the spit bucket on the floor.

I took a sip and held it in my mouth for a while then spit it out. "Well, some winemakers would probably bottle it."

"What do you think?"

"It's not ready yet."

He nodded, closed the barrel, and jotted a note in his book. He pointed at the bucket, and I picked it up. He moved on to another numbered barrel, and I followed. He took the first sip then handed the glass to me. This wine was darker. He spit into the bucket. I took a sip and used the bucket. He waited for my response.

"Another six months?"

He nodded, made a notation in his book, and capped the barrel. I peered around his shoulder to see his notes, but he snapped his notebook shut. "But why another six months?" he asked.

"It's a little harsh. It has to sit down and mature more. But not much."

"I have one more to test today."

I picked up the bucket and glass and followed Phillipe. We went deeper into the cellar. New barrels and old barrels rested side by side. All the aging wine, the aroma, the potential, made me long for Harmonie. I wished Tom hadn't gotten our harvest this year. Phillipe stopped midway up an aisle, and I nearly bumped into him.

He opened his notebook and checked the barrel number. He gave me the first taste, and I handed the glass back. This time I swallowed. So smooth and well balanced. I wasn't going to waste this spectacular nectar. Phillipe eyed me, waiting for my verdict.

"It's ready, and it is magnificent."

His laugh boomed through the cellar.

On the walk back to the front of the cellar I told him about my theory. "If the vines are naturally sustained with the biodynamic preparations, the yeast stays with the seed and fruit on into the wine making. Yeast additives aren't needed. Chemically treated vineyards kill the natural yeast, so yeast has to be added back in."

He nodded. "That makes sense."

"I want to test the native yeast content of grapes from both types of vineyards."

I had my research project. I was overjoyed, but I kept my calm.

"*Merci*, Phillipe." I wanted to give him a kiss on each cheek, but I didn't. I climbed the stairs and walked outside, squinting into the bright light, the sun a fireball in the sky. Heat waves rose off the ground. I headed to my cottage to shower and change. How hot did it get in August?

Seven cars were parked outside the tasting room. I felt a bit like an intruder walking around the property, but Lili had said to come. I slipped through the large door and let my eyes adjust. A crowd of about fifteen people lined the tasting counter. Another group sat on the couches and chairs around the center table.

A stunning young woman with cascading brown hair poured a taste for a group of four. Nicole. Tall with full lips, too skinny but gorgeous. I took in the scene, searching for Lili. A moment later she appeared from the back room, pulling an antique cart stacked with two cases of wine. She stopped behind the counter, wiped her brow with a small pink handker-chief, and poured two customers another taste while describing the wine. She noticed me standing by the door and smiled wide.

"Olivia!"

She came out from behind the counter and kissed me three times, like a long-lost friend.

"Come," she said. "Do you want to taste?"

"No, *merci*. Is there something I can help with?"

"*Oui.*" Her eyes shone in thanks. She waved me back behind the counter. The sink was full of wineglasses, the service counter messy and chaotic. Luckily the customers couldn't see that aspect. Lili pointed to the two cases on the cart. "Can you please restock the rack?" She handed me a box cutter.

I nodded. Lili carried a bottle to the customers on the couches. I started my task.

"I need two bottles of the 2017 rosé."

I turned to see Nicole addressing me. She was even more beautiful up close. Her makeup perfect. Too much, for my taste, and in this heat—but perfect anyway.

"*Bonjour*," I said, staring up at her, six feet tall in heels.

"*Bonjour.* I need two bottles of the 2017 rosé," she repeated.

Why didn't she get them herself? I walked down the rack, pulled the two bottles, and handed them to her. She examined me up and down, taking in my fringed skirt, sleeveless silk top, the bangles on my wrists and the leather sandals with straps wrapped around my ankles. She took the bottles and walked off without a word.

I finished my task and started to wash glasses. Lili returned and nodded to the other near-empty rack. "Can you go in back and bring out whatever we need and restock? You can keep track of each case here." She pointed to a notebook on the counter.

Two couples entered the tasting room. I made note of which wines to stock and took the cart and went into the back, where I'd never been before. Cases of wine were stacked in an orderly fashion. I found what I needed and finished restocking the racks.

"Let me wash the glasses, Lili," I said.

She nodded, taking another bottle of wine to the group on the couch. I heard someone call out Luke's name. Nicole rushed out from behind the counter and gave Luke three kisses. "I hoped you'd come in today."

"*Bonjour*, Nicole," Luke said. He caught my eye and waved me over.

"I've been looking for you." He flashed his smile at me. "It's past two. We have to go."

"Go? You just got here. And you can't go, you're working," Nicole said to me.

"You've met?" Luke asked.

I shook my head. Luke introduced us. "Olivia is here as our guest. She's from California. She's doing research."

"When do you go back?" Nicole asked.

Luke and I looked at each other and back to Nicole. Luke shrugged. "She just got here. Come, we have to go."

"Luke," Nicole said, her pink lips pouting. "I hoped to spend more time with you."

"We're bottling tomorrow." Luke shifted his gaze to me. "A Domaine blend. Ninety percent Mourvèdre, five percent Grenache, and five percent Cinsault."

We left Nicole in a sulk. I waved to Lili. She placed her hands together on her chest, bowed her head in a thank-you, and blew me a kiss.

Luke drove the van, which was filled to the brim with cases of wine, the Domaine Laroche name and crest prominent on both sides. I hardly remembered the beautiful road winding down to Bandol. Luke reached over and squeezed my thigh ever so lightly. A gentle wave flowed up my body. Yes, let this feeling last forever.

"You visited the winery today," Luke said.

"Yes. And I came up with an idea for my research project." I went on in a rush about the idea.

Luke looked my way and back to the road. "Yes, Phillipe told me. We have theories about it, but I don't think it's been tested in a lab."

The sea, a deep blue today, seemed to go on forever beyond the red-tile roofs of Bandol.

"He was testing you today," Luke said.

"Phillipe?"

"*Oui.*"

"Did I pass?"

"*Oui.*" He squeezed my thigh again, and I sucked in my breath. "I tasted the same barrels this morning, and all four of us agree. We all keep separate notes and compare after."

"Four?"

"Bernard."

Bernard, of course. I wanted to get to know him better. Talk to him about wine.

In Bandol, cafés and shops lined the crowded streets, definitely not the sleepy village I'd imagined. The promenade, shaded by pine, oleander, and palm trees, was crowded with families, boaters, and beachgoers. Farther on were beautiful villas, all with a view of the sheltered bay, cradled by hills and protected from the wind.

One block off the water, Luke drove down a backstreet, stopped at the back of a restaurant, and knocked on the door. He opened the van doors and unloaded three cases of wine onto a cart.

A man opened the door and greeted Luke. "They didn't tell me the boss is delivering." The man laughed, and they exchanged a greeting, one kiss on each cheek. Luke returned to the driver's seat and repeated the deliveries around town. With the van now empty of wine, Luke declared our errands complete.

"Are you hungry?" Luke asked.

I nodded. I hadn't eaten lunch.

"Good. I know just the place," he said.

He parked on a side street, and we walked toward the water hand in hand. I loved his affection. Across from the harbor we walked up a flight of stairs into a small restaurant. A waiter greeted Luke warmly and led us out to a small balcony with three tables. Lavender spilled from old pots nestled by the wrought-iron railing. The bay glistened before us, its graceful curve filled with hundreds of boats.

Luke ordered a white wine. I leaned over and inhaled the scent of lavender. Everything was sublime. The waiter returned and poured the wine, and he and Luke spoke rapidly in French. Something about grandparents? Luke ended in English. "We are going to go see them today. My grandparents."

"Give them my regards," the waiter said.

Luke ordered mussels and frites and the waiter retreated to the kitchen.

"We are?" I said, surprised.

"*Oui.* They don't speak English, but I want them to meet you. Do you like the wine?"

I took another sip. "It's good, I taste white flowers and citrus. But what is the grape?"

"Ugni Blanc."

"It's good. Crisp and cold for a hot day."

Luke described the grape and growing conditions.

The waiter brought steaming pots of mussels and plates of french fries and poured more wine.

"Tell me about your grandparents. I'm curious why they don't live at Domaine Laroche?" I said.

"They did, but as they aged they wanted to be in town, near all of their friends. They can walk to the morning market, stop and talk to friends, sit outside and watch the world go by."

I took a bite of the steamed mussels in garlic and dipped a french fry into the nectar as I'd seen Luke do. "What do they know about me?"

"I told them I've met the girl of my dreams." Luke raised his glass to me.

I laughed. "The girl who doesn't speak French."

"It'll come. You're trying, and you're doing fine."

"I get the feeling your mother wishes I was French."

"She has ideas for me that are not my ideas."

We each took a bite of the mussels. They were delicious.

So, the vibe I got from Marguerite was real. She wanted Nicole and Luke to be together, and I was in the way. I had been an unwanted surprise.

Luke parked the van in a driveway outside a beige stucco home that overlooked the harbor and bay. The house had turquoise shutters and a red-tile roof, the same color scheme as the manor. The front porch was welcoming and shaded under graceful arches. An older couple sat on wooden chairs padded with French print pillows. A large tan dog with a black saddle marking and beard lay on the cool terra-cotta tile at their feet.

"Oh, an Airedale Terrier. My grandparents had one. She was my baby," I said.

The Airedale bounded to Luke, tail wagging and the typical Airedale smile on its face. "This is Pepin," Luke said. He bent to scratch her ears.

I crouched low. "Pepin, you are the cutest. Oh, I miss mine so much. She died when I was at college." I gave Pepin a big hug. "Yes, you are a good one." I ruffled her curly black and tan fur.

Luke had joined his grandparents on the porch. They all watched me, Luke with a smile. I went over, and Luke introduced me to Henri and Isabelle. I responded in French and kissed them both on the cheeks. Luke and I sat near them on chairs. Pepin sat between us, and I stroked her head and neck.

In crude French, I attempted to tell them my grandparents had an Airedale years ago at their vineyard. "How old is she?" I asked.

"Six," Henri said.

"Oh, she's still a baby," I said.

"*Oui*," Henri agreed. "She is bored here in town. She loves the vineyard."

Luke filled them in on the happenings at Domaine Laroche. Isabelle and Henri glanced my way from time to time. Luke spoke about the vintage we were bottling tomorrow. Both Henri and Isabelle listened to him with interest. They exuded warmth and love for him. I mirrored the feeling. I thought I might burst. I heard Isabelle mention Nicole Gravois. What had she asked Luke? He responded, but the words were too fast for me to comprehend.

Luke noted the time, stood up, and patted Pepin and told his grandparents we'd see them Sunday. Pepin followed me to the van.

"Olivia," Isabelle called. "You have a new friend."

I laughed and nodded. I gave her a last pat before we drove off. "What a nice surprise," I said, "meeting your grandparents and Pepin."

Luke reached over and stroked my cheek, his endearing habit. "That was not the surprise."

"No?"

"No."

Luke drove south on the coastal highway and parked the van at a pull-out overlooking the sea. "We're going on a hike." He took out a backpack. "Put your bathing suit in here."

I'd forgotten all about the swim. I walked behind him on a narrow footpath that followed the coastline. Far below, people swam in coves or lay under beach umbrellas. The women were topless in the French tradition. I had brought my two-piece suit. Now I panicked. Should I go topless? We turned onto a steep side path and made our way down. Around a small curve we came upon a deserted aquamarine cove with a sandy shore. I pulled out my cell phone and snapped a photo. I'd never seen anything as beautiful.

Luke laid out a beach blanket and handed me a towel. He pulled off his shirt and wrapped a towel around his waist. I couldn't take my eyes off his muscular chest. I wanted to touch him. He slipped off his pants under the towel and tugged on his bathing suit.

"Well, what are you waiting for?" Luke asked as he walked to the water's edge and dove in.

I wrapped the towel around my waist, slipped out of my skirt and into my bathing suit bottom, dropped the towel, pulled off my top and bra and followed him in.

The sea was so salty, I floated effortlessly. Luke and I smiled at each other but didn't speak. We didn't need to. Our future seemed as vast as the sea.

Chapter Thirteen

After twenty-four months aging in oak casks, the Bandol red was ready to bottle. Luke invited me to join them in the cellar and help. Phillipe, Bernard, and Luke were standing around the bottling machine when I walked in.

"*Bonjour*, Olivia," Bernard said.

I greeted him and returned Phillipe's wave of the hand. Luke came over, kissed me on both cheeks, and instructed me on my job: cart the finished bottles to the boxing area and place them in the cardboard wine cases.

Marguerite arrived with the labels. I picked one up. An artist's modernist rendition of the manor and vineyard. "These are beautiful. They will sell the wine," I said. "Who did the design?"

"It's my design," Marguerite said. "Domaine Laroche doesn't need a fancy label to sell our wine. Our reputation does that."

Had I insulted her? She had talent as an artist. Phillipe turned the switch and the bottling machine whirred into action. Once the bottles were filled, corked, and labeled, I pushed the ancient bottle cart and quickly placed them in the boxes. Marguerite joined me by the boxes and sat on a low stool. She worked silently as she sealed the boxes and affixed the Domaine Laroche seal on the side.

"I didn't know you were an artist," I said.

She nodded.

"When do you have time to paint?"

"In the winter."

We lapsed into silence and focused on our tasks as the bottles flowed off the rack.

At lunchtime, we stopped for a break. Angelica had set up lunch on the patio by the pool. Large umbrellas shaded the tables, yet the heat still punished. I wanted to dive into the pool. Luke sat across from Marguerite, and I joined him. Cheeses, bread, olives, onion quiche, two salads, and fruit were passed around the table. Bernard poured a crisp rosé from a wine jug.

"Bonjour."

I turned to see Nicole walking onto the patio. Marguerite motioned to the seat next to her. In a miniskirt, high heels, and sleeveless pink top, she resembled the epitome of cool and refreshed. She smiled at Luke. "We need to catch up," she said.

He nodded and took a bite of quiche. Nicole regarded me for an instant. My mouth full, I could only smile. Marguerite and Nicole began a jovial conversation I tried to follow. Maybe Marguerite wasn't talkative with me as it took too much effort. But everyone else did. I needed to learn French. Nicole had Marguerite in fits of laughter. Marguerite was pretty when she laughed. Everyone at the table smiled except me.

Luke leaned over. "She visited my mother's parents in Paris, and she accidently started a little fire in the garbage can with her cigarette."

I nodded and took a sip of wine. So, Nicole visited the grandparents. I thought of Nana. I needed to text Cody about when he was going to stop by. I worried about her alone at Clos de l'Harmonie. But I'd only been here a week. It seemed like a month.

We finished bottling late that afternoon. Everyone was jovial about the effort. The new bottling machine Luke had insisted on had been a wise investment. The old machine, "the cranky one," sat in the corner until Bernard was satisfied. We bottled 277 cases of wine from the small barrel. Tomorrow we'd start on the medium barrel.

After dinner, Luke and I sat on the back patio of my cottage. The night sky sparkled above the shadow of the mountain.

"In November," Luke said, "we'll go to the Paris wine show. We'll show off Domaine Laroche wines and have a blast. The show is work, but the after-parties make it all worthwhile."

I gazed up at the stars. But I wouldn't be here in November. Professor Clark had approved my project, and I needed to complete it by the end of August. I had to get back to prepare for the biodynamic certification. I didn't know the future of Clos de l'Harmonie, but I was determined to get it certified.

Luke kissed me for a long moment. I swept back his hair and melted into his strong body. "I'm in love with you more each day, Olivia."

I love you too, I wanted to say, but his lips were on mine again, soft and warm.

The bottling continued the next day. Angelica replaced Marguerite. Bernard, satisfied with the new bottling machine, gave Lili a break in the tasting room. Saturday afternoon was her Bandol day. Luke turned on music, and the whole dynamic changed. Angelica put in her earbuds to listen to her audiobook.

At lunch, Nicole joined us again. I guess she did have to eat. I stiffened when she brushed Luke's hair from his face. Marguerite smiled at them.

"Come for dinner tomorrow, Nicole," Marguerite said. "Isabelle and Henri come on Sundays. I'll invite your grandparents."

"We'd love to," Nicole said.

Nicole went back to the tasting room, and Bernard appeared and filled up a plate.

"She's a lovely girl," he said.

"I don't think we can leave her alone in the tasting room," Luke said.

Bernard waived him off. "The customers love her."

"Talk to Lili about her," Luke said. "I'll go in until you get back." He rose.

"No, I'll go," Angelica said, glancing at me. "Go bottle."

We left Marguerite and Bernard on the patio and went back to the cellar. An hour later Angelica returned, shaking her head and throwing her arms up. I guessed things hadn't gone so well in the tasting room.

Chapter Fourteen

*L*ili appeared at my front door Sunday morning, her basket brimming with fresh food and supplies. She wore flats and a blue paisley dress. Her skin glowed from time at the beach. After three kisses, she breezed through the cottage, replacing supplies. "Next Saturday night I'm taking you and Luke into Bandol. The town is booming with summer people. The bars are hopping."

"Sounds like fun. I love your dress, by the way."

She twirled around. "I got it yesterday."

"Oh, take me where you got it. I love the style."

"Of course. On Saturday, we'll go shopping. I thought of you when I bought it. It is your style. Bohemian chic. A cool hippie chick."

I laughed. "My nana is the hippie chick."

"What are you looking at?" Lili peered over my shoulder.

I had Nicole's Instagram page open. "Do you know she has four million followers? Four million," I said.

"And they're all fluff, like her. Has she posted one thing of importance? No. If I had four million followers I'd be promoting climate change initiatives."

I nodded and shut the page.

"I met a guy at the beach. He's coming to taste today. He's from California!" Lili said.

"What time? I want to meet him and make sure he is who he says he is."

"I don't know. We were out late. I'll text you when he gets here. But yes, come and meet him."

"*Merci*, Lili!" I called. She was already out the door, bounding down the road, a ball of energy. The inner smile and gratitude I got from her brief visit lasted all morning.

Slathered in sunscreen, wearing a sun visor, shorts, and tank top, I met Luke at the barn. We planned to spray the Grenache plot with nettle tea, a biodynamic preparation that enlivens the earth and stimulates soil health. I hopped on the small tractor next to Luke and monitored the spray as he drove. I could do this all day despite the heat. The sea glimmered below, and the terraced vines climbed up to the mountain. I told him about Lili and her plan for next Saturday. He smiled and shook his head.

"She met a guy from California, and he's coming to the tasting room later today. I'm going to go met him."

"Yes, go check out this guy. I hear Californians can be wild and crazy."

I kissed him on the cheek as we turned down the next row. When we finished the plot, we were drenched in sweat.

"Go shower and meet me at the pool," he said.

I was definitely wearing my bathing suit top here.

After we swam, Luke stayed to talk with Bernard. I went back to the cottage and changed for the early dinner. I slipped on my white dress with the embroidered bodice. The white enhanced my skin, which was now bronzed despite all the sunscreen.

My phone chimed with Lili's text. "He's here."

I dashed on dark pink lipstick, grabbed my purse, and walked down the road to the tasting room. Still shy about walking into the main house even though welcome, I entered the tasting room through the main visitor door.

My eyes adjusted. I saw Nicole on the visitor side next to a tall blond man. Lili waved me over, gave me my three kisses, and poured me a taste of a rosé of 100 percent Mourvèdre. Nicole and the man were talking about Hollywood.

"Jon, this is my friend, Olivia. She's the one from Santa Barbara."

He reached out his hand to shake mine. "Nice to meet you," he said.

71

I shook his hand and turned to Nicole. "*Bonjour*, Nicole."

She raised her glass to me but said nothing. Jon and I began to talk about what had brought us to France. Nicole crowded by his side, listening.

He lived in Los Angeles and worked in film production. This trip he was scouting the area for film locations. "Bandol is perfect, and the countryside is magnificent," he said. "It's a small version of Santa Barbara."

I nodded. There were likenesses. I told him about Clos de l'Harmonie.

"I've filmed in the valley. We spent six months there. Spectacular scenery, and the food and wine were a bonus. I'm sure I've been to your vineyard. I went to every winery in the area at least once."

I pulled up a picture of Clos de l'Harmonie on my phone.

"Ah, yes. I spent an entire afternoon there talking with the vintner. The ambiance of the vineyard was so relaxing. Exactly what I needed after a week of filming with touchy actors."

"I want to go there someday," Lili said.

"You will," Jon and I said in unison. The three of us laughed. He liked her as much as I did. Jon leaned in and asked Lili something.

I scrolled through a few more pictures, warmed to think of my grandfather.

Nicole came around to my other side. "So, you are infatuated with Luke, yes?"

Infatuated? Well, yes, but it was more than an infatuation. I didn't know what to say.

"It won't last. It never does. He's all about the wine," Nicole said. "Our families go a long way back." Nicole smiled at me triumphantly. "By the way, I have a beauty tip. You're getting too much sun. It's not good for the skin."

Lili saved me with a pour of the Bandol red. "Your favorite," she said.

At closing time, I took my wineglass behind the counter and started washing glasses. Nicole walked through the back door to the kitchen, her heels clacking on the tile. Lili sighed and shook her head.

On the back patio I found the family starting to gather. Luke, Phillipe, Nicole, and Bernard were there. Luke's eyes found mine, and he winked. Bernard introduced me to Nicole's grandparents. They didn't speak English. I moved to the far side of the pool and gazed down at the sea in the distance. Lili and Jon stood talking by his car in the parking lot. A car came up the drive. Luke's grandparents. I waved.

Henri opened the back door, and Pepin jumped out. "Pepin!" I called. She trotted over to me with a bounce in her step and a big Airedale smile. I crouched down to snuggle her. "I missed you."

Luke called for Pepin, and she bounded over. Playful, she started to nudge everyone for attention. Nicole jumped up and moved away. "No, no." Nicole held her hand out to fend Pepin off.

I laughed inwardly. Pepin wouldn't hurt anyone unless you needed her to. Marguerite and Angelica started to bring out platters of food. "Where is Lili?" Marguerite asked.

"I'll find her," I said. I walked out toward the parking lot. Lili saw me, and I motioned her to come.

I sat silent throughout dinner. No one seemed to notice. Pepin lay between Lili and me. Luke somehow got seated by Nicole. Would I ever fit in here? Angelica got up and started clearing platters and plates. I got up and helped. Marguerite gave me a faint smile and stayed seated. Bernard went to open more wine.

Pepin followed me back and forth to the kitchen as I cleared the table. As we washed the dishes, Angelica asked, "You like the dog?"

"I love her."

"She loves it here. This is her home. She seems sad in town, but nobody here wants the responsibility."

"I'd look after her while I'm here."

"Hmm."

We joined the others on the patio. Luke lit citronella candles in glass jars. It appeared everyone planned to stay awhile. I sat down next to Lili. Pepin lay at my feet, her head on my sandals. Bernard got up and poured me a glass of wine. I surmised they were talking about people they knew in town.

I started to daydream about a life in France. Despite all the people around me, I felt alone. Angelica was speaking to her grandparents. I heard my name and Pepin's in the same sentence. I turned to Luke, trying to figure out what Angelica had said. Henri and Isabelle looked at each other, and I made out something about a good idea for the summer. Henri scrutinized Bernard, Marguerite, and Luke. "Okay?"

Bernard and Marguerite both shrugged and nodded. Luke smiled at me. "Pepin will be staying with you this summer."

I jumped up and hugged Henri and Isabelle while Pepin bounded around us. "*Merci, merci!*" Lili laughed. Nicole's eyes narrowed, but Angelica wore a conspiratorial grin.

Chapter Fifteen

The summer advanced with punishing heat and Pepin at my heels. I worked all aspects of the vineyard and winery, learning more and more about running Domaine Laroche. While Luke brought in workers at harvesttime, as we did at Harmonie, the day-to-day work was a family affair, and they appreciated my help.

Luke was always in command and always had a plan. I admired him for it. He knew what to do and took charge. I'd seen him with his father, thoughtful and not overbearing, trying out new ideas and methods. He was diplomatic and usually right, as in the case of the new bottling machine he'd purchased to save numerous hours of downtime and frustration.

I accompanied Luke on trips to nearby villages on wine errands. Errands anyone could have helped him with—but he wanted us to get away. We hiked the bluff top paths and swam. We ate seafood in small cafés. Occasionally we went into town with Lili on Saturday nights. Monday nights, my favorite, Marguerite and Bernard went into town for dinner, and everyone scattered to do their own thing. Luke and I traded off cooking at each other's houses. I wanted to be with him all the time. My French improved slowly, and except for Marguerite, I seemed to have been accepted as Luke's girlfriend. They all knew, however, that I'd be gone when the summer drew to an end.

In mid-August, Luke told me we were going to a two-day wine and food event in Marseille. "We're spending two nights. It will be work, but only from one o'clock to six o'clock."

He drew me into him and kissed me. Two nights. We had taken it slow and had only kissed so far, but all I could think of was making love with him. And now we had two nights alone and away from Domaine Laroche.

The day before we left for Marseille I was headed into the kitchen in the main house, Pepin at my side as always, when the sound of Luke and his mother in a heated debate stopped me. I heard Nicole's name.

"I'm not interested in Nicole," Luke said.

"But she is a beautiful girl."

"Her only desire is to shop or sit in outdoor cafés, sipping champagne and being seen. I can do that for about an hour and then I get bored."

"Okay, what about another girl… from Bandol, or Provence, or anywhere in France? You can't find a French girl?"

"Olivia and I are in love. Do you believe in love at first sight?"

Marguerite didn't answer.

"I know you do. You and Papa met that way. So, trust me on this."

I turned to retreat and almost ran into Angelica, who had also stopped to listen. She shook her head. Heat flowed to my scalp. I'd been caught eavesdropping on her family.

"She'll come around," Angelica said quietly. "I got the same thing with Phillipe."

"You did?"

"*Oui*, she had someone else in mind for me. But that's not how love works, is it?" She smiled and opened the screen door. I turned and walked up the road to the vineyard and sat on the first terrace to collect my thoughts. Did Bernard and Luke's grandparents think the same way? Was I only a summer girlfriend to them? I pulled out my phone to check the calendar. I needed a final push on my research paper. I noticed an email from Jameson.

Olivia,

I can communicate via email now. So, you flew away to France. Good for you. I wish I could fly away somewhere, anywhere, but I don't know where to go. I need a plan for when I get out of here. Send me your news.

J

I smiled and gazed at the sea below, today a piercing blue. I didn't even know my own future. How could I help plan his? Pepin poked me with her nose, panting. The heat burned like a fever. The grapes before me swelled on the vines, and the flowers and herbs bloomed bright in the carefully tended beds, their heady scent floating in the air. Could I be part of this? I tried to envision living in France, but Clos de l'Harmonie always pulled me back to California. Perhaps I shouldn't go to Marseille with Luke. I shouldn't start anything so serious when Nana needed me at Harmonie. But my pull toward Luke was strong. Stronger than I was.

In the morning, Phillipe helped Luke and me load the van with cases of wine and boxes of engraved wineglasses. Lili threw in stacks of tasting notes.

"Have fun," she said.

"Why aren't you going?" I asked.

"I've done it two years in a row. And Jon is back." Her eyes sparkled when she said his name.

Pepin jumped in the van with us. We were dropping her off at Isabelle and Henri's on the way to Marseille. The ocean shimmered in the morning sun as we drifted around the curves toward Bandol. I couldn't stop smiling, anticipating our two nights away from Domaine Laroche, but also nervous and conflicted. Had Luke booked two rooms or one? I wanted one, but shyness was getting the best of me.

"I like to see you smiling," Luke said, resting his hand on my thigh. "You seemed sad yesterday. I worried you were getting tired of me."

I squeezed his hand. "I could never get tired of you."

"Why were you sad?"

"I heard you and your mother talking in the kitchen yesterday."

"Ah, sorry you had to hear that. She's old-fashioned. My father is more open minded. Angelica told me you heard, actually." He squeezed my thigh. "Wait until my mom finds out Lili is going out with a Californian also."

Angelica had told him? They were a very close family.

We dropped off Pepin at Henri and Isabelle's and took the coast road to Marseille. Rocky inlets and sunbaked beaches were on the left and terraced vineyards climbed up the slopes to the right. Forty-five minutes later we were in Marseille, winding around the old port that cradled the city.

Luke parked at the waterfront near a huge white tent. Luxury yachts flanked the docks across from the boardwalk. Winemakers were setting up their tasting booths. A Domaine Laroche banner hung behind a large rectangular table covered with a white linen tablecloth. A young man called out to Luke and hurried over with a cart. We unloaded the wine and glasses and made numerous trips to our table. The voices in the tent were jovial.

"See you at one o'clock," Luke said to the young man and slipped him a tip. Then he took my hand and led me back to the van. We drove along a street that hugged the harbor. Luke parked in front of a stunning villa. "Our hotel."

A valet greeted us and took our bags. We followed him through an interior courtyard where bright rose-colored bougainvillea and pink-throated jasmine were planted in huge ceramic pots. A colorful tile fountain in the center was surrounded by five tables set apart for privacy.

The front desk attendant handed Luke two key cards. Luke handed me one, and we followed the valet up a flight of wide tile stairs. Luke opened the room for the valet. Momentarily confused, I waited in the doorway. Was this my room or his? The valet set our bags down and opened French doors that led out onto a balcony. An antique filigreed wrought-iron table and chairs were set among more flowers in pots. Luke tipped the valet as he departed and raised his eyebrows, seeing me still standing by the door.

"Aren't you coming in?"

"Well, I, um…" I glanced at my key card.

Luke picked me up and carried me outside to the balcony. He set me down and hugged me from behind. A spectacular scene of the *vieux port* and the sea lay below. "Welcome to Marseille." He kissed me on my neck. I closed my eyes and leaned into him.

Interrupted by a knock, Luke went to open the door. The valet brought in a tray with two café au laits and a basket of pastries. He set them on the patio table and quietly disappeared.

"I'm in heaven," I said. "I'm going to wash my hands." I stepped inside. The large four-poster bed with a luxurious white bedspread invited a touch. My hand sank into the feather-soft bed. Massive carved antique furniture and tapestries were reflected in two large mirrors. The marble counter in the huge bathroom gleamed, and a double-size soaking tub was built into the corner. An array of Provençal olive oil soaps lined the counter. I washed my hands with an orange blossom bar and went back onto the patio. Luke sat surveying the port. Behind him, I wrapped my arms around his neck and kissed his hair. The hair I loved so much.

"Did you jump on the bed?"

I laughed. "I wanted to."

He took my hand and breathed deeply. "You smell so good."

We sipped our coffee and gazed at the *vieux port*. "Ships have been sailing into this port for twenty-six centuries."

I tried to imagine twenty-six centuries. California had been discovered five hundred years ago—except of course for the Native Americans.

"We have reservations for dinner tonight. We're going to the best restaurant for Marseille's specialty, bouillabaisse."

"I remember the bouillabaisse we had after you picked me up at the airport. I'll never forget the flavors."

"Ah, that was more like a fisherman's stew. This is Marseille's signature dish. It requires a two-day notice to get the right ingredients."

Luke had put some thought into this trip. I thought of the clothes I'd packed from the shopping trip with Lili. Mom would approve.

We walked to the wine fair through the lively Avenue du Prado marketplace. Strung out along a tree-lined boulevard, an array of stalls sold bread, fruit, cheese, Provençal soaps, olive oil, ceramics, and specialty items. Jostled along by the crowd of shoppers, Luke took my hand, and we threaded our way through the throng.

The wine fair went by quickly. Luke introduced me to many people I'd never remember. Our tasting table was continuously swamped with buyers placing orders. I was able to converse in French and enjoy myself. I poured wine and took orders. Waiters served food on trays, and the tent swelled with wine aficionados. Two other biodynamic winemakers were present, and our three tables had the biggest crowds.

At one point our table quieted. Luke whispered in my ear, "I'm going to make love to you all night."

I sucked in my breath and watched as a new horde of tasters with notebooks descended upon us.

Luke held my hand as we walked to dinner at the elegant Michelin-star restaurant he'd selected for us. In the swanky dining room, I felt kissed by the French sun in my strapless black dress.

Luke's dark hair shone against his white linen shirt. He ordered a crisp white wine from Cassis. I loved it here with him, in France. But how would this work? Nana needed me. There was so much work to be done at Clos de l'Harmonie. I forced my mind to be in the moment, here with Luke.

The waiter first brought the broth, rich with saffron, fennel, and tomato. He followed with the cooked fish, which he deboned tableside and served on a platter. He placed rouille, a thick garlic and chili pepper mayonnaise, with croutons and grated Gruyere cheese on the side. My eyes grew wide. How did one go about this? I needed guidance.

Luke ladled broth into my bowl. "Add fish to the broth, spread the croutons with rouille, top with cheese, and float them in the soup." He demonstrated, and I followed suit. The flavors were unforgettable. I lifted my glass, and we toasted.

After dinner, Luke ordered two café au laits. I sat back and enjoyed the restaurant ambiance, starched linen tablecloths, modern white hanging lamps, and ocean view. It was noisy but intimate. I thought of going back to the hotel, and my stomach fluttered. Luke watched me with a serious face. Maybe he was nervous too.

We strolled back along the waterfront hand in hand. Under a streetlamp he paused to kiss me. I hungered for his body as I pressed against him. We had waited so long.

I emerged from the bathroom in a short silk robe tied at the waist and joined Luke on the patio for a cognac. He pulled my chair close to his and motioned for me to sit. The evening was warm, and the harbor glittered below. Laughter and voices drifted up. I took a sip and coughed.

"It's too strong for me."

"Ah, wait here. Don't move." He jumped up and returned with a small glass of red wine. "Ninety-five percent Mourvèdre."

"Thank you." I held up the glass, swirled, and sniffed. I took a sip and held it in my mouth and finally swallowed. I tipped back my head and closed my eyes. "Heaven." I opened my eyes and regarded Luke. "Domaine Laroche?"

He nodded. My dream was to make wine like that, and it all started with the grapes. I would, someday. "This has been a perfect night," I said.

Luke reached over and began stroking my leg. The silk robe rose high on my thigh. "It's not over yet."

Desire clung thick on his words, and I ached for him. How did he have so much self-control? He took my hand and led me inside. A candle flickered, and the intoxicating scent of frankincense filled the room. Luke pulled off his shirt and wrapped his arms around me, his chest and arms solid against me. Slipping off my robe, he placed me on the bed. He hummed appreciatively and stroked my midnight-blue lace bra and panties. I had never felt so feminine or aroused.

His hands swept slowly between my thighs and up to my pressure point. Hooking his thumb under my panties he slipped them off and slid a finger into my wetness.

"Hmm."

Massaging me, he leaned over and kissed my breasts and unhooked my bra. This time he moaned. I put an arm around his neck and tried to bring him to me, but he gently removed my hand. I wanted him. His strokes were perfection. I couldn't hold out. A pink lotus flower spread through me, filling my entire body with such pleasure and release, unlike anything I'd experienced. I opened my eyes to Luke's steamy smile, and this time he relented to my pull.

Luke stayed true to his word. We made love all night.

I woke to sounds from the harbor below. Luke's arm was around me, my back to him. He had shut the French doors sometime in the early morning, and a soft light filtered in. I closed my eyes and leaned into him. I wanted to wake up in his arms every day. Did that mean I should move to France? Or would he come to California? No, he wouldn't leave Domaine Laroche.

But I was getting ahead of myself. Maybe his feelings would change now that we'd broken the built-up tension. Would he see me off to California without a thought?

Luke stirred and held me closer.

Chapter Sixteen

We returned to Domaine Laroche with a record number of wine orders. Without a pause we dove into work at the winery in a somewhat heightened state. It was late August, and some varietals were ready for harvest on fruit days. Barrels still needed to be bottled on flower days. Luke and I were often separated, working where needed, on different production processes. While the work forced a distance between us, the magic of our two nights stayed with me.

Every night, after dinner with the family, I spent the evenings in my cottage finalizing my research paper. A week after our trip to Marseille, lab results backed up my premise. I thought of how to explain the research and results to Mom to interest her. Dad would get it right away. I'd send them a copy when I finished. The culmination of my degree. Now I could focus on growing grapes and making unique, sought-after wines at Clos de l'Harmonie for as long as Nana was alive. I didn't want to leave Domain Laroche and Luke. But it was time for me to go home.

A knock on the back door brought me out of my daydream. Pepin bounced to the door.

"Come in," I said.

Luke entered with his endearing smile. "Are you avoiding me?"

"No! Of course not. You've been bottling late, and I just finished work on my paper. Now I can move on with my life."

His brow briefly furrowed. He pulled me to my feet and kissed me on the lips. "What does that mean?"

"I'm free. I'm done with school. Thank you for the internship."

Luke pulled back a step. His eyes clouded in confusion. Finally, he smiled. "We need to celebrate. Will you join me at my house?"

"Right now?"

"*Oui*, right now." He led me up the road in the darkness, my hand cupped in his.

We sat on his back terrace. Luke lit a candle and poured glasses of wine. "To your future," he toasted.

I raised my glass and drank. I wish he'd said to our future. I stared at the mountain in the distance. The heat had subsided, and the contours softened in the moonlight.

"Will you stay?" Luke asked.

I considered him. I wanted to stay with him always, but there were barrels and barrels of wine at Harmonie that needed to be bottled this fall and winter. And Harmonie needed work for the certification inspection.

He reached for my hand. "I want you to stay. I want to marry you."

"You do?"

"Yes. I knew it the day after I met you. When I offered to take you out to lunch at the best restaurant in the valley and you said you'd rather get a picnic and take me to the Pacific Ocean."

I laughed. That seemed like such a long time ago.

"I want to propose properly, after I ask your father."

I squeezed his hand. He did everything with such feeling. He was never indifferent.

"But I need a sign," he said.

I leaned over and kissed him, and he kissed me back. He tasted of berry, cinnamon, and a hint of eucalyptus. We pulled away to look at each other. I knew Mom would sell Harmonie as soon as she inherited it. Was my future here? But I doubted Bernard would let me make my own wine, even a small batch.

"Can I make my own wine here?"

He laughed and stretched his hand out toward the vines that crept up the mountain. "Of course. There is no shortage of grapes."

He pulled me up and led me through the house to his bedroom. His warm callused hands undressed me. His strong arms wrapped around me. Our bodies entwined. The way we moved, we were perfect together. Supple, tender, melting.

Before the first light, he walked me back to my cottage. I fell into bed with Pepin nearby.

I awoke wondering if I had dreamed the night before. Did Luke really want to marry me? I jumped up and started some coffee. The reality of it made me queasy. What would his family think? Would I be welcomed or resented? Nana wouldn't want me so far away. Who would run Harmonie? What would Mom and Dad think? Would Jameson like him? That was important to me. If I worked here, would I get a small salary for living expenses? Did Luke get a salary? I loved Luke, but I couldn't abandon Harmonie. How would I decide?

Chapter Seventeen

I walked to the winery with Pepin at my heels. I'd sent off my research paper to Professor Clark. Instead of feeling free, my heart was heavy. I needed to make plans to go back to California. That meant saying goodbye to Luke.

The September light shone golden, and the sea below was flat as glass. There was no sign of anyone. The barn door was closed, the tractor parked outside. The winery door was shut. I eased it open. The lights were out. The tasting room wasn't open yet. I walked through the back door to the kitchen. No sign of anyone. Usually Marguerite was whipping up a delicious treat.

I heard Bernard's voice, low and serious. Luke's voice boomed in disagreement. At the dining room door, I stopped. The entire family and Phillipe sat at the dining room table. Bernard stopped talking. Everyone stared at me, not smiling, except Luke. "Business meeting." He cocked his head apologetically.

"Oh, sorry." I retreated through the kitchen. Outside I inhaled deeply and breathed out slowly. They were so serious. Was everything okay with Domaine Laroche? Had Luke mentioned our plans?

I walked back to the cottage and sat out front with another coffee. I stroked Pepin's ears. She was so silky. I pulled out my phone. I wanted to call Nana, but it was too early in California. Even Cody wouldn't be up yet. There was a voice mail from Mom from the night before.

"Olivia, call me immediately."

She hadn't called me the entire time I'd been here. Dad and I talked, but Mom and I only exchanged emails. I pushed call.

"Mom?"

"Olivia, you must come home. Nana…"

"Mom, what about Nana? Is she okay?"

"No, Livie. She passed away yesterday."

"What?" I gripped the phone. "What happened? She was so healthy!" Tears filled my eyes, and the sea below blurred.

"Honestly, I think she died from a heartbreak. She missed Papa so much."

Tears flowed down my checks. "I'll be there as soon as I can. I'll call you back with my flight. Take care, Mom."

Inside, I lay on the bed and wept. Nana gone? Inconceivable. First Papa, now Nana, and soon, the end of Harmonie. Mom would sell the farm. Sorrow wound through me like a whisper of smoke.

After no more tears would come, I got up and booked a flight from Marseille to Los Angeles and on to Santa Barbara for four o'clock that afternoon.

I packed my suitcase and cleaned the cottage. I could leave some things like books with Luke perhaps. I heard whistling from the open door as I swept the tile floor. Luke peeked in. His eyes landed on the suitcase.

"Olivia?" His eyes questioned mine.

Tears welled up and began to flow down my cheeks again.

"That was a business meeting we have every quarter. In time we'll include you. Come here, *ma chérie*." He held me in his arms. "What is this suitcase? I told the family our plans." He kissed my forehead and stoked my hair. "They like you. My mom will come around. They know you are a passionate vintner."

I leaned into Luke to absorb his strength. "It's not that."

"What is it?" He lifted my face to see my eyes.

"Nana passed away. I've booked a flight for this afternoon."

"Ah." Luke sighed and held me close. "I am so sorry."

My tears flowed. Luke led me to the back terrace and we sat, his arm around me. "Do you want me to come with you?"

Yes. I didn't want to part with him. But I thought of the backlog of bottling and the upcoming harvest. "No, you have too much to do here."

"You'll be back soon, yes?"

I nodded.

"I'll buy your ticket back. How long will you be there?"

"I know Mom will sell Clos de l'Harmonie, so there won't be much to do. The funeral and cleaning out the farmhouse. She'll probably sell it to Tom. He already acts like he owns the place." I broke down in sobs. Luke held me tighter. Nana gone, and now the end of Harmonie.

Chapter Eighteen

*D*ad picked me up at the airport, and for the next few days I moved in a fog. I wished Jameson could be with us.

We buried Nana next to Papa, and the finality of it made me numb. My loss was immense. Guilt racked me for going to France in the first place. I should have stayed with Nana.

The morning after the funeral I sat with Mom on her patio, staring at the ocean. I checked my messages. My heart ached for Luke. Lili sent me news that Nicole had gone back to Paris. I let out a sigh of relief. She did vie for Luke's attention.

"We're going to the reading of the will this morning," Mom said. "I want you to be there."

"Oh, Mom. I can't do that. It's too sad. I just want to go up to Harmonie, check on the vines, tend the flower and herb gardens, and stay there." And mourn. I needed to mourn.

"We can go after. I need your support, and besides, the attorney requested your presence." She paused. "I'll go to the farm with you after. I don't want you to go up alone, and Dad is back at work. I'll stay the night, and Dad can pick me up tomorrow after work."

I opened my mouth but couldn't speak. Of course she wanted to go to Nana's house. She grieved for her mother and maybe her childhood home. She would have to start sorting things out to sell it. Nana would want us to be together.

The attorney's office was somber, like the man himself. We sat in leather chairs facing his desk and stared blankly at massive bookshelves on the back wall. Did anything happy ever happen in an attorney's office? A musty smell arose when Stan, the attorney, opened a file cabinet and brought out a file.

"I'm sorry for your loss," Stan said. "I knew both your parents since before they bought the farm. I helped draw up the purchase agreement, and I became one of their best customers for wine. We had many wonderful afternoons on the porch."

Mom nodded and smiled. "I remember, Stan."

He cleared his throat and opened the file. He handed us each a copy of the will. I had never seen one before. The language was very formal. "Your parents prepared their will two years ago."

Mom nodded.

The words on the legal document blurred, rambling on and on and not saying anything. I thought of Nana, buried next to Papa. They were together now. That was what she wanted. I thought back to a conversation we had on the porch right before I left for France. She said her heart ached for him and she wouldn't be happy until they were together. Maybe she had died of a broken heart. It was a scientific fact people can die of heartache.

Stan set about reading the main points. "Jameson has been bequeathed ten percent of the stocks and bonds from the Merrill Lynch account. Eve, they have bequeathed you ninety percent of the stocks and bonds from the Merrill Lynch account. Olivia, they have bequeathed you the property, buildings, and all equipment that make up Clos de l'Harmonie and one hundred thousand dollars, of which fifty thousand is to be used to pay off your school loans."

Mom inhaled and started coughing. I snapped out of my daze.

"Pardon me, I apologize, my mind was elsewhere. I heard something about school loans?"

Stan rose and brought Mom a glass of water. Her normal facial glow had paled to white.

"Are you okay, Mom?"

She closed her eyes. Stan sat down and reread my part.

Mom's eyes were still closed. Clos de l'Harmonie was mine? Stan watched me and waited for me to speak.

"I don't know what to say. I had no idea," I said.

"No, of course not. I questioned them about this, and they were adamant and confident you would 'know what to do,' is how they put it. They knew you would take the reins and carry on."

I began to sob. They had been so generous. They had faith in me. Now I knew why Nana had been so adamant about knowing how much my school loans were. They had wanted to help pay, but I had refused. I had no idea how much money they had. Clos de l'Harmonie was mine?

Stan brought me a glass of water and a tissue. I regained my composure and turned to Mom.

"Honey, we will help you sell it. It's too much of a burden for a young girl. That old farm. Don't cry."

"These are tears of happiness. This is my childhood dream. Clos de l'Harmonie will stay in our family." Plans started to form. I'd continue to work on the biodynamic certification. My head burst with potential plans for Harmonie. Thank you, Nana and Papa. Thank you, thank you. I won't let you down. I couldn't wait to call Luke. But, how was this going to work? Now my dreams were on opposite sides of the world.

Chapter Nineteen

I drove Mom in the MINI Cooper to Clos de l'Harmonie. We were both silent, alone in our thoughts. I went over what I'd say to Luke. It was pretty simple. I had inherited the vineyard.

Mom's sunglasses hid any emotion. She had lost both her parents in less than a year, and Jameson and I had lost our grandparents.

"Are you resentful I got the vineyard?" I asked.

"I'm processing it. I have to let it sink in."

"Me too." My world had been turned upside down, but in a good way. I would bring Harmonie back to life with new vitality and spirit.

We descended the mountain pass on Route 154, past Lake Cachuma, or what used to be a lake and drinking water reservoir before the long drought. It was parched and down to 8 percent of its usual volume. The highway carved through the valley. Vineyards and oak trees dotted the landscape. I breathed in and exhaled. This felt like home.

"Mom, I don't want you to be resentful."

"You're my daughter. I want to be happy for you and for you to be happy. I think it's too much of a burden."

"It's not a burden. When I think of Harmonie, it's all sweetness and light. It's a living organism."

"I just remember chores. Endless chores, mean roosters, and manure piles."

"You mean compost. The heart of organic farming."

"Well, it didn't do anything for my heart. I couldn't wait to get out of there."

I eased up the driveway. Tall weeds and grass engulfed the car on either side. I needed to get out the mower.

In the distance Tom and his crew harvested grapes. Our grapes. Stan had given me a copy of the contract before we left his office. After a quick review, I asked Stan to write Tom that we would not be renewing the agreement and remind him that remuneration for the grapes was due next month as soon as he finished the harvest.

The house stood lonely atop the knoll. "I'm glad we're here together," I said, unlocking the door.

Mom walked through the rooms silently. She ended up in the kitchen and made chamomile tea. I walked through the house, opening windows. We sat on the porch drinking tea, both unsure of what to do. The vineyard and flower beds stretched out below.

"It is peaceful here," she said. "Won't you be lonely? By the way, how was France? And Luke? I'm sorry we didn't get to come visit due to the circumstances, and now you're back."

"Oh, I'll be going back."

But as soon as I said it I wondered when? How? Now that I had Harmonie to revive, the two parts of my life seemed incompatible. My phone vibrated. It was Luke. "Excuse me, Mom."

I answered and walked around the back of the house and sat on the back porch steps.

"I miss you," Luke said. "Where are you, and what are you doing right now? I want to picture you."

"I miss you too. I am sitting on the back porch steps of Clos de l'Harmonie. They're harvesting grapes."

"I wish I could say the same. We'll start the Mourvèdre harvest mid-October. The grapes are taking their time this year. You'll be back by then. Back in my arms."

I smiled. How I loved being in his arms. Closing my eyes, I could smell his scent, lavender and rosemary from the Marseille soap he used.

"Olivia?"

"I'm here. Thinking of you."

"How is everything going? Is your mom okay?"

"It's been an interesting day. Mom is okay. She's here with me for the night."

"Good. When can you come back?"

"Luke, something incredible has happened."

"Yes." He laughed. "We're going to get married."

"Yes, that too." It hadn't really sunk in yet about the vineyard.

"What incredible thing has happened, *ma chérie*?"

"Clos de l'Harmonie is mine now. My grandparents left it to me."

Silence on the line.

"Luke?"

"I am happy for you."

There was not a trace of excitement in his voice. "Happy for us," I said.

"What are your plans?"

"I'll get certified in January and next year start making biodynamic wine."

"So, you're not coming back?"

"Yes, of course I am. I have to sort everything out here. I love you, Luke."

"I love you too."

We worked out the soonest feasible time we could see each other. Luke would come to California after the Mourvèdre crush. That seemed like a lifetime away.

Chapter Twenty

In the morning I stood on the front porch surveying the farm. It didn't feel right without Nana. There was so much to do, I was momentarily overwhelmed. At least the orchard was in good shape thanks to the orchardist I'd hired before leaving for France.

Hailey walked toward the porch from the side yard, her long dark hair shining in the sunlight. She held a bouquet of flowers and a basket of eggs.

"I'm sorry about your grandmother." She handed me the flowers.

"Thank you. Do you want to come in?"

"No, I can't stay. The school bus will be at the mailboxes in a few minutes. Here are some eggs."

"Thanks for minding the chickens."

"I enjoyed it. It gave me an excuse to get away. I can still do it, if you want. My dad really likes them. He said he's never tasted better eggs."

"Well sure. I'll be staying here now."

"Really?" A smile lit up her face. "Your grandmother talked a lot about you. She said you already were a good winemaker. That's so cool. Ciao! I have to run. See you tomorrow."

"Ciao."

Inside, I put the flowers in a vase and smiled. The flowers, valerian and yarrow, were from the flower beds I grew for the bio preparations.

I joined Mom in Nana's bedroom. She was methodically packing Nana's clothes, as if in a trance.

"You don't have to do this now," I said.

"I want to. Everything is a memory. Besides, it's best to do it sooner than later."

"Hailey, the young girl next door, stopped by. She's quite nice."

"The opposite of her father. Call the sheriff if he bothers you, okay?"

"He won't bother me."

Over the next week, the enormity of my inheritance sprang from every corner of the farm. The barn and tasting room needed repair, the flower beds begged to be weeded, the house paint flaked, the vines required compost and biodynamic applications as soon as Tom finished the harvest. I created a spreadsheet and prioritized.

Luke was quiet on the phone when I talked about my plans. He didn't have much to say. When I asked about Domaine Laroche, he said they were busy and everyone missed me. Especially Pepin, who sat outside my cottage waiting for my return.

I called Cody frequently to talk. He'd started working at a winery in Paso Robles for minimum wage. I invited him to come to the biodynamic cow horn ceremony at the autumn equinox the following week. A ceremony needed more than one person. The farm needed more than one person.

The evenings were lonely. I thought of Luke and his family, eating together in the massive dining room, in contrast to the quiet of Nana's kitchen. I emailed Jameson every other night. He didn't respond. I assumed he also resented me getting the farm.

While tired from the day's work outside, in the evenings I sorted out the house. I wanted to keep the antique furniture but update the decor with my style. I went room to room and boxed up memories. Mom didn't want anything but maybe Jameson would. I moved my belongings to my grandparents' bedroom, large and airy with French doors opening to a porch. The view of mature oak trees, the old Indian wall, and the undulating hills was peaceful. A small swath of vineyard was also visible.

Saturday morning, at dawn, I walked through the vineyard with my notebook, tasting the grapes. A sea of gold and red leaves clung to the vines. The Sauvignon Blanc and Malbec had been harvested, and the Cabernet Franc would be next. In the distance, I watched Tom's truck stop at the corner of the plot. He and a field hand got out.

"Have you ever seen anything like these?" Tom said. He took a grape and tasted it.

He surveyed the plot, and his eyes finally rested on me. "You're up early. Olivia, I'm sorry about your grandmother."

I stared at him. He hadn't been sorry enough to go to the funeral service. Everyone else we knew in the valley attended. Christ, they'd lived here since the sixties.

"How are my grapes?" Tom said.

Heat rose to my face. Contractually they were his, but we'd grown them. "I'd give them another week. Let them lose a little water. Next Thursday is a fruit day, your best day to harvest."

"We're harvesting today. We'll be done this afternoon."

"They're not ready."

"Listen, missy, I'll harvest these grapes whenever I like."

I looked out over the rows of grapes, and my stomach somersaulted. A tractor, pulling a long trailer stacked with grape containers, drove up the driveway followed by a van full of workers. He was making a mistake. One couldn't force Mother Nature. I turned and strode back to the house.

Later, Hailey stopped by with the daily egg delivery. At least the chickens were one thing I didn't have to worry about. "Come in," I said.

Hailey stopped in the entry. "Wow, it's so… different."

"I've been cleaning out fifty years of stuff. I'm taking some of it to the Salvation Army in town today."

"I can help."

"Are you sure? I've got a bunch of other errands too."

"I'll go tell my dad."

She bounded out the door. I followed with the truck keys.

The old truck turned over after three tries. The column shift creaked as I put her in gear and parked next to the front porch. I loved the old truck. Papa called her Old Red.

Hailey returned practically skipping. We loaded up the truck and drove into town.

Hailey talked nonstop. Within the first mile I learned she would turn eighteen in December, her dad was overly protective, and living in town with her mom was not an option.

"What do you want to do after graduation?" I asked.

"I'm going to get a job, save my money, and go to college in the fall."

"Where do you want to go?"

"Same place you did. UC Davis."

"How did you know I went there?"

"Everyone knows everything about everybody in the valley. And your grandmother told me all about you. She was so proud of you. How you graduated with a master's degree, went to France, and were living at a winery with a handsome Frenchman and doing research. It sounds so idyllic."

I laughed and shook my head. Not anymore. The Frenchman hardly called me these days. Clos de l'Harmonie had wedged a divide in our path.

"And what do you want to study?" I asked.

"The same thing you did. Viticulture and enology."

"I'm impressed."

We passed a billboard. "Protect our water and way of life. Don't frack," I read out loud.

"Oh, Dad talks about that all the time. He says there's big money in it."

"Nobody is fracking in the valley. We're all farmers."

After we dropped off the truckload of clothing and household donations, I pulled into a parking space in front of Violet's Café. "Let's get lunch. I'll buy."

"Here?" Hailey stared at the restaurant.

"Yes, my friend owns it."

"I've always wanted to come here."

"Your dad doesn't go out to eat?"

"Not to an organic place."

"How about your mom?"

"Never, she's too preoccupied with getting stoned, and she's always broke."

We were seated by the window. Violet came out of the kitchen to greet us. Her petite frame was out of proportion to the long auburn braid swaying down her back.

"It's about time you came into town," Violet said.

I hadn't seen Violet since the funeral. "This is my neighbor, Hailey. Hailey, this is Violet."

"Nice to meet you," Hailey said.

"The pleasure is all mine." Violet winked at her.

"I have news," I said.

"Congratulations on the vineyard," Violet said.

"How did you know?"

"The whole valley knows. When you didn't renew Tom's contract for future grape harvests he whined for sympathy in the tavern." Violet's brown eyes danced over me.

"Those grapes are coming into their own. They're going to keep getting better," I said. I thought of the next preparation I needed to spray and the cover crops to be planted this month. "I can't bear to watch his crew drive off with our grapes. He's got the Cabernet Franc left and then he's done, hopefully today."

"I need to get cooking, but I'll be back to talk. Today's menu is on the wall." Violet pointed to a large sheet of butcher paper tacked to the wall as she hurried back to the kitchen.

"Everything is organic and grown within fifty miles of here. Violet is a serious locavore," I said.

Hailey studied the menu. "What's a locavore?"

"A person who only eats locally grown food."

"I have no idea what any of the dishes are," Hailey said. "What's rocket salad?"

"Arugula. A spicy green. Everything is delicious here."

Annie, the waitress, appeared. "Sorry about your grandmother," she said. "I didn't get a chance to talk with you at the funeral, there were so many people."

"Thanks for coming, Annie." Tears welled up, and I tried not to cry.

"They will be missed in the valley. They were good people. Always willing to help others," Annie said.

We ordered iced tea, two different salads, and a Gorgonzola pizza with caramelized onions and pears.

"I've never had pears on a pizza," Hailey said.

"They're from our orchard," I said.

I pointed out the glass case filled with pastries made with fruit from Clos de l'Harmonie.

After we finished eating, Violet came out and handed me a bag of pastries.

"Come over some evening," I said.

"Ha! You know I get up at three in the morning to bake. Two of the hotels are serving my pastries. I can barely keep up."

We hugged goodbye. "The apples are almost ready," I said. "Oh, I meant to ask you for your contractor's phone number. I'm going to start remodeling."

"He moved up north. Let me know if you find one. I'm thinking of adding on here."

Back in the truck we made a few stops for supplies. Our final stop, the farm supply store, was for chicken feed. I stopped and read the bulletin board. Various livestock were for sale, short-term laborers were needed, and lots of hay was for sale. I pulled off two cards for remodeling contractors.

"Let's go. I have a hundred things to do at Harmonie," I said.

We drove back to the farm. Hailey picked up the two business cards. "My dad knows a good contractor. He can build anything."

"I'll have to get his number."

I drove up the long driveway to the house. The wheels crushed the wild chamomile, and the sun-kissed scent spiraled in the air along with dust.

"Oh no, now what?" I said. Tom's truck was in the driveway, and he sat on the porch like he owned the place. I backed the truck into the carport.

Tom stood as we approached the porch. "You two look like trouble."

"I don't have time for trouble," I said. Or you.

"No, I guess you don't." Tom peered around at the farm. "You've certainly got your hands full here."

"What can I help you with?" I asked.

"You're all business. I won't beat around the bush, then. I want to buy the farm."

"It's not for sale."

"Olivia, we all know you're in over your head here. You won't be able to manage this operation."

"I have some things to repair and update, but I'm managing just fine."

"I'll give you a week to reconsider. By the way, we completed the harvest today."

"Good. Bring me the grape spoils as soon as you can."

"You really want the grape spoils?"

"It's in the contract. We compost them. Have a nice day, Tom." I unlocked the front door, and Hailey and I went inside.

We watched him drive down the driveway, and instead of turning onto the road toward town, he turned up the Haywards' driveway.

"Have a nice day, Tom," Hailey mimicked and burst out laughing.

I had to laugh too, but not for long. I had work to do with the harvest complete. The planets were aligned for an application of preparation 500, a rich humus, one of the nine biodynamic preparations. It was made from cow manure stored in female cow horns and placed in the ground over winter. I would bury this year's cow horns next week when Cody arrived.

Hailey followed me out to the barn. The previous spring, I had dug up the cow horns I'd prepared and placed the rich humus into glazed earthenware jars and stored them in the barn in a box lined with peat.

I measured a small amount of the rich, sweet smelling powder into a ceramic vessel, added water, and began to stir.

"What does it do?" Hailey asked.

"I'll spray it at the base of the vines, and it will enhance the soil and allow the vines to receive planetary forces."

"What?"

Hailey's expression made me laugh. "Okay, in short, it acts on the vines' central nervous system, and the roots grow vertically downward."

I continued to stir the mixture. "Next week it will be time to bury next year's horns. My friend from school is coming for the ceremony."

"The ceremony?"

"When we bury the cow horns we thank the earth and the stars."

"My dad is right."

"What do you mean?"

"He calls you a voodoo vintner."

"Ha! Tell him there is no matter without spirit and no spirit without matter. It's not voodoo, it's biodynamics."

Hailey pondered this as I methodically stirred the liquid.

"How long do you stir?" she asked.

"About an hour, until it's fully dynamized."

"I'd like to stay, but I've got chores," Hailey said. "I'll see you tomorrow."

Methodically stirring was like meditation. A calm came over me, and my thoughts became reflective as I focused on the vortex created by stirring.

I emptied the contents of the vessel into the sprayer and hooked the sprayer to the back of the old quad, the vineyard workhorse. I hopped on the quad and began to spray row after row of vines, periodically checking my phone. Luke hadn't called. I'd left him a message yesterday but had heard nothing back. The harvest kept him busy, and the nine-hour time difference didn't help. In Bandol, it was already the middle of the night. I'd try him in the morning. At dusk, I parked the quad. Tomorrow I planned a full day of spraying.

Inside, the house loomed bare and deserted. I picked up the two contractor cards and sat on the front porch with my notebook. The list of projects grew.

I called the number on the first card.

A man's voice answered. "Yeah?"

"Hi, I'm looking for someone to remodel a tasting room and do structural improvements to an old barn."

"What's your timeline?"

"I need to be finished by December, for the holidays."

The man laughed. "Listen, sweetie, I'm booked till June."

"June? Wow, okay, thanks."

I dialed the next number. "This number is no longer in service."
I sat in the dark and thought of Luke, so very far away.

Chapter Twenty-One

*I*n the morning, I sent Luke a text. "I miss you! Call me when you can. XXOO." I sat on the porch with a cup of coffee and ate one of Violet's apricot pastries. The flaky crust melted in my mouth and the apricot was tangy. Perfection. She was a master baker. I added the orchard to my list. I would try and share the orchard tasks with the orchardist to keep the costs down, at least in the near term. I knew I couldn't do everything myself.

I walked over to Leroy's to get the name of the contractor. The moment I stepped onto his land the hair on my arms stood on end. What was it about his property? Harmonie had the opposite feeling. It enveloped you in peace.

I pulled the rope to ring the bell on the door, and Leroy stepped onto the porch.

"Good morning," I said.

"Hailey's still asleep. What do you want?"

"Hailey mentioned you know a remodeling contractor. I wanted to get his number."

"Are you really going to stay here? Why not sell to Tom and get on with your life?"

"This is my life. I'm going to make the best wine this region has ever tasted."

"Well, I have big plans too."

"What are they?"

"I'm going to expand my cattle ranch and more, much, much more."

I smiled. People loved their land here.

"Listen, Olivia, sell your farm to Tom and save yourself some heartache."

"Can I get the number of the contractor?"

"Hold on." Leroy went inside and came back with a business card.

"Thanks. Good luck with your plans, Leroy."

I walked back to Harmonie as quickly as I could without running. The vibes from Leroy and his property made me uneasy. Poor Hailey. No wonder she needed excuses to get away.

My phone rang, and I almost dropped it. It was Mom. I'd hoped to see Luke's picture pop up.

"Olivia, we haven't seen you in weeks. Come down to the boat today for a picnic. You can spend the night."

"Too much to do here. I'm spraying the vines. The planets are aligned."

"The planets? Do you really believe that hocus pocus?"

"I do. Speaking of hocus pocus, do you think Leroy is a little crazy?"

"More than a little. Why?"

"Never mind. Hailey is a good kid though."

"Why don't you bring her down sometime? Dad can take you sailing."

"Maybe this winter. I have too much to do here."

"Can you pencil us in sometime?"

"I'll come down next month. What do you hear from Jameson? He doesn't respond to me. Is he upset over the will?"

This was met with silence.

"Mom, are you there?"

"Well, to be honest, we are all still surprised. If my parents had at least talked to me, I would have changed their minds."

"Mom, this is my dream. I'm living my dream."

"Well, it sounds like a nightmare to me."

"Bye, Mom. Tell Dad hi for me."

I slumped in the chair on the porch. No one was happy with me. Not Mom, not Jameson, and not Luke.

I held out the contractor's business card and dialed the number. I had to keep moving forward.

Chapter Twenty-Two

The contractor showed up late afternoon. I stopped spraying and walked over to his pickup truck.

He held out his hand. "I'm Peter."

"Olivia." I shook his hand and winced from his strength.

Peter was a burly man with curly red hair. His eyes sparkled as he took in the vines, house, and barn. "Nice little spread you have here."

"It needs a little help," I said.

I led him to the barn and laid out my plans. "I want to change the layout of the tasting room after the structure is shored up." I handed Peter the rough drawing. I had gotten ideas from Domaine Laroche for a better flow for wine tasting. I had big plans for the tasting room. My future relied on quality wine and sales.

He nodded. "No problem."

I led him through the wine storage and wine-making areas to a large unused area at the back of the barn. "And back here, I want to create sort of a dorm with three rooms for sleeping, a bathroom, and communal kitchen with a separate entrance out the back."

"For workers?" Peter asked.

I nodded.

"That's a lot of expense for workers."

"They'll have an option to stay over on our long days or harvest nights and not have to drive fifty miles each way. You probably know better than anyone there is no affordable housing in the valley."

"I can start the tasting room, but this will need a permit. Is your father on board with this plan?"

"My father is not involved. I own the farm."

Peter studied me intently, his green eyes locked with mine. "You own the farm?"

"That's right."

"You're a lucky lady."

I smiled and nodded. "When can you start?"

"I have a small window before I start building a new house. I can start Wednesday. In the meantime, I'll draw up the plans for the permit."

"Thank you, Peter." I reached out my hand to shake his. This time I expected his vise-like grip. "I have to finish spraying."

Back on the quad, I watched Peter go down the driveway and turn into the driveway next door to Leroy's house.

Oh boy, my life here was an open book.

On the morning of the autumn equinox, the day of the cow horn ceremony, Cody arrived. I watched him bounce up the rutted driveway in his Toyota pickup. He sprang out, his brown hair cut short and neat as usual. Sunglasses hid his eyes and he wore blue jeans and a faded Neil Young concert T-shirt. He loved music. Any music. We had talked by phone and messages. He was sad about Nana passing away and incredulous I inherited the farm.

We got into Old Red and drove to a neighbor's organic beef farm. I needed fresh cow manure for the horns. We shoveled fresh cow patties into a barrel and drove back to the farm. Hailey sat on the porch, reading a book.

"Cody!" she called.

"You know each other?" I said.

"I met her last summer when I stopped by. She hung out with your nana."

We carted the barrel to the side of the barn, and I retrieved six female cow horns from the shed where the biodynamic preparations were stored.

"Here's what we do," I said. "Take a horn and tamp the manure into it."

"I don't know about this biodynamic stuff. This seems kind of wacky," Cody said.

Hailey stood watching, her eyes wide.

"After we bury these for six months it turns into spiritual manure," I said. "Full of enzymes and organisms, a life-giving fertilizer."

I walked the tray of horns to the side of the pasture where stakes marked a spot and set them down. Cody held the shovel and began to dig a square in the area where I had buried horns for the past two seasons.

Peter, who had been at work in the tasting room, stepped outside and came over. "What in the world are those?"

I set the horns in the bottom of the pit.

"Spiritual manure," Hailey said.

"Spiritual manure?" Peter repeated.

"We'll dig them up in six months at the spring equinox. Steiner, a leader of the biodynamic movement, called horn manure a living oil for the biological wheels of life," I said.

"I can't imagine how these six horns will have any effect on all these vines," Cody said.

"I don't know," Peter said. "Tom is secretly raving about his harvest here. He's vying to get next year's too."

"Ha! Not on my life," I said.

Cody and I took turns with the shovel covering the horns with dirt. I thought of Luke. He too would have buried cow horns today at Domaine Laroche.

Peter went back to work in the tasting room.

"Now we're on to the orchard," I said. "The apples are starting to fall."

"I'll help," Hailey said.

"I smell an apple pie in my future," Cody said.

Hailey laughed. "All right. I'm trying to perfect Nana's recipe."

"She taught you to bake?" I said.

Hailey nodded.

"Wow, she really liked you. Her recipes are sacred," I said.

"She didn't write them down. She just showed me," Hailey said.

We picked apples and packed boxes as Cody and I caught up on the past few months.

"Have you found any leads for a permanent job?" I asked.

"I made appointments at two wineries while I'm down here. I'd like to find a place here and establish roots. No one wants to hire an outsider. When Molly graduates in May, she wants to set up her veterinarian practice here in the valley."

I stopped and stretched. "You can stay here and help out. I could give you room and board, but until I get the tasting room up and running again I can't pay you. My only income is from wine sales to restaurants around the county and loyal Harmonie customers."

"Really? You've got yourself a deal." Cody reached over and gave me a high five.

Hailey made a pouch in her T-shirt and loaded it with six apples. "I'm going to make a pie. Okay if I use your kitchen?"

"Of course," I said. "I need to deliver these to Violet."

"I'll go," Cody said.

"Okay. Have her sign a receipt for the six boxes." I needed to invoice customers but hadn't had the time. Money matters were still handled loosely in the valley.

My phone rang. Probably Mom again. Luke's picture smiled at me from the phone.

"*Bonjour*, Luke!" I waved at Cody and headed to the porch.

"*Bonne nuit, ma chérie.* How are the cow horns?"

"Properly buried for next spring. And yours?"

"In the ground under the ascending moon."

"I miss you," I said. "It's so lonely here."

"You're lonely. I'm lonely. And Pepin is lonely. She still sits outside your old cottage and waits for you."

That made me smile. "Are you still coming in November?"

"Yes, but now not until after the Paris wine fair. I could come for your American turkey day."

"Oh." Thanksgiving seemed like an eternity away. "Cody's here. He's going to stay on and help for room and board until he finds a permanent job."

"Cody's there? He's going to stay in the house?"

He sounded wounded.

"Yes."

"I don't like that arrangement, Olivia."

"I need some help."

"I know you need help, but does he have to stay with you?"

"That's his form of payment."

"Geez, Olivia. I miss you so much and can't stop thinking about you. Now I have to worry about him getting to you."

"You have me, Luke. No one else will get to me, as you put it. He has a girlfriend in Davis."

Silence. I could picture him brooding. He was possessive, but he knew what he wanted.

"Luke?"

"I'm here. I don't know how this is going to work. My vision for our life in France is falling apart."

"It's not falling apart, it's changed. When you're here in person we'll figure it out. The tasting room remodel is almost done, and the permit for the workers' living quarters should be approved soon. Everything is going well."

I continued to fill Luke in on the goings-on at Harmonie, and he listened in silence. I stopped. "How's your family?" I asked.

"Angelica is pregnant, and my mother is ecstatic. Lili is entwined with the California guy. He's back in Los Angeles, and she's moping around."

I laughed. "I know the feeling. I'll send her a message."

"Good night, *ma chérie*."

"Do you have to go?" I wanted to hear his voice a bit longer.

"I'm not much of a phone talker. I'd rather hold you in my arms."

I closed my eyes at the thought. I would rather be in his arms. "*Bon nuit*, Luke. I love you."

"*Bonne nuit.*"

The call had ended. I sat back with my eyes closed. I felt wretched. Wasn't love supposed to make you happy? He hadn't said he loved me back, and now I wouldn't see him until late-November.

Chapter Twenty-Three

The roosters woke me at dawn. I heard Cody in the kitchen. My mental list flashed before me. I needed to spend time on invoices and bills. I was still sorting through the farm paperwork. But first up today we were planting the cover crop between the vines: mustard, peas, and fava beans.

I sat down on the front porch with coffee and checked my messages. I hoped for something from Luke, but there was no response to my late-night message. Lili had responded though.

Olivia, happy to hear from you. Jon went back to California to start a movie. I'm so lonely! I hope to come out to visit him this winter. Speaking of lonely, in the evenings I see Luke and Pepin sitting in front of your old cottage staring into the night. We are all so happy about your inheritance, but we miss you. Kisses, Lili

Luke told me Pepin sat there, but it was both of them. I put my head in my hands and closed my eyes, picturing them. What was I trying to prove here? My heart torn between this farm and Luke.

The screen door creaked open. "What's the matter? Money woes?" Cody asked.

I sat up and shook my head. He handed me a plate of pastries Violet had sent home with him yesterday. "These will cheer you up."

I took one. "Thanks. Are you ready to plant?"

"Just waiting for your lazy bones to get up."

I laughed. It was six thirty a.m.

The planets lined up in root days for the next two and a half days. We had our work cut out for us. Cody brought out his speaker and played music as we walked up each row sowing seeds with a seeder. Midmorning, I heard a loud rumble. A semitruck, loaded with large well casings, slowly rolled up Leroy's driveway. He must be drilling a new well. He had recently dug two huge ponds. Ponds attracted wildlife. It was a good thing.

I continued with the seeding. In the spring, we'd till these plants into the soil to fix nitrogen. Spring seemed a long way off. I counted the days until November when Luke would come for Thanksgiving. I envisioned his handsome face smiling from the opposite end of the dining room table, across from Dad. Thanksgiving at Harmonie was a tradition, and I intended to keep it. The one trip to the farm Mom put up with was Thanksgiving at Harmonie. Peter promised the tasting room would be finished by mid-November. I could open for the holiday season.

I was determined to make my grandparents proud, and maybe even Mom. This time next year the farm would be certified, the tasting room thriving, and my first batch of certified bio wine aging. I envisioned Violet catering wine dinners in the summer. I smiled, but it was short lived. I was in a fairy tale. Everything around me needed updating. The house paint peeled, the fence needed repair, the driveway a washboard… and the list kept growing.

That night at the big desk in the living room I worked through bills. Everything was organized but the accounting had been recorded by hand in a ledger. It clearly needed automating. There was a box with unopened mail I needed to go through. What surprises did it hold?

Cody bounded down the stairs, his hair still wet from the shower. "I'm going to the tavern. Do you want to come?"

"No thanks."

"You work too hard."

"Nothing I do here ever feels like work."

"Well, I'm going to hang out with the locals to try and network a job."

"Don't try too hard. I need you around here for a little while! Can you mend fences?" I asked.

"Sure."

"Network an accountant who will trade for wine," I called.

I found the wine inventory ledger and studied it. We kept separate inventories for the barrels and bottled wine. I knew all the vintages from working beside Papa over the years. A lot of wine was ready to bottle this winter. Our first 100 percent biodynamic grapes were aging in barrels. These vintages would need good labels to honor them even though we couldn't label them biodynamic.

I added labels to my list. Getting labels approved took time and patience. Nana, who had overseen the labels, probably had designs started somewhere. I could only hope, as I was no artist. Jameson was the one who took after Nana in that way. I hoped he was sketching in prison to pass the time.

I filled the bath, poured a glass of wine, and sank into the hot water. I drifted off to sleep thinking of Luke and Pepin sitting outside my old cottage.

Chapter Twenty-Four

On Friday, Cody headed up to Davis to spend the weekend with his girlfriend. I walked up to the oak trees on the highest point of the property and began collecting oak bark. I planned to make the bio preparation 505 to prevent vine disease. Tomorrow I would bury it in a pit until next spring. A loud rumble from below grew louder. A large piece of equipment on an oversize truck moved up Leroy's driveway. Now what? It resembled a well drilling rig. I needed to find the water right paperwork for the Harmonie well, our only water source. Leroy's new well better not interfere with our well's production.

I scraped off another chunk of bark and added it to the basket. Below, a small white pickup truck turned up the Harmonie driveway and slowly made its way to the parking area by the tasting room, out of view. It was probably one of Peter's workers. He had a large job to start and wanted to get Harmonie finished. He had gutted the worker housing area to build it out once the permit was issued. I made a mental note to call the building department again and see what was taking so long.

After I had collected enough bark I made my way down to the house. I came around the side of the house, and a man in his late twenties was seated on the porch, his brown curls shining in the afternoon sun. I stopped. He hadn't seen me approach.

The screen door creaked open and another young man with longish blond hair appeared.

"Jameson?"

"There you are. You really should lock your door out here."

I ran up the porch steps. He stood smiling. I hugged him tight.

"Geez, see I told you she'd want to see me."

"You're out." He appeared healthy. A bit thin and pale, but his eyes sparkled.

"I am," he said. "This is my college buddy, Caleb."

Caleb stood up and reached out his hand.

"Nice to meet you," I said.

"The pleasure is mine. I've heard all about this wine-making sister."

I turned back to Jameson. "You're out early."

Jameson shrugged. "Time off for good behavior, and then there is the problem of overcrowded jails."

"I'm glad you're here," I said.

Jameson pointed to my bucket. "What's that?"

"Oak bark. I'm going to place it in a cow skull, bury it over the winter, dig it up next spring, and add it to the compost."

"What's the point?" Jameson said.

"It provides healing forces to combat plant disease," I said.

"Mom is right. You are practicing witchcraft in the vineyard."

"It's not witchcraft. It's biodynamic farming."

"A cow skull?" Jameson said.

"Yes, it's out in the freezer in the barn. You need to keep the membrane lining fresh before you pack it. Preparation 505 is the brain of compost."

"Jesus, Olivia. Do you howl at the moon too?" Jameson said.

"Sure," I said. "Whenever I feel like it. But mostly when the moon stands in Ram, Lion, or Archer." Did Jameson's chip on his shoulder have to do with me inheriting the farm?

"No, there is something to it," Caleb said. "When I worked as a chef we got our best produce from a biodynamic farm."

I sat down in one of the rockers. "So, what are your plans?"

"Well, that's just it. I don't have a plan other than I need to find work, as does Caleb. He's taking a break from the Bay Area."

"Have you been to Mom and Dad's yet?"

"We stopped by this morning. Mom means well, but she makes me nervous with all her questions. Questions I don't have answers to."

"I'm sorry you couldn't make it to Nana's funeral," I said.

Jameson stretched out his hands and stared at them. "Yeah, me too."

"How do you feel about me inheriting the farm?"

"I'm fine with it. You're the only one in the family who really cares for it. I mean the idea of owning a winery and vineyard is cool, but I wouldn't know the first thing about what to do here," Jameson said.

"Do you want to stay and find out? I can feed you, and your old room is the way you left it."

He squinted at Caleb. "What about my buddy?"

"What about it, Caleb? Do you want to stay and work here?" I said.

Caleb scrutinized the orchard and vineyard. "That would be awesome. Really awesome. Thank you."

"You'll have to sleep on the couch, but I'm building a bunkhouse in the barn. So, you were a chef?"

"A chef, handyman, orchard hand, gardener, poet, you name it, I've probably done it."

Caleb's clear blue eyes held mine. They were beautiful. "Well, I could use all of those," I said, though I wasn't sure where the poet fit in.

At the end of the driveway the school bus pulled away. Hailey walked toward the house. She had been making a habit of hanging out on Fridays and weekends. Jameson watched her as she approached. "Who's that?" he asked.

"The girl next door."

Hailey paused at the bottom step. She took in Caleb and Jameson. Except she kept taking in Jameson. I could feel the energy between them. Finally, Hailey met my gaze. "Are you busy?"

"Come on up. I want you to meet my brother, Jameson, and his friend Caleb."

Jameson stood and reached out his hand. "I'm Jameson."

"I know; I can see the resemblance." She shook his hand for a long moment. Time seemed to stand still, and the light over the vineyard seemed clearer.

Chapter Twenty-Five

I went out to the porch to call Luke. The morning mist settled, coating the valley with a whisper of white.

"Olivia," Luke said.

"I have good news."

"You're at the Marseille airport and need a ride?" he said.

"Jameson is here. I'm so happy."

"He's out? How is he?"

"Feisty, resentful, and he thinks I'm a witch, but he's good. He's going to stay here for a while."

"I'm happy. He'll keep you company."

"Oh, and he brought a friend."

"A friend?"

"Caleb. They met in college. He's going to stay too."

This was met by silence.

"Luke?"

"I'm sorry, Olivia. I don't know how to say this politely, but what are you doing? Opening a boardinghouse?"

"He's my brother." I tried to swallow, but the lump in my throat had swelled.

"And this Caleb guy?"

I took a deep breath and exhaled. "They want to work, and they don't want to be in the city. Caleb is a chef, a handyman, gardener, orchard hand. I need all those skills here. His dad owns an orchard up north. So now I have three workers, not including the girl next door."

"The girl next door?"

"Hailey. She wants to be my apprentice."

"I can't picture this."

"I can't do everything. I need help."

"I know. I'm worried about you. I wish I was there or better yet, you were here, but I'll see you in six weeks, *ma chérie*."

"I can't wait that long."

"Me either, but you're in my dreams, both day and night," Luke said.

I closed my eyes. "What are you doing right now?"

"We're harvesting the Mourvèdre. I'm standing in the middle of the plot."

I could smell the Bandol earth, the piney shrubs and spicy flowers, and felt the warmth of the sun.

"*Au revoir*, I have to keep picking."

"Tell everyone hi."

The screen door squeaked open. I needed to oil it.

Jameson stepped out on the porch. "You're up early."

"I could say the same for you," I said. In the recent past, he had never gotten up before noon.

He sat next to me. "Mom called me last night. They're coming up tomorrow. She said they'd bring lunch."

She was coming up for Jameson. She hadn't been here since the first time we came up together after the funeral. "I'm glad she's bringing food because I have a hundred things to do tomorrow."

"On a Sunday?"

"A biodynamic farm is governed by celestial rhythms. The lunar cycles, solar cycles, the constellations, and the movement of the planets."

The screen creaked, and Caleb appeared with two cups of coffee and handed one to Jameson. "Thanks. Celestial rhythms?" Jameson shook his head, grinning.

"We plan vineyard tasks around the position of the sun, moon, stars, and planets. Life comes from the whole universe, not just the earth."

Jameson's laugh boomed through the vineyard. "So, my little sister, what is your task today, besides burying a cow skull filled with oak bark?"

I started laughing too. It did sound cultish. "I'm spraying horn silica, one of the nine bio preparations, on some of the vines."

"Why, pray tell?" Jameson asked.

"Silica contains forces that originate with distant planets, the warm planets, Mars, Jupiter, and Saturn. Silica allows the cosmic forces to be absorbed by the earth and gives plants the ability to assimilate sunlight and be pulled from above. Cosmic matter into matter."

"Silica? Forces? Distant planets? Cosmic matter? I'm worried about you," Jameson said.

"It's spiritual science. The soil where light reaches the earth needs to be receptive to cosmic forces for plant growth. Will you at least read about it, because that's what we do here?"

"I'll read about it," Caleb said. "Do you bury the silica too?"

I nodded. "In cow horns."

"Hmm," Caleb said.

I didn't mention the dandelion 506, the chamomile 503, or the yarrow 502 preparations, which all were buried in animal organs. Caleb was a chef. I could enlist his help with those.

Hailey appeared with a basket of eggs. What was going on? Everyone was up so early.

"Well, if it's not the girl next door," Jameson said.

"She has a name," I said.

"Hailey, Hailey, Hailey. A song in my heart," Jameson said.

Hailey smiled and dipped her head. I'd never seen her shy before. Jameson could be so charming when he wanted, but with me he had an attitude. I stood up. "I've got to spray."

"Pluto is calling," Jameson said.

"Actually, today it's Virgo."

Caleb reached for the eggs. "Omelets?"

"Yes, thanks," Jameson said.

I glanced back as I walked. Jameson and Hailey sat talking on the porch.

In the barn, I mixed the silica and hooked the sprayer on the old quad bike. I drove through row after row, spraying silica upward in a fine mist, and thought of Luke picking grapes in France, a world away from Harmonie. I smiled, imagining what he thought of my new workforce. Cody had a master's degree in viticulture, he just didn't know biodynamics. Caleb could help in the orchard, fix things, and I could put him to work on the bio preparations. But Jameson? Well, I'd try him out everywhere.

I drove back to the barn to refill the sprayer. I had to hurry, it was warming up. The trio walked toward me.

"What do you want us to do?" Jameson said.

"We need a load of manure to start a new compost pile. I've made arrangements with an organic farm in Los Alamos to pick it up today."

"You're kidding, right?" Jameson said.

"The keys are in Old Red," I said. "I know you know how to drive it." He used to coast down the driveway after he thought Papa was asleep. He'd start it at the road and be back by dawn.

"I'm not picking up a load of shit," Jameson said.

"I'll go with you," Hailey said. "I know the farm. Wait until you taste the honey they sell."

Jameson glowered at me and turned back to Hailey. "Okay. You're on Hailey's comet."

Caleb and I exchanged a smile. "What can I do?" Caleb asked.

"You get to pick apricots and deliver them to a local café."

"Apricots?" Jameson shook his head and headed for the truck. "He gets apricots and I get shit."

At noon on Sunday I stopped work and cleaned up. I got out the new French-print tablecloth I'd bought at the Bandol outdoor market. I set it on the picnic table out back, under the shade of a giant oak tree. I placed a vase of flowers in the center and arranged the plates and glasses and set out a large bowl of apricots.

I stepped out on the front porch with my notebook to wait. Caleb sat reading a biodynamic farm manual, but Jameson just stared down the driveway. "There are books and magazines in the house," I said.

"Yeah, I saw them. The *Farmers' Almanac* and *Wine Spectator*. Not too exciting," Jameson said.

"I've got a stack of novels you can read. They're in my bedroom."

"Your bedroom? You mean our grandparents' bedroom."

"Jesus, Jameson," Caleb said.

"Sorry, Olivia. I'm, well—still getting used to things."

"I get it," I said.

"No, you don't. You have no idea what months in prison was like. It makes me edgy."

"One day at a time, buddy," Caleb said. "So, Olivia, tell me about this Violet woman I met yesterday. She owns the café?"

"Oh God, here they are," Jameson said.

Mom and Dad's convertible Mercedes coupe eased up the driveway. Of course, the top wasn't down. Mom stepped out with her hair perfectly coiffed, wearing a white tailored shirt, legging jeans, and a peach-colored floral silk scarf that flowed around her neck, setting off her golden hair. Dad fit right into the valley, wearing well-worn jeans, a jean shirt, and cowboy boots. He carried the picnic basket up the steps. Mom followed.

"Where's your horse, Dad?" Jameson asked.

"At the marina, Son." He set the basket down.

I laughed. I would have never asked him that.

Caleb stood and shook his hand. "Good afternoon, Theo." He nodded to Mom. "Nice to see you, Eve."

"How are you boys doing out here in the boonies?" Mom asked.

I turned my gaze to Jameson. He mouthed the word *boys*.

"It's awesome," Caleb said. "I stuffed and buried a cow head for the spring, picked apricots, and shoveled cow manure for the new compost pile."

Mom wrinkled her nose. "Ew."

"That's what I said," Jameson agreed.

"Well, there's no shortage of things to do around here," Dad said.

"Come on, Dad. I'll show you the remodeling, and we can pick out some wine. Mom, do you want to see the soon-to-be new tasting room? I could use your advice on decorating it."

"No, I'll stay here with the boys. I don't do rustic."

I turned and walked down the porch stairs. Tears stung my eyes. She had no interest at all. I'd envisioned us working together on ideas to decorate the tasting room. And *rustic* was not the theme. Dad caught up with me and put his arm around my shoulder, and the tears really began to flow.

"What's the matter, Livie? Are you sad about Nana?"

I nodded. He handed me a white handkerchief with his initials.

"Come on now, I want to see this new tasting room."

We stepped inside. "Wow, beautiful design and workmanship. You can fit forty people in here."

"Fifty, actually. There's going to be seating in the middle where tasters can take their pour or buy a glass or bottle and relax. And I can hold events. I took some ideas from Domaine Laroche."

"Ah, speaking of Domaine Laroche, Luke called me."

"Luke? He called you?" He hardly called me lately.

"Yes, he seems very serious about you. He wanted to let me know he's coming over in November. How's this relationship going to work, Livie?"

"I honestly don't know. Right now, we have parallel lives, but I want to be with him."

"Well, Mom thinks you should sell and get on with your life."

"I'll never sell Harmonie. Never."

He followed me into the barrel room. Half of the room held barrels of wine and the rest held boxed cases. I flipped open the notebook.

"I have a 2013 Grenache Blanc in the fridge. You get to pick a red."

He ran his finger down the ledger. "How about the 2011 Grenache Syrah?"

"Perfect."

We gathered at the picnic table, and Dad opened the wine. Jameson poured iced tea. Caleb, Dad, and I sipped the Grenache Syrah, Mom the Grenache Blanc.

Dad had gone all out at the gourmet deli with the picnic. We passed around the food and made small talk. It was pleasant under the big oak.

"You should see the house I'm working on," Mom said. "Spectacular views, and they've given me free rein with ideas. There are two living rooms, and I've ordered gorgeous fabric from Schumacher."

"Who needs two living rooms?" I asked.

"Everyone has two living rooms now," Mom said.

"I thought people were downsizing, smaller is better, less of a carbon footprint," I said.

"Not in Montecito," Dad said.

Hailey walked around the corner in white shorts and a Minnie Mouse T-shirt. "Oh, sorry. I didn't know you were entertaining."

"Join us," I said.

She hesitated. Jameson moved down the bench. "There's room," he said.

"You remember my parents?" I asked.

"Of course I do. Nice to see you." She slid in next to Jameson.

He poured her a glass of tea. "Food?"

She nodded, and he handed her a plate.

"Caleb, tell me what you taste in the wine?" I said.

He held it up and sniffed. "Vanilla bean, some kind of baking spices, maybe an herb." He took a sip. "Definitely boysenberry and some other fruit."

"Not bad," I said.

Hailey's plate of food was piled high, and she ate quickly. She seemed insatiable. Did Leroy buy any healthy food? I imagined boxes of mac and cheese, the refrigerator chock full of beer, and not the local craft brew, but Bud Light.

After more small talk Mom and Dad stood to leave.

"Can't you stay longer?" I asked.

"Cocktail party at the Larsens'," Mom said.

Jameson smirked. "Do people still have cocktail parties?"

"I want to have Thanksgiving here, like always," I said.

Mom and Dad exchanged a glance.

"Luke will be here. His first American Thanksgiving," I said.

"We're looking forward to it," Dad said. "And let me know when you're ready to bottle. I'll take off work to help."

I smiled. For some reason, all seemed well with the world. I walked them out through the house. "Mom, I have a bunch of Nana's things in boxes I want you to take sometime. Or Jameson can drive them down."

"Can I talk to you about Jameson?" she said.

I nodded. Here goes.

"Keep an eye on him. And keep him busy."

"Anybody staying here is going to keep busy," I said.

"And one more thing. Can you talk to Hailey?"

"About what?"

"She shouldn't wear white after Labor Day."

"Geez, Mom. We're in the valley in the backyard of a farmhouse, not at the yacht club."

"Well, I can see you two have a bond, and she needs some guidance. Her parents sure won't be any help there."

"Sure, Mom."

I walked back through the house. In the kitchen, Caleb and Hailey were putting away the food. Jameson sat alone outside at the picnic table studying the wine labels.

I walked out and sat down.

"Okay. Give it to me straight. What did she tell you to do with me?" Jameson said.

"Nothing."

"Come on, she always has the last word of advice."

"She told me to tell Hailey she shouldn't wear white after Labor Day."

He squinted at me and cocked his head. His laughter boomed. It was contagious. We both laughed so hard we cried.

Caleb and Hailey came out. "What's so funny?" Caleb asked.

"My mother," I said. We started laughing again and couldn't stop.

Chapter Twenty-Six

*E*arly Monday morning I tiptoed into the living room, but Caleb was already up waiting for the coffee to brew in the kitchen. I sat at the desk in the living room and recorded the past week's bio preparations and applications.

Caleb brought me a cup of coffee. "Thanks."

"What's all that?" he asked.

"For certification you have to keep records of every preparation made and every application. They're stringent."

"You're really serious about this, aren't you?"

"Harmonie will get certified in January. That will be two full years of bio farming. My grandfather let me give it a go after I was so enthusiastic about it." I took a sip of the steaming brew. "I brought him a bio wine to taste from another vintner up north, and he was hooked."

Cody and Jameson came through the screen door, wearing running shorts and shoes, their T-shirts wet with sweat. And I'd thought they were upstairs sleeping. Cody had gotten back Sunday night and been surprised to find new roommates, but they all seemed to hit it off.

"I didn't know you run," I said to Jameson.

He shrugged. "I'm trying a lot of new things."

"I'll come with you next time," I said.

"What's the plan today, boss lady?" Cody asked.

"Tom is bringing back the grape spoils from the harvest. The moon is descending, so everything is aligned to build a new compost pile. Caleb can help me measure the bio preparations, and you two can build the pile."

"Great," Jameson said. "I'm going to go take a shower so I can shovel shit."

"Violet's coming over for dinner. She's going to help me finalize the tasting room decor," I said.

"The chef from the café?" Caleb asked.

I nodded.

"I'll cook," Caleb said.

"I don't mind cooking," I said.

"Let me cook. I want to try a recipe I've been perfecting in my head," Caleb said.

"Okay," I said. This might work out fine to have a chef in residence.

A half hour later we started to construct the new compost pile into a long windrow alongside last year's. Cody worked the small tractor and scooped the manure into the row. Jameson added straw on top.

A large flatbed truck with wooden sides rumbled up the driveway with the Oak Valley Winery sign on the doors. Tom parked the truck and got out. Three more trucks followed.

"Right on time," I said.

"Looks like you've got some help here," Tom said, eyeing the three men.

"That's right. You remember my brother, Jameson, and this is Cody and Caleb."

"Yes, I remember Jameson, I haven't seen you in a while. What have you been up to?"

"A little of this, a little of that. Just keeping it real," Jameson said.

"Just keeping it real?" Tom repeated. "Real what?"

"You can dump the grape spoils over there." I pointed to a spot next to the windrow of cow manure.

Tom got in the truck, backed it up, and tilted the bed. The grape spoils swooshed down into a heap. I grabbed a rake and got the last of them from the truck bed. Their heady scent swirled in the air.

Tom put the bed down and drove out of the way of the other trucks. He returned to talk. "Those grapes were different from any I've worked with. What do you put in your compost?" he asked.

"Cosmic matter," Jameson said.

I laughed. "Organic manure, straw, grape spoils, dried seaweed. And I add six bio preparations."

"Bio preparations?" Tom said.

"Flowers, buried over the winter in cow skulls, intestines, or bladders," I said.

Tom looked at Jameson. "She's kidding, right?"

"No," Jameson said.

"Why bury them?" Tom asked.

"It concentrates the forces," I said.

"The forces?" Tom's eyebrows raised in a question mark.

"Growth forces. Each preparation has a different force," I said.

"Like what?" Tom asked.

"The oak bark combats vine disease, stinging nettle absorbs iron forces, chamomile stabilizes nitrogen…"

Peter drove up and parked. He got out and waved a bright green paper in the air. "I got your permit."

I smiled. "Finally."

"It had to go through zoning review," Peter said.

"What's the permit for?" Tom asked.

"I'm adding a bunkhouse," I said.

"For workers?" Tom said.

I nodded.

"What are you trying to do, make the rest of us look bad?" Tom asked.

"It has nothing to do with you. I'm providing the option for workers to stay here during the busy seasons and not drive fifty or more miles to work," I said. "Some of the varietals we pick at night."

Tom shook his head and looked at Peter. "What do you think about this loony bio stuff?"

"The cow horn ceremony was interesting," Peter said.

"Cow horn ceremony?" Tom said.

"Never mind. We have to get back to work here," I said. I instructed the other truck drivers where to dump the spoils along the row.

"The cosmic compost calls," Jameson said. "I want to try the tractor."

Peter posted the permit on the barn as Tom drove off.

"I'm going to get building supplies," Peter said as he hopped in his truck.

"Remember, no treated wood," I called.

"I know, I know, but it'll cost you more."

All morning we worked on the compost build. We repeated manure, straw, grape spoils, and seaweed.

In the afternoon Caleb and I went into the barn through the side door to the winery. I stored the bio preps in a protected area of the barn. Some were in clear glass jars, and others, like the valerian tincture, were stored in bottles without air or light. I got out the six needed preparations.

"We're going to measure out ten units of each, and when the compost pile is done, we insert these along the compost row. The valerian we dilute with water and spray on the top of the pile at the end."

I measured a teaspoon of prepared oak bark, misted it with water, and rolled it into a ball. "Ten of these is all you need for ten to fifteen tons of compost."

"For real? Ten little balls?"

I nodded. "Here, you can make nine more. I'll do the chamomile." I handed him the jar and a small glass tray to put the balls on.

When the five preparations were ready, I diluted the valerian tincture with water, stirred, and filled the backpack sprayer.

Jameson and Cody sat in the shade, talking. They stood and walked over. At ten intervals down the row, I made five holes with a rake handle and dropped in the preparations. The balls of oak bark and stinging nettle were set in the center hole.

"I'll spray," Cody said.

"No, I need to do it," I said. "There is a close tie to the farmer and the preparations at this stage."

Jameson rolled his eyes. "A compost connection. Now I've heard everything."

I walked down the row, misting the pile to stimulate the compost. I finished with a surge of energy, a distinct lightness of being.

"That's it. Enough work for you guys today. Thanks. It's a really fine row," I said.

Caleb scanned the compost row and nodded, seeming pleased with the work. "I'm going into town for groceries," he said. "Anyone want to go with me?"

He had no takers.

When Violet arrived, I went outside and waved her over to the tasting room.

"I thought you'd be in the kitchen," Violet said.

"Caleb is cooking."

"Caleb?"

"He's the guy who delivered the apricots. He's a friend of Jameson's."

"So that's his name. He can deliver my fruit anytime," Violet said with a smile that wouldn't quit.

"He's staying here, working. He used to be a chef."

"Used to be?" Violet asked.

"He took some time off. He worked at Boulevard in San Francisco."

"Impressive," Violet said.

We stepped through the door. "Wow, this is amazing. You have much more room. I love the skylights," Violet said.

"It was too dark before. We used too many lights. I need help with the wall color. I'm not sure what I want."

"Why isn't your mom helping with this? She's the interior designer."

"She said she doesn't do rustic."

"Well this isn't rustic anymore. It's got really clean lines and the lighting is so soft," Violet said.

"I'll display wine in these cases, and there's another case for local wine items. You know, corkscrews, coasters, T-shirts."

"The cases and countertops are beautiful. Who built them?"

"Peter. He's a master carpenter. I was thinking of staying with two colors. Off-white walls to set off the dark wood counters. I'll get some local photographs for the walls. Brown couch and chairs set around a large coffee table, like a living room. But I want a different color for the back wall. I just can't envision the color."

"Peach or apricot. It will bring it all together and bring the orchard inside," Violet said.

"That's perfect," I said.

"That was easy. It's going to be stunning. Your mom will flip."

"I hope she likes it. Let's get some wine and have a glass on the porch."

I grabbed two bottles from the cellar behind the tasting room, made a note of them, and we walked into the kitchen.

Caleb was putting nasturtium flowers on the salads. His hair was tied in a man bun, but his curls still escaped. A sauce was simmering on the stove.

I reached in the drawer for a corkscrew and startled him. He had been in his own world.

"Something smells heavenly," I said.

I pulled down three glasses. "Violet, this is Caleb, and vice versa." I was too tired for a lot of formalities.

"Violet. It's nice to see you again." His eyes sparkled.

"Hi again. I didn't know you were staying with Livie."

I handed them both a small pour of wine. "Cheers to today," I said. Glasses clinked.

"I understand you're a chef."

"I was."

"Once a chef, always a chef," Violet said. "It gets in your blood."

He smiled and nodded at her.

"Can we do anything?" I asked. "I can set the table."

"Jameson already did. I'm good here. Dinner will be ready soon."

Jameson set the table? I had to see this. Out the window to the backyard. Jameson, Hailey, and Cody were playing cards at the picnic table under the old glass chandelier that hung from the oak tree.

I picked up the wine, and we walked through the dining room to the porch. The dining room table was set with a tablecloth, Nana's hand-embroidered napkins, water glasses, and a vase of the valerian flowers I grew for preparation 507. I had to smile.

"Wow," Violet said. "I expected pasta and eating on the porch."

We sat on the porch and sipped the 2013 Malbec, a dark beauty with an aroma of coffee and chocolate and a concentrated taste of black and red fruit.

"I envisioned you lonely out here by yourself."

"I'm not lonely. But I do miss Luke." My heart ached for him.

The screen door creaked open. "Time to eat," Hailey said. "Jameson invited me to stay."

"If he hadn't, I would have," I said.

A smile lit up her face. She was so pretty.

Jameson and Cody greeted Violet with a hug. Cody had gotten to know her over the years, and Violet knew Jameson from when we were kids.

Caleb served us each a small game hen, which he drizzled with a dark berry sauce. He passed a bowl of new potatoes cooked with herbs and placed an exotic salad by each plate. My mouth watered.

"This is a feast," Cody said.

"It's like a holiday dinner," Hailey said.

I took a bite of the game hen dipped in the sauce. I closed my eyes to taste it. "Oh my God. This is good. What's in the sauce?"

"Blackberries and Merlot, mainly," Caleb said. "I'm still trying to perfect it."

"You could bottle this sauce and sell it," Cody said. "It's really good."

"Caleb studied at the Culinary Institute of America in Napa," Jameson said.

"You did?" Violet asked. Her head tilted as she studied him.

Caleb nodded. "You've got a sweet café going there. I checked it out on the web. You're sort of leading the locavore movement in the valley, it sounds like."

"What in the world is a locavore?" Jameson said.

Hailey giggled. "They only eat locally grown food," she said.

"What defines local?" Cody asked.

"You can set your radius. Some choose twelve miles, others one hundred, or some, the whole state," Violet said. "For the café, I source from a fifty-mile radius to capture seafood in the mix. By the way, this is delectable."

"Delectable." Hailey repeated the word. "I like how that sounds."

We ate in silence for a minute, savoring the tastes.

Hailey's cell phone buzzed. She silenced it. "Just my dad. I'll call him back later."

"You can go into the living room and call him back," I said.

Hailey shook her head. I exchanged a glance with Violet.

When we finished dinner, no one made a move to get up. An easy calm hung in the air. Violet and Caleb were talking cooking schools. Violet had been to a cooking school in France, which was evident in her baking skills. My thoughts drifted to Luke.

A loud banging and a shout came from the front screen door. "Hailey! Are you in there? Get your butt out here."

Hailey's eyes widened. "I've got to go." She leaped up, knocking over her chair. "Thanks for dinner."

Jameson stood and righted it. I got up and went with her. Jameson followed.

I opened the screen door. "She's right here, Leroy. We were finishing dinner."

His figure stood large under the porch light. "I don't want you hanging out here at night."

"I was invited for dinner, Dad."

Leroy glowered at me. "She's a witch."

"Dad, she's not a witch."

"Tom tells me you're out burying cow horns. Tell me that's not witchy. And I saw all those things hanging from the trees all summer."

"Leroy, cow horns and the things hanging are part of biodynamic farming. Bio farming heals the earth."

Leroy glared at Jameson.

"My brother, Jameson, is working here now," I said.

"Evening Mr. Hayward." Jameson stepped forward and reached out his hand.

Leroy studied Jameson before reluctantly shaking it. He turned toward the steps. "Come on, Hailey."

Hailey followed him down the porch stairs, looked back, and waved. "Good night, guys."

"Is she safe over there?" Jameson asked.

"I've wondered the same thing, but she said he isn't violent, just protective and a little rough around the edges."

"You think?"

I laughed.

"I'm going to watch some baseball," Jameson said.

Violet and Caleb sat talking. Cody had cleared the table and started the dishes.

"I'll finish. Jameson has the Dodgers on," I said.

"I think you should get a dishwasher," he said.

"Good idea." Another thing to add to the list.

Chapter Twenty-Seven

Jameson, Caleb, Cody, and I sat on the porch drinking coffee, our morning ritual. It was late October. We started our days early and each morning talked about what was on tap for the day.

We had accomplished a lot. The four of us had applied last year's compost to the vines. The cover crops Cody and I planted poked up between the rows of vines. Caleb had painted the tasting room walls, teaching Jameson how to paint. And now they scraped the old paint off the house when they had a few hours to spare. The house looked worse by the day, but Caleb assured me that when the prep was done, he would rent a sprayer and in three to four days, the house would have a new coat of paint. The vineyard was alive and well, improved every day, and soon the earth would be ready to breathe in for the winter, the growth forces concentrated underground, with sap flowing to the roots.

I still had a mountain of paperwork to sort through, but winter was coming. There would be time. I had the farm covered for now. If I could get reliable workers when needed for the harvest and pruning, I knew I could manage the farm.

"I want to finish the house painting prep today and start painting tomorrow. The weather is cooperating," Caleb said.

"Really?" I said. "Painting tomorrow?"

"I don't know," Jameson said. "I like the Halloween look. Decrepit house, witch in residence."

"Cody and I are going to apply compost to the orchard and bury the valerian, chamomile, and dandelion preparations. The moon is descending," I said.

Jameson got up and began to chant and dance around looking skyward, waving his fingers in the air. "Valerian, chamomile, dandelion, ho ho, valerian, chamomile, dandelion, ha ha. They're coming to take you away, ho ho, ha ha, he he…"

Caleb laughed.

I rose. "Just wait. The wine will be magical."

Cody stood and stretched. "Let's go shovel some cosmic dust."

I turned to Caleb. "Anything you want to add?"

He shook his head. "Nope."

An engine started up next door, and the clanging of the drill rig began. It would go on all day once again.

In the orchard, Cody and I picked the last crop of apples and stored them in boxes in the wine storage area. David Bowie emanated from Cody's speaker as we shoveled the orchard compost, rich in wood chips, into wheelbarrows. In the orchard, we spread it on the base of the trees.

"My grandfather planted these trees fifty years ago," I said.

"Hardy stock," Cody said, "just like you."

I laughed. I didn't feel so hardy. For every one thing I crossed off the list, two more were added.

We finished and broke for lunch. At the house Caleb and Jameson were in the kitchen making sandwiches. Caleb's was piled high with bean sprouts, a local smoked cheese, and avocado.

"Yum," I said.

Caleb put it on a plate and handed it to me.

"Thanks!"

I took the sandwich, sat at my desk, and pulled out my phone. No calls or messages from Luke. It would be after nine p.m. there. He'd said he'd call me this morning. Our communications had become more infrequent. I missed him more than ever, but did he miss me? I typed a text: *What's up?* I deleted it. Too informal. I typed: *I miss you.* Too whiney. Delete. *Descending moon. Burying 502,503, and 506 today.* Delete. *Thinking of you. Were our two nights in Marseille only a dream?* I pressed send.

I ate and flipped through a stack of yesterday's unopened mail. There was a letter from Stan, the attorney. I slit it open with Nana's antique pearl letter opener.

Dear Olivia,

Tom stopped by my office with an offer to buy the farm. I'll drive up Saturday to review it with you. I also want to stock up on wine while I'm there.

Sincerely,

Stan

Tom wasn't giving up. Well, Stan was welcome to come and buy wine, but the answer to Tom was no.

Cody and I went to the oak tree where the preparations had been hung to dry since spring. The gourd-like concoctions swayed in the light breeze.

"You have to admit these are odd," Cody said. "What is this one?"

"502, the yarrow. It's sealed in a stag's bladder."

"What?"

"That's the recipe. The 503 chamomile preparation is stuffed in cow intestines, and the 506 dandelion is stuffed in a cow's stomach lining."

"Where in the world do you get them?"

"The local butcher. The first year he thought I was crazy, but last spring another vineyard and a farm also wanted them."

We loaded the preparations carefully into a wheelbarrow and headed out to the plot behind the barn. The previous year's pits were marked with stakes. I dug in the yarrow area and uncovered the brick-lined pit.

Peter stopped work in the barn and came over. "Now what are you burying?"

"Yarrow," I said. I placed the dried bladder into the pit. "In a stag's bladder."

"Yarrow in a stag's bladder," Peter said.

"That's right," I said.

Peter stared into the wheelbarrow at the little chamomile sausages and dandelion pouches and raised his eyebrows.

I explained the preparations as Cody shoveled dirt back into the pit.

"Well," Peter said, "it must work. Tom can't stop raving about those grapes."

Tom. I shook my head and smiled. We walked to the next stake, and Cody began to dig a pit. Peter went back to work. I wished my grandfather were still alive. I wished Nana hadn't signed the contract with Tom for the harvest. I wished a lot of things. I had tried to dissuade Nana from letting Tom enter a contract for the grapes after Papa died, but she wanted me to focus on college. But next year's harvest would be even better. The soil and vines were improving every day. I knew in my heart I could not have managed the harvest and wine making this year without help. So, one harvest got away. Next year the vineyard would be certified, and the grapes would be all mine for making fine wine.

Jameson and Caleb drove up in Old Red. Jameson glanced at the pit and the wheelbarrow. "They're coming to take you away, ho ho, ha ha, he he…"

"We're going to buy paint and rent a sprayer," Caleb said.

"Can you stop and get groceries?" I said.

Caleb pulled a list from his pocket. "I've got it covered."

I smiled. "You're the best, Caleb."

"What about me?" Jameson said.

"Needs improvement," I said.

He laughed at our childhood joke. His report cards were full of *Needs Improvement* comments from his teachers. Except for art. He excelled in art.

I watched them drive down the rutted road. I needed to get a load of new gravel on the driveway before the tasting room opened. The school bus stopped at the mailboxes. Hailey got off and walked to the driver side window. Jameson got out to let Hailey hop in, and then they drove off.

Cody stood watching. "Puppy love," he said.

We finished burying the dandelion and chamomile preparations, and I marked them with stakes for the spring. Cody went off to repair a fence, and I went into the barn. At the end of the long oak work counter a space was dedicated to paperwork. An old wooden file cabinet anchored the end, making a cozy office space off the fermentation room. I sat on a stool, recording the day's activities in the log. I checked my phone. No messages from Luke.

I searched the file cabinet for new labels for the wine silently aging in the cellar. Were there new labels? I had been so preoccupied at college I hadn't paid attention. Nana always designed them when the wine was racked. I found the notebook with all the previous labels in plastic sleeves. Some years her artwork was abstract, some years more formal, using only the Clos de l'Harmonie logo. I paged through every label. Over forty years of wine making. I had been a part of the last twenty-five years at Harmonie. I had spent every summer here trailing after my grandfather. He had called me his shadow. I swiveled to take in the barrels that held Papa's and my last vintages. A sadness sifted through me. Why did they have to go so soon? We had been the perfect team. But now I wasn't a shadow. I needed to find the new label designs, if they existed, or start designing them. I had wine to bottle in the coming months.

I went into the house and sat at the big desk in the living room to search for label designs. Nothing to be found. I opened the box with paperwork and held up a rubber-banded bundle of mail with a return address from Texas: ERG Operating Company, LLC. That wasn't it. Nana used a California company for the final proofs and printing.

I had to find her sketch pad. I thought I'd seen it on the bookcase, but it wasn't there.

I heard Jameson, Hailey, and Caleb come through the kitchen door.

"Ah owww," Jameson howled like a wolf. "Ow, ow, ow."

Never a dull moment with Jameson around. I moved toward the kitchen. On the coffee table by Papa's overstuffed chair was Nana's sketchbook, opened. The left page had an intricate sketch of the oak tree with the bio preparations hanging like lanterns glowing in the dusk. On the right page a sketch of the barn and vineyard. At the tasting room entrance, an enchantress stood gazing skyward at a sliver of a moon dangling by a string. A luminescent aura wafted toward the moon from the vineyard.

They were both titled *Life on the Farm - Series one.* They were beautiful, delicate, and magical. The sketches drew me in for more. This was not Nana's work. Her style was very different. Jameson?

"Big barn dance Saturday night," Jameson said.

I jumped. Jameson and Hailey had entered the room.

"Are these yours?" I asked.

"Yeah, just killing time."

"They're really good. I mean it. I was searching for Nana's new labels, hoping beyond hope that she'd designed some."

"Oh, they're in there." Jameson flipped the pages, and there they were. Four new labels. Lovingly drawn and hand colored.

I put my head back and closed my eyes. "Thank you, Nana." We were still a team.

"Are you coming with us to the barn dance?" Hailey asked.

"Barn dance?"

"Saturday night. It's a full moon too," Jameson said. "Violet and Caleb and Hailey and I are going. You should come with us."

"Violet said there are lots of bands playing, and there is a rumor of a special guest," Hailey said.

Music sounded fun. I knew there were a lot of celebrities and musicians with getaway ranches in the valley. "Sure, I'll go with you. The Indians call the October full moon the hunter's moon. This year it's also a supermoon."

"Aw oww," Jameson howled. "You'll be in your element."

Chapter Twenty-Eight

*C*aleb and Jameson were busy painting the house. Caleb manned the sprayer while Jameson followed with a brush. The old farmhouse was miraculously transformed with robin's-egg blue paint. They worked quickly, and on day three they painted the trim a darker blue and the window trim white. I stood in front of the house and watched in awe. An old station wagon with two men pulled up the driveway.

"Oh shit," Jameson said.

He said something to Caleb that I couldn't hear.

"Who's that?" I said.

Jameson stared at the car. "Some jailbirds I have no need for."

Caleb put down his paintbrush. "I'll take care of this."

He walked to the driver's window and put his hands on his hips. We couldn't hear the words, but his voice was terse. The driver backed around and tore down the driveway, leaving a cloud of dust, reminding me I needed to order the gravel for the driveway.

"I wonder how they knew I was here," Jameson said, gazing at the wake of dust.

"They won't be back," Caleb said, picking up his paintbrush.

Saturday morning Hailey brought over a basket of eggs. I peeked in on the chickens every day and brought them scraps to eat, but Hailey was their keeper. She liked her role and the excuse to stop by the house every day.

She practically lived with us on weekends, but she respected her father's rule to be home before dark, unless he was away in the evening. She didn't like to be there alone at night. I didn't blame her. The vibe of that property creeped me out.

Caleb was starting to make us omelets when my phone rang. Luke. My heart warmed to his photo on the screen. "Don't wait for me," I said and walked out to the porch. We had been messaging frequently the past few days. Short but sweet, and that was all I needed.

"*Bonjour*, Luke."

"What are you doing right now? I want to picture you."

"I just walked out to the porch of a newly painted house. Caleb did such a good job. It doesn't even resemble the old house."

"I mean before I called."

"In the kitchen. Caleb is making omelets. He's the best cook. I'm going to have him taste the wine and help fine tune the tasting notes for the labels."

"Caleb, Caleb, Caleb. He's all I hear about."

"That's not fair. I don't even pay him. He gets room and board."

"Oh, and whose room is he in?"

"Luke, please. Don't be jealous. We are working hard here. It's coming together."

"I can't imagine that, with the crew you have."

His words stung. Tears welled in my eyes. "I have a fine crew," I whispered.

"I'm sorry. I'm frustrated. You're over there, I'm here. I want you in my arms tonight."

I swallowed. "I want you too, every night."

"I can't wait to see you. I'm flying out of Paris right after the Paris show."

That was the best thing I'd heard in weeks. "That makes me so happy."

"What are you doing today?"

"My attorney is coming up to buy wine. He also is presenting an offer from Tom to buy the farm."

"Really? What do you think?"

"I'm happy to sell him some wine, but the offer is a no."

"You should think about it."

I held out the phone and looked at it. Maybe we didn't really know each other.

"Olivia?"

"Luke, I'll never sell Harmonie. I want you to know that."

I heard a big sigh.

"Olivia, *ma chérie*, what are we going to do?"

"We're going to see each other soon and figure it out. So, tell me. Where are you at this exact moment?"

"Pepin and I are sitting out front of your cottage gazing at the biggest full moon of the year and missing you."

"I thought she went back to your grandparents."

"That lasted two days. She moped around, and they called me to come and get her."

"Put the phone to her ear." I paused. "*Bonjour*, my sweet baby Pepin. I miss you."

I could hear Luke laughing. He came back on the phone. "You should have seen her face, and her tail is still wagging. She's looking all around for you."

I started laughing, and tears came to my eyes.

"Good night, my love," Luke said.

"Good night. I love you."

In the kitchen I slid my omelet onto a plate, still warm from the pan, and joined the others at the picnic table. Jameson, Caleb, and Hailey were finishing breakfast. Cody had driven to Davis Friday morning for the weekend.

"Were you crying?" Hailey asked.

"Tears of joy," I said, smiling about Pepin.

"Joy about what?" Jameson said.

"You'll think I'm crazy."

"That box has already been checked, Sister. Come on, tell us."

"I was talking to my dog in France."

"You have a dog in France?" Hailey asked.

Jameson bent over in laughter. He sat up and tried to be serious. "You were talking to your dog in France," he repeated. "And did your dog in France talk back?"

"Never mind. We have chores to do. A local photographer is dropping off framed photos to sell in the tasting room, and Caleb is going to hang them. Then we have tasting notes to fine tune for the labels. A load of gravel is being delivered for the driveway, and Stan, the attorney, is coming up to buy wine." I paused and turned to Jameson. "I need you to take the truck to the coast and get three barrels of seaweed."

"You're kidding me, right?" Jameson said.

"No, you know the place. They used to let you surf there. They'll recognize the truck. If you don't want to take the barrels, just load it into the truck, but that's how much we need, three barrels or more if you can get it."

"No. I'm not doing that," Jameson said.

"What does seaweed do?" Hailey asked.

"It's rich in magnesium. We'll compost it and use as a soil amendment. The soil in the Merlot plot needs it," I said.

"I'll go," Hailey said. "There are always dolphins along there."

"One of your old surfboards is hanging in the carport," I said to Jameson.

"All right. Come on, Hailey. I need to get off this funny farm," Jameson said.

A Volkswagen bus rumbled up the drive, creating a dust trail. Violet's photographer friend had arrived on time. His work hung in galleries in the valley. He'd agreed to let me hang some photographs in the tasting room to sell. We'd both benefit. I needed art, he needed sales.

I picked out the photos to hang and bought two for myself. A photo of the outside of Violet's Café and one of a sea of gold poppies and blue lupine wildflowers on Figueroa Mountain.

The gravel truck arrived. I went out to talk with the driver and watched while he skillfully dumped and graded gravel on the driveway and parking area. Things really were coming together.

"Where's Hailey?"

Startled, I turned to see Leroy striding toward me. "Good morning, Leroy."

"Where's my girl?"

"She went to get seaweed with Jameson."

"You let her go off with that convict? Listen, Olivia, she's all I have."

"He was saving a young woman from an assault. After she got away, the guy started fighting Jameson. He was only defending himself but he was the one that was charged."

"She tells me she's going to the barn dance with him. If anything happens to her, I don't know what I'd do. I'm holding you responsible."

"Why don't you go too?"

"I don't do crowds."

"It might be good for you."

"The only good thing in my life is Hailey, and don't you forget it." Leroy stormed off toward the gate in the fence by the chicken coop.

"Have a nice day, Leroy."

I stood in the doorway of the tasting room. Caleb hung the last photograph, a view of Violet's Café's neon sign glowing in the twilight. The room was completely transformed, modern and sleek. The couches and chairs that had arrived were inviting, the wall colors calming, and the photographs enhanced the ambiance. I arranged the stemware and put out tasting notes. The notes needed a new design. We weren't officially open, but Stan was welcome to taste.

Caleb adjusted the Violet's Café photograph. "This one's my favorite."

"Ready to taste some wine?" I asked.

"Yep."

I got out the pipette and two glasses. Caleb followed me into the barrel storage area. "So, you and Violet hit it off?" I asked.

"Do you believe in love at first sight?"

"It seems like there's a lot of that going around."

"Except I'm not worthy of her."

"Why do you say that?"

"Look at me." Caleb held up his arms. "Ex-chef with no job"

"You do have a job. Everything you've done around here is amazing.

Painting the house and the tasting room. As soon as I get the tasting room open I can start paying you."

"I want to start over and be part of something, and be part of the community."

"Like what?"

"I'd like to grow my own food and cook for people. The valley needs a good dinner spot."

"Well, I need a part-time orchard manager. And there's an old garden plot you can use." I handed Caleb the two glasses and opened the top port of the barrel. "Violet might let you use the café to open up for dinner on the weekends since she's only open for breakfast and lunch."

I dipped the glass pipette into the barrel and released a small amount of the deep-ruby liquid into each glass. "This is one hundred per-cent Grenache."

"I'm honored to taste this with you," Caleb said.

"It's an honor to have you." I swirled my glass and held it to my nose. "Raspberries, rose hips, and what else?"

"Allspice?"

"That's it." I took a sip. Silky smooth, concentrated berries. I made a note in the notebook.

"Berries, plum, dried strawberries," Caleb said.

"There is something on the finish," I said.

"This is weird, but it's like hibiscus tea?"

I took another sip. "You nailed it." I made another note. "We'll bottle this in December."

"Were you serious about needing an orchard manager?"

"Yes, I want to focus on vines, grapes, and wine."

"I'd like that job."

We clinked glasses just as the tasting room door jingled. I closed the top of the barrel and we went into the tasting room. Stan and his wife stood at the door.

"Olivia, you remember my wife, Dolly?"

"Yes, of course." She had been at Nana's funeral. "This is Caleb, the orchard manager."

Caleb shook their hands. Stan surveyed the room. "You've been busy. I don't recognize the place. You painted the house, and you're fixing the driveway. The grader almost ran me off the road."

"Oh, sorry. It's coming together," I said.

"Well, let's start with business. Can we sit?" He motioned to the couches and table.

Caleb said he'd be back later, and Dolly moved around the tasting room, studying the photographs. Stan set his briefcase on the table and opened it.

"I'm not interested in Tom's offer. I already told him the vineyard isn't for sale."

"First things first. Here is Tom's check for the harvest." He handed me the check and pulled out a letter. "I need to at least present the offer to you."

I reached out and accepted the letter. "The answer is no. Are you ready to taste some wine?"

"I think you've got a little bit of both of your grandparents in you," Stan said.

"I do, and I'll take that as a compliment."

"Honestly, Olivia, driving up here I planned to recommend you seriously consider the offer. But seeing all this…" He waved his hand around the room at the rich wood tasting counters and display shelves and the new tasting area where we sat. "I know why they put their faith in you."

"Thanks, Stan." I rose so he wouldn't see tears forming. "I want you to try our 2010 Bordeaux blend."

Stan and Dolly left with two cases of wine and promised to come back for the grand reopening. Caleb and I finished tasting the other three barrels, and I revised the notes. In the tasting room, I logged into the Alcohol and Tobacco Tax and Trade Bureau website and uploaded my information into the Certificate of Label Approval section of the site. The government had made it easier than before to submit and get label approval, but they were strict on the content.

Jameson and Hailey came through the door, laughing. Jameson stopped and scanned the photographs on the walls. He nodded his approval. "We got your seaweed. Where do you want it?"

Hailey walked around the room examining the photos. "This is like an art gallery."

"Your dad was looking for you. You should check in with him."

Hailey rolled her eyes. "I better go finish my chores. See you tonight."

Jameson and I unloaded the seaweed and kelp into a pile to compost. "I love the smell of seaweed," I said.

Jameson stabbed his pitchfork into the seaweed and shook his head. "You're really into this, aren't you?"

"Yes. Hey. I need your help on something," I said.

"What now, boss lady?"

"Please don't call me that. We're all a team here."

"Don't be so touchy. You need to lighten up."

"I need you to design new tasting room notes and create a flyer for the reopening. You're the artist around here."

"Sure. That's way better than compost duty."

"And start thinking about labels for next year. We've got six wines aging. I'll get you some preliminary descriptions. Try and capture the bio theme."

"You know Hailey wants to follow in your footsteps," Jameson said.

I nodded. "I like a girl with a plan."

"Me too."

"Be careful with her. She's seventeen."

"Geez, you think I don't know that?"

"Young girls are vulnerable, and you two seem to have hit it off."

"I wouldn't do anything to hurt her, you know that."

Chapter Twenty-Nine

That evening I worked in the house on bills and paperwork. Hailey arrived wearing a short tunic, cowboy boots, and a black cowboy hat, her long dark hair shining. She didn't bother to knock anymore.

"The hat suits you."

Hailey's smile lit up her face.

Jameson came down the stairs and bowed to Hailey. She replied with a curtsy. Mom would have liked that.

"Aren't you coming?" Hailey asked.

I hadn't changed yet. "I'm going to shower and meet you there."

"Caleb already left to pick up Violet, but we can wait for you," Jameson said.

Jameson was actually being considerate? "No, go on ahead. I need to finish a few things."

I heard Old Red's tires crunch on the newly graveled driveway. We'd done a lot that day. Jameson honked twice like Papa always did. I had to smile. Maybe he would settle in here. I certainly needed his help. I opened the laptop and began to search for accounting software. I needed to automate the finances here. I'd decided not to hire an accountant except at tax time. I wondered what software Bernard used at Domaine Laroche. Did he use software?

After showering, I slipped on a denim skirt and plaid blouse tied at the waist, a proper cowgirl. I opened the French doors and lay on the bed watching the full moon rise and thought of Luke. This same moon would still be out in France. The hunter's moon stayed in the sky until dawn.

I heard my phone ring from far away. I opened my eyes in the dark. The moon lit the sky. I sat up and turned on a light and found the phone.

"Olivia, where are you?"

"Violet? I fell asleep, I guess." It was eleven o'clock.

"Are you still coming?"

"No, not now. It's too late." I heard the band in the background.

"Okay, we won't worry anymore."

"Thanks, Violet."

I went out to the front porch and sat in one of the rockers. The moon lit up the orchard and vineyard. I played Adele from the music library on my phone and waited for Hailey and Jameson to return. Around midnight, I heard Old Red pull into the Haywards' driveway and watched the headlights cast light through the hedgerow in front of Leroy's place. The truck door clanked shut, and Jameson waited until Hailey was inside the house before turning around, honking twice, and driving back to Harmonie.

Jameson came up the porch steps and sat in the other rocker. "Party pooper."

"I know."

"Caleb's staying over at Violet's."

"Hmm."

"I know, right?"

We sat in silence, watching thin feather-like clouds dance around the moon.

"Mom's bugging me to come visit," Jameson said.

"You can use my car."

"I don't want to go. I like it here. The valley is growing on me. Let her come up here."

"She won't though. Why don't you take Hailey down some Sunday and Dad will take you sailing?"

"Yeah, maybe on her birthday. That's all she talks about. She's counting the days."

I was counting days too. Thirty-seven to be exact. I envisioned Luke getting off the plane at the Santa Barbara airport and smiled.

Chapter Thirty

One Monday morning in November, Jameson and I were working in silence in the office. The sound of the drill rig next door was incessant. Clank, clank, clank as the steel was driven into the earth. When would he be done drilling? The sound grated on my nerves.

I had downloaded software for winery management and started inputting the wine inventory. It wasn't my favorite thing to do, but it would pay off in the long run. There was a lot of wine stored and more to bottle. My grandparents had opened the tasting room less frequently over the years and virtually never this past year. Nana's heart hadn't been in it after Papa died. I needed to sell wine and get customers to reorder to keep the winery afloat. I set aside two hours a day for entering data into the new software.

Jameson was revising the tasting notes with mystical artwork. The flyer he'd produced for the grand reopening was a modified sketch of the tasting room with the enchantress gazing skyward at a sliver of moon dangling from a string. At first, I'd thought he was making fun of me, but I liked it. It could also be a good label for next year.

The tasting room door jingled, and Violet appeared in the office doorway. "I thought I might find you here," she said. "I'm making the rounds on my day off."

She walked in and peered over Jameson's shoulder at a drawing. "Wow, that's good. A new label?"

"It's a work in progress," he said.

"Can I hire you to do my seasonal menus?"

"Hire me?"

"I could send you the menu, and you could do your magic."

"Okay, I'll try it. But I won't take your money. I'll work for food."

"We've got a deal." Violet reached out a hand to shake, and Jameson stood up and gave her a hug.

I smiled. He was coming out of his shell more and more. And now he had an outside gig.

The side door to the office opened, and Caleb stepped in. "I saw your car out front," he said to Violet. "I was going to call you. Can you join us for Thanksgiving?"

Violet glanced at me. "Good idea," I said. "Caleb is cooking. He's banned me from the kitchen except to bring the wine."

"You won't have to lift a finger," Caleb said to Violet. "Well... could you bring the pies?"

"Of course. For how many people?" Violet asked.

"My folks, Cody and his girlfriend, and the four of us," Jameson said.

"And Luke. Don't forget Luke. He's at the International Wine Show in Paris, and after it's over he's flying here. I'll google it. Let's see what they do at this show."

I typed "International Wine Show" in my browser and event photos popped up. Caleb, Violet, and Jameson stood behind me. I scrolled through photos and froze. Luke and Nicole Gravois stared back at me, his arm around her, in front of the Domaine Laroche booth.

"Wow, she's gorgeous," Jameson said.

Nicole impeccably made up with her long hair worn on the right side. She wore a skintight dark blue dress and high heels, not a stray hair out of place.

"A perfect couple. Who are they?" Caleb asked.

I couldn't speak.

"It's Luke and a *Vogue* model. I recognize her from when I went to cooking school there and read French *Vogue*," Violet said.

I had sent Violet pictures of Luke and me in France, so she recognized him.

"That's Luke?" Jameson asked. "I'm going to punch his lights out."

I scrolled through more event photos. Nicole, a magnet for the cameras. Luke stood tall, handsome, and relaxed, with a glass of Bandol red in his hand. He had wanted me to go to the Paris wine show and stay on to enjoy a romantic weekend in Paris. A jealous rage spread through me, and I snapped the laptop shut.

"I need to check on some things," I said.

I slipped out the back door and walked to the oak grove, the highest point of the property, my spot to come and think. From here I could see the entire farm and the valley below. I sat in the meadow under an old oak and closed my eyes. I'd lost Luke to Nicole.

You still have the farm, a voice inside me said.

But I wanted them both.

Chapter Thirty-One

I woke with a weight on my chest. I opened the French doors and got back in bed. Luke and Nicole's picture was burned into my mind. I was such a fool. His mother had won. She had pressed them together.

But could I blame him? I was here and he had a life and family and a winery there.

A knock sounded at my door.

"Come in."

Jameson entered with a cup of coffee. He set it down on the night-stand. "You're late for your appointment with Peter. He said the building inspector is on the way."

"Oh geez." I jumped up. The final inspection of the bunkhouse. "Thanks."

"You're always up at dawn. Are you okay?"

Tears welled up in my eyes and slid down my cheeks. No, I was not okay.

"Is it Luke and that model?"

I nodded.

"Is there anything I can do?"

I shook my head.

"Put a spell on her."

I half smiled. I wished I could.

"Well, pull yourself together. Caleb's tired of sleeping on the couch and can't wait to move into the bunkhouse."

Yes, I needed to pull myself together.

Jameson shut the door. I dressed quickly, washed the tears from my face, and brushed my teeth. I took my coffee and walked to the bunkhouse. Peter stood talking with Caleb and Jameson on the newly constructed back porch.

"Good morning, sunshine," Peter said.

"Morning," I said.

"Big day. Final inspection. We should be fine though," Peter said.

I nodded and tried to smile.

"What's the matter? I thought you'd be swinging from the rafters," Peter said.

"Guy trouble," Jameson said.

"Ah," Peter said. "Matters of the heart. They're complicated."

The building inspector pulled up and parked by Peter's truck. With clipboard in hand he came up the porch steps, eyes darting to every surface, already examining the work.

"Morning, Peter." He nodded to the three of us. "Where do you want to start?"

Peter led him into the bunkhouse. I followed. Caleb and Jameson went back to whatever chores Cody had assigned them.

The building inspector checked off items on his inspection sheet. The three rooms for sleeping were large enough for a bed and furniture, like a hotel room. Peter had hardwired smoke and carbon monoxide detectors. Caleb and I had worked with Peter to add another kitchen. Caleb planned to get licensed and sell his products at local wineries and groceries, and so a separate kitchen was required by the Health Department.

The two kitchens opposite each other were well laid out. Peter had built an island work space and a large oak rectangle dining table. The living room area was off the kitchen. The large bathroom was next to a laundry area. The rooms were light and airy, with skylights and tall windows. The building inspector turned toward me. "This is some bunkhouse."

"Thank you," I said. "Peter does nice work."

The inspector signed and dated the report and handed it to me. "You're in business."

I took the report, and we watched him leave. I walked over to the window and removed the bright green permit.

Peter handed me the keys to the bunkhouse doors. "Well, I'm off to my other job."

"Wait, I have some wine for you, and I'll pay you."

He followed me to the tasting room, and I unlocked the door. We stepped in, and Peter whistled. He hadn't seen it since the building inspection last month. Now it was painted and furnished and the photographs hung.

"This is one of the nicest tasting rooms in the valley." He walked around perusing the photographs.

I pulled out my phone and sent Peter his final payment.

"Thank you," Peter said. "Do you know how hard it is to collect payments? I usually have to send my wife out to hound people."

"I really appreciate your work. I put together a mixed case for you."

"You don't have to do that."

"Your reward for a job well done and ahead of schedule. Come to our reopening this Sunday. Bring your wife."

"I'll do that. And Olivia... if your guy did you wrong, he's an idiot."

I swallowed. The tears started to come again. Peter picked up the case of wine, and I let him out.

I went to the desk and studied the calendar. Today was Wednesday. Luke had planned to come Saturday; the tasting room preopening was scheduled for Sunday. Thanksgiving and the grand reopening were the following week. I would have to slog through it and try to smile occasionally. What excuse would he give me for not coming?

I called the furniture store in town to request delivery of the new beds. Keep moving through your list. Move forward. Don't think about Luke. But the pictures of Luke and Nicole together left me raw.

A truck rumbled up the drive with two dark brown leather couches in the bed. The Craigslist guy. I went out and directed him to the back. Caleb and Cody walked over.

"Sweet," Cody said. "We may never leave."

"Hotel Harmonie," Caleb said.

"The beds are on their way," I said. "Can you tell them where to set them up when they arrive?"

I walked to the top of the property. I didn't want to talk to anyone until I could get a grip on my emotions, my tears ready to spill. I sat under the oak tree and surveyed the valley.

Down at Leroy's a cement truck idled. Two small figures guided the pouring of a large twenty-by-twenty-foot foundation. Now what was he doing? Building a water tank?

I watched the cars on the road. How would I get through Thanksgiving dinner with Mom and all the questions? I wish I'd never met Luke. No, that's not true. I had found real love. Short lived but real. Real love and real pain. He had rushed in with his declaration of love, and I reciprocated. It happened so fast.

I thought of our two nights in Marseille, swimming in the turquoise sea, pruning the vines together in an unspoken contest with Phillipe and Angelica, walking through the vineyard holding hands, Pepin bounding ahead. At least I had memories.

I checked my phone for messages. Nothing. It would be evening there. Luke would be at the after-parties he loved so much, with Nicole at his side. I opened the picture on my phone Dad had taken of us on his boat. We were good as a couple. Our hair ruffled in the breeze and both of us smiling at Dad. I opened Nicole's Instagram page and scrolled through the posts of her glamorous life. Two posts were photos of her and Luke at the wine show. The perfect Paris couple. I turned off my phone and let my tears flow.

An hour later, when no more tears would come, I rose and walked back to the house. Find your list and do two things on it. Keep moving forward. I repeated my new mantra... keep moving forward.

Nana's linen closet was filled to the brim with sheets, towels, blankets, and madras bedspreads. I stacked an assortment, put them in two large bags, and lugged them to the bunkhouse.

Caleb and Cody were unpacking boxes Cody had brought down from Davis. Jameson unpacked the boxes I'd set aside from cleaning out the house; kitchen utensils, plates, pots, and a lamp. Peter had installed lighting throughout, but the lamp added a homey touch.

"Linen delivery," I said.

"Where were you? You disappeared," Cody said.

"Up communing with the oak tree," I said.

"Witchy woman. She's conjuring a spell," Jameson said.

"Do you do that too?" Caleb said.

I tried to smile and shook my head. I went into the bedrooms and made up the beds. One set of sheets, printed with large multicolored flowers, must have been from the seventies. I put the towels in the bathroom.

"I'll be back with more stuff, like cleaning supplies. You guys are on your own to clean."

Inside the house my funk returned. Keep moving forward. Keep moving forward.

Chapter Thirty-Two

*a*t dawn on Thursday morning, I went out to the last two plots that had been harvested. The timing was right to spray the 501 silica preparation. There was no trace of wind as the sun rose. I stirred and stirred to dissolve the silica. When it was dynamized I filled the backpack sprayer. Silica had the same forces as the distant planets, the warm planets. It enhanced the light metabolism of the vine and influenced the color, aroma, and flavor of the grapes.

Two deer stood on the edge of the plot nibbling the new growth of the cover crop. I turned down the next row and saw Cody and Jameson starting down the driveway for their morning run. I'd go with them tomorrow. A run might help pound Luke out of my head. Maybe I would get a dog since I wouldn't be traveling so much now. I'd get an Airedale terrier puppy.

The silica spray caught the sunlight and illuminated the vines as I went row to row. Cosmic matter into matter. It was calming. I finished and went to the house to brew coffee. This would be another long day. How long would it take to stop feeling bad?

I took my coffee out to the porch and checked my messages. My stomach whirled. A message from Luke. His breakup announcement via WhatsApp.

"I can't wait to see you and hold you in my arms. Two days to go. Love, Luke."

I reread it. Anger flooded me. If he thinks he can have us both he's wrong. I typed a response. "You're still coming?" I hit send.

I should have said, "Don't bother."

My phone rang. Luke's photo on the screen.

"Hello."

"What do you mean, are you still coming? I can't wait."

"I saw the photos."

"What photos?"

"You and Nicole at the wine show."

"Oh, that. She had a photo shoot for an article. The theme was something about a night on the town, and she stopped at the show. They were only there fifteen minutes. But we'll get some publicity when the article comes out."

It sounded plausible.

"Olivia? Are you there?"

"You had your arm around her, and you looked so happy."

"That's ridiculous. I put my arm around my mother and sisters for photos. And I am happy. I have you, and I'll be with you in two days. I'm incredibly happy. Aren't you?"

"Well I was, until I saw the photos."

"Olivia, you're letting your imagination run away. I don't have any interest in Nicole. Listen, tonight is the winemakers' dinner. Tomorrow I'm spending the night with my grandparents, and the next morning I'll be on the plane. I'm bringing you a surprise."

I confirmed I'd pick him up Saturday. What a fool I was. He'd repeatedly said Nicole was not his type, too high maintenance and no interests in common. I had let my jealousy run wild. The weight seeped out of my chest. He'd be here in two days. I needed to get my act together.

In the house, Jameson came down the stairs with his suitcase, his hair still wet from the shower.

"Going somewhere?"

"I'd rather stay in the bunkhouse. I like the idea of being a farmhand."

"And artist," I said.

"Yeah. The bunkhouse is closer to my work space. Plus, you'll need your privacy to sort out the love triangle."

"I just talked to Luke. It wasn't how it looked. It was publicity for some magazine article."

"Right. I'm still going to have a heart-to-heart with him. Hey, I have to go. We're replacing stakes in the Sauvignon Blanc plots."

"Can you repaint the sign by the road? We're changing the tasting room hours from by appointment to our new schedule of eleven to five Wednesdays through Sundays. A new sign for this Sunday would be fitting."

Jameson bowed. "But of course, my lady."

I laughed, feeling better. I played Arcade Fire on my phone and cleaned the house till it shone.

Chapter Thirty-Three

*H*ailey drove to the Santa Barbara airport with me. I was nervous about seeing Luke after so long, and Hailey asked if she could go. I couldn't say no. She loved to get off her dad's property.

We waited at the outside baggage claim for the plane to touchdown.

"I've never met a Frenchman before," Hailey said.

"You're in for a treat." Nervous energy surged through me. I'd never felt so hyper.

The plane taxied in and stopped. The steps were attached, and the passengers descended. I scanned each male face for Luke. He finally strode down the steps. He saw me and waved, and his smile melted my heart.

The line of passengers came through the gate to wait for their baggage. I walked toward Luke and caught a glimpse of Lili right behind him. Lili! For a moment, I wasn't sure who to hug first. I ran to both, and Luke picked me up and twirled me around. Corny, but I soared with his warmth, his love. I didn't want to let him go.

Luke set me down. "I brought you a surprise."

I hugged Lili. "Welcome to California."

While we waited for the bags to unload, I introduced Hailey. Luke grabbed his bag and Lili's enormous red suitcase, and we walked to the car.

Luke sat up front with me and Lili and Hailey in the back on either side of Luke's bag. Lili's suitcase had filled the entire cargo space.

Luke and I exchanged glances every minute or so, his hand resting on my thigh as I drove. Lili told me her California boyfriend, Jon, was going to drive up from Los Angeles on Wednesday. They would stay until Friday and then go back to Los Angeles.

"You're both welcome to stay with me. Invite him for Thanksgiving."

"We're staying at a dude ranch with private suites. I can't wait. A real Western ranch. But we'd love to come for Thanksgiving."

"Ah, that would be Alisol Ranch. It's beautiful there. I'm not sure if it qualifies as a real dude ranch. There's a day spa, pool, restaurant, and golf, and you don't have to work for your dinner." I smiled at her in the rearview mirror.

"We're going to go horseback riding."

"Get a picture of that," Luke said. "I can't imagine you on a horse."

Hailey sat quietly, observing, probably enamored with the French accents. Their voices were music to my ears.

I pulled into Clos de l'Harmonie past the newly painted sign Jameson had finished. He'd kept the Harmonie logo but added two planets and some constellations. I was nervous about Lili's reaction to the house and winery, so different from the grand Domaine Laroche.

Caleb worked in the orchard as we drove past, and he tipped his hat. I drove beyond the tasting room and parked in front of the house.

Luke glanced from the tasting room to the house. "Is this the same place?"

Hailey laughed. "She's on a mission. There are no slackers here."

"What does 'slacker' mean?" Lili asked.

"It's someone who is not working hard," Hailey said.

"I'm not that bad," I said. "We just have a lot to do."

Luke struggled up the porch steps with Lili's giant suitcase, and I took his. Hailey went off to find Jameson. I showed Lili her room upstairs and the bathroom. I gave her my old room, the guest room now. Luke set her suitcase down.

"Are you tired?" I asked Lili.

"A little. Let me shower, and I'll feel fine," Lili said.

"If I had known you were coming I would have gotten special soaps like you had in the cottage for me."

She patted her suitcase and smiled. "I brought plenty."

"More than plenty," Luke said.

Luke followed me downstairs. "Do you miss her?" he asked.

"Lili? Yes, of course."

"No, I mean Nana."

"Yes, and Papa. I had to pack up a lot of their things. It made me too sad to be here with all the memories. But she's together with Papa now. That's what she wanted."

I took his small bag into my bedroom.

"And we're together now," Luke said, drawing me into his arms. He kissed me, long and hard. Hunger radiated from his body. How could I have doubted him?

When Luke and Lili finished showering, I made coffee. The best thing for jet lag was to stay up until bedtime and then sleep. We sat on the front porch talking.

"When do I get a tour?" Lili said.

"Relax. Let's finish our coffee," Luke said.

Lili stood up and took her coffee cup to the railing and looked out over the vineyard, the deep red and gold leaves shimmered in the breeze. The late afternoon light was gauzy.

Jameson came around the corner and stopped at the bottom of the stairs. He glanced from Luke to Lili to me and back to Lili, dressed in legging jeans, suede ankle boots, black T-shirt, and large sunglasses.

"This is my brother, Jameson. Jameson, this is Lili, Luke's sister, and this is Luke."

Jameson walked up the stairs and offered his hand to Lili. She set her coffee cup down. "No, no. In France, we greet like this." She kissed him on each cheek three times. His color reddened. Luke stood to shake his hand.

"Hello Luke. We need to talk," Jameson said. He motioned to the screen door.

Luke shot me a puzzled look and followed Jameson into the house.

"He's so handsome," Lili said, "but so serious."

"There was a misunderstanding." We could hear their voices in the living room, firm and low. I told her about the photos of Luke and Nicole.

"Ah," she waved her hand. "He barely puts up with her. I'm still trying to reconcile our inventory after she worked in the tasting room. She never entered any sales."

The screen door squeaked open. Luke smiled at me behind Jameson. How I loved his smile.

"I'm ready for the tour," Luke said.

Jameson accompanied us. I unlocked the tasting room, and we stepped inside. Light poured in from the skylights, and the room glowed.

"Wow," Lili said. "*C'est magnifique!*"

"We're opening tomorrow for a trial run," Jameson said.

Luke took my hand and pulled me into a kiss. "What a transformation."

Lili walked around studying the photographs. She paused at the one I had hung the day before of my grandparents, standing in front of the old tasting room raising their glasses to me, behind the camera lens. Lili smiled. "This is my favorite."

"Mine too," Jameson said, staring at the photo.

I glanced at him, surprised. He never shared any family sentiment. Except for when he had apologized to me for not being able to attend Nana's service. We continued through the tasting room. Behind the counter at the register, I flipped open the laptop, and up popped the accounting system.

"I automated the paper trail of inventory, accounting, and expenses. Eventually I'll input payroll and orchard sales."

"You have to show us this," Lili said. "We use three systems, and they're not connected."

"That will be your battle," Luke said. "Papa is quite stubborn about his systems."

"We'll see," Lili said. "You got the new bottler."

I took them through the barrel room and case storage area. In the office, Jameson's latest drawing lay on the long worktable and a sketch of a wine label was tacked to the wall.

"Who is the artist?" Luke asked.

Jameson stood by quietly. I pointed to him.

"Jameson?" Lili said. "These are good. I thought Mom did nice designs, but these are… magical." She waved her hands through the air.

"They're really good," I agreed.

"Ready to see the bunkhouse?" Jameson said, trying to change the subject.

"Bunkhouse?"

"We call it Hotel Harmonie. A deluxe hotel for workers," Jameson said.

We walked out the side door to the back of the barn.

"This barn is so big!" Lili said.

"It used to be a covered horse arena," I said.

On the porch, Hailey sat cross-legged on a chair reading a book. We walked up the porch steps.

"Hailey!" Lili said. She bent and kissed her three times on both cheeks like she hadn't just seen her two hours ago. How I loved Lili.

Inside, Jameson showed them around. Caleb came out of his room, showered from the workday. Introductions were made. Luke stood aloof after shaking Caleb's hand, checking him out before turning his attention to the rooms.

"This is like a house," Lili said.

Luke took my hand and squeezed it. "This is amazing."

"Peter did all the work. You'll meet him tomorrow."

We moved to leave. "Nice to meet you both," Caleb said. "I'll see you soon up at the house. I'm cooking for everyone tonight."

"He's a chef," I said.

Lili's eyes sparkled. "I love a man who cooks."

"You sound like my nana," I said.

We walked back to the house, Luke and Lili on either side of me. The sunset glowed pink and gold across the clouds in the sky. "I can't believe you're both really here."

Luke put his arm around my waist. "Your brother is quite protective of you."

"As you are of Lili and Angelica," I said.

"You're right, that's fair."

After dinner Lili went up to her room to call Jon and get some sleep. Jameson went to the bunkhouse, and Caleb and Cody were meeting Violet at the tavern for a beer.

Luke and I lay on my bed, talking, my head on his shoulder. I stroked his face and hair. His five-o'clock shadow was dark.

"We'll make beautiful wine together and babies," he said.

"Babies?"

"Yes, my love. I want to have children with you."

We hadn't talked about children. I was so young. "We have all the time in the world." I leaned in and kissed him.

Luke slipped off my shirt and began kissing me. I closed my eyes and lost myself in his love.

Chapter Thirty-Four

Sunday evening, Luke, Lili, Jameson, and I sat on the couches and comfortable chairs in the tasting room. I poured wine for Luke and Lili. Jameson sat with his head down, his pencil moving swiftly over his sketch pad.

"That was successful," Lili said. "How many people came to taste?"

"About eighty," I said. "A smooth trial run. We're ready for next Friday's official reopening."

"You sold a lot of wine," Luke said.

"Everyone is stocking up for Thanksgiving. They drink more when relatives get together," Jameson said.

Lili laughed. "I can't wait to experience this American Thanksgiving."

I went to the counter and flipped open the laptop. I had sold a lot of wine. The software had worked. With regular hours, I would be able to start paying the bills and salaries. My cash reserve had been almost depleted by the remodel.

I sat down next to Luke and took a sip of wine. "Jameson, why don't you design some Clos de l'Harmonie T-shirts? You could keep the proceeds after the costs. Customers asked at least five times if we had shirts."

"I'll think about it. Why didn't Mom and Dad stop by?"

"She's allergic to the valley. They'll be up on Thanksgiving," I said.

"Allergic?" Lili said.

"Not exactly allergic. She doesn't like the countryside and small towns even though she grew up here—or maybe it's because she grew up here," I said.

"How long can you both stay?" Jameson asked.

I glanced at Luke and Lili. I never wanted them to leave.

"I'm going to Los Angeles with Jon on Friday. He's taking me to Hollywood, Beverly Hills, and the movie studios. Luke and I fly back Tuesday."

"Tuesday? So soon?" Jameson said.

My chest grew tight.

"I've got barrels to bottle and wine fermenting," Luke said, reaching for my hand.

I awoke to clattering in the kitchen. It was Thanksgiving morning, and Caleb had started early. I rolled over to hug Luke, but his side of the bed was empty, his inner clock still on European time. I found him in the kitchen, drinking coffee, watching Caleb stuff the turkey. I hugged him from behind. I never wanted him to leave. The thought of it left me heartsick.

"I've never seen such a large turkey," Luke said.

"Welcome to America," Caleb said.

"What's on the menu? Luke and I will pick out some wines," I said.

"For starters, butternut squash soup, turkey and stuffing, rainbow chard with chanterelles, potatoes with sage and brown butter, and roasted beets with garlic and chestnuts."

"Wow. Can we help?" I asked.

"I've got it covered. Can you set the table?"

"Of course," I said.

Jameson and Hailey came through the kitchen door with a basket of eggs.

"Wow, look at that bird," Hailey said.

"What are you doing for Thanksgiving?" Caleb asked.

"Nothing. My dad's not into holidays and it's just the two of us, so he said why bother."

Caleb glanced at Jameson with raised eyebrows.

"Do you want to join us?" Jameson asked.

"Just me?"

"No, your dad too, of course," I said.

"He'd never come. Besides, he'd think you were putting a spell on him with some exotic ingredient."

I laughed and looked at Luke. "Hmm. A little valerian juice in horsetail tea?"

"The witch and the warlock," Jameson said.

"I'll go over and ask him," I said. "Jameson, want to come with me?"

"I'm not exactly on his favorites list."

I set down my coffee cup and went out the kitchen door. The grass glistened with dew and the air smelled crisp like autumn. I inhaled deeply. I loved the valley. I went through the gate to Leroy's and immediately got a bad vibe. A shiver ran up my neck. Something was off about this place.

I surveyed his property as I walked up the drive. Behind the house the drill rig still loomed over the well. Shouldn't they have reached the aquifer by now? I knocked on the door. No response. I knocked again, harder.

"Hold on." Leroy opened the door. I could hear a country song coming from the back of the house. "Now what?"

"I'm inviting you and Hailey for Thanksgiving dinner."

"No."

"Are you going somewhere else?"

"No."

"My folks will be here. And Hailey wants to come."

"She does, does she?"

"Yes, she does."

He glanced toward my property, frowning. "Well, I suppose it wouldn't kill me. What time?"

"Four o'clock. Are you almost done drilling?"

"It's none of your business," he said, shutting the door.

He was nothing like his father. I walked back through the gate and instantly felt calm. I walked into the kitchen, and the conversation died.

"Add two more guests to the table," I said.

"You're kidding me," Hailey said. "How did you get him to come?"

"He's doing it for you," I said.

Luke helped me move another table into the dining room. I set the tables with Nana's tablecloths, wedding china, and silver, and brought the china serving bowls into the kitchen.

"Fancy," Caleb said.

"Let's go pick out some wine, Luke," I said.

I unlocked the tasting room door, and we went into the storage area. I grabbed an empty case box.

"Sauvignon Blanc, for starters." I put four bottles in the box.

"Syrah would be good." Luke added more bottles to the box.

"And some Grenache."

Luke came over and kissed me. "This is a special day."

I nodded and kissed him back. The tasting room bells jingled on the door. I listened for a moment, not wanting to let go of our embrace.

I heard a woman gasp. "It's absolutely beautiful. Look at this."

"Mom," I whispered to Luke.

He kissed me again, and I took his hand and led him into the tasting room.

"Hi, Mom and Dad."

They turned to see us. Luke went over to them and kissed Mom on both cheeks and held out his hand to Dad.

"Good to see you," Dad said.

"We can't wait to meet your sister. Olivia is so enthusiastic about her." Mom turned to me. "Olivia, you did this? The design?"

I nodded.

"It's so well planned and tasteful. I love the photographs."

Stunned, I murmured, "Thanks, Mom." I turned toward the counter. "We revised the tasting notes, and here's the flyer for the grand reopening tomorrow." The art popped off the page.

"Decidedly unique," Dad said.

"They're gorgeous. Who is the artist?" Mom said.

"Jameson."

Mom stared at the artwork and back to me. "Jameson?"

"Nana's prodigy. Have a seat. Let's taste some wine."

Mom moved toward the couches, taking in all the details. Luke, Dad, and I got out wine glasses and popped a bottle of chilled Grenache Blanc.

"Mom actually threw me a compliment," I whispered to Dad.

"And well deserved," Dad said.

I brought Mom a glass and sat next to her on the couch. Luke and Dad stood by the counter talking in low voices.

"How is Jameson?" Mom asked.

"He's good. He's staying busy."

"He's living in a bunkhouse out back?"

"I'll show it to you and Dad. It was his choice. He says it's closer to his work space where he does his artwork, in the office."

"There's an office?"

"There always was a small one, but I expanded it, and it feels roomier with skylights."

She stared up at the natural light coming though. "Those were a good idea. And the house is painted. I love the color."

"Caleb and Jameson painted it."

She took a sip of wine and shook her head. "Jameson?"

"I want to see this bunkhouse," Dad said.

We went out the side door of the office and around to the back of the barn. Cody and his girlfriend, Molly, sat on the porch listening to music and reading.

"You remember Cody and his girlfriend, Molly. She's down from Davis for Thanksgiving."

"Of course. Thank you, Cody, for being so kind to my mother," Mom said.

"Mind if I give a tour?" I said.

"Make yourself at home," Cody said.

Inside, it was clean and bright. Jameson had tacked up some of his drawings. "My, my," Mom said.

"Some bunkhouse," Dad said. "If I ever get into hot water with your mom, I know where I'm coming."

I laughed. "There is plenty of room in the house. Speaking of which, we'd better get up there. Lili and Jon are coming." I felt like we were intruding on their space and wanted to keep it brief.

"Thanks, Cody. We're serving wine at the house," I said.

"We're there," Cody said.

Luke scooped up the box of wine, and I locked the tasting room. The wine must have gone to his head. He was smiling a lot. Good. Today was a special day.

At the house, Violet had arrived with the pies, and Jameson and Hailey played cards at the kitchen table, in the middle of the cooking fest. Dad and Luke opened bottles to breathe. I went into the bedroom to change. I knew Lili would arrive soon in full holiday style.

I put on a dress I'd bought with Lili in Bandol and Nana's vintage Indian belt. The intricate beads shimmered. I always felt some magic when I wore it. I could hear the noise level in the kitchen rise a notch. Lili and Jon had arrived. I slipped on Nana's turquoise necklace and went out to greet them.

Lili squealed when she saw me like she hadn't seen me for a year and came to kiss my cheeks even though I had said goodbye to her yesterday when Jon picked her up. She wore a clingy silk dress and high heels, so classically French and beautiful. Cody and Molly stood with glasses of wine, watching with amused expressions.

Lili fingered the belt. "I love this. Jon, we have to find one for me."

"It's almost an antique," I said.

"There is a store in Santa Ynez that specializes in Native American stuff," Violet said.

Caleb opened the oven door and pulled out the turkey to baste it.

Lili put her hand over her mouth and let out a small scream. "It's huge! Luke, have you seen this bird?"

Luke laughed. He slipped his hand though my belt at the back of my dress. I leaned into him. I wanted to be connected to him all the time.

"Let's give the chef some space," I said and tried to get the group to move into the living room.

Luke, Mom, Dad, Lili, and Jon followed me. The others stayed put, watching Caleb perform his culinary alchemy. At exactly four o'clock, there was a knock at the door. Dad went to answer it and returned with a strange expression on his face and Leroy. I'd forgotten to tell him he'd been invited. Leroy had dressed in brown corduroy pants, a blue plaid cowboy shirt with pearl snaps, and polished cowboy boots.

"Would you like a glass of wine?" I asked. I immediately remembered Hailey said he didn't drink wine because it confused him. "Or a beer?"

"I'll try a wine. I want to taste those grapes Tom talks about."

Dad poured him a glass of Grenache. Leroy eyed it warily, sniffed, and took a big gulp.

"Not too bad," he said.

How had I gotten him to join us? It was Hailey. He'd do anything for Hailey. Mom watched him from the corner of her eye then turned to Lili and Luke.

"What does your mother think about you and Luke both dating people from California?"

"She's old-fashioned and would prefer to play matchmaker with locals, but Dad says it's a small world and wants us to be happy," Lili said.

Cody and Molly brought in a steaming soup tureen and bowls and set them on the dining room table. Violet appeared with a basket of fresh-baked rolls.

I moved people to the dining room table and made seating suggestions.

"We have a tradition," I said. "Everyone gets a turn to say one thing they're thankful for." We went around the table.

"I only get one?" Dad asked. "Then it's our family."

"I'm thankful to be here right now with all of you," Lili said.

Jon repeated the sentiment.

"I'm thankful for Clos de l'Harmonie coming into my life," Caleb said. "To Harmonie." He raised his glass.

"To Harmonie," everyone toasted.

"Please, start eating the soup," Caleb said.

Jameson raised his glass. "I'm thankful for forgiveness." He took a drink. "My grandfather had all these clichés that are still in my head. One of them was 'you can do anything you want as long as you don't hurt anyone.' Well, I hurt a lot of people, and I'm sorry."

My eyes teared up. I wanted to hug him.

Leroy spoke next. "Hailey, I'm thankful for Hailey."

"Here's to Hailey," I said, raising my glass.

Dad got up to pour more wine.

"I'll go," Mom said. "I am thankful for my talented son, beautiful daughter, and loving husband."

Everyone raised their glasses. I felt a light kick on my shin. Across the table Jameson grimaced at me. He knew her remarks could hurt. A beautiful daughter. That's all she saw in me. Not the fine wine we were drinking and not the work I'd done reviving the winery.

"I'm thankful for everything in my life," I said, locking eyes with Luke.

Finally, everyone had spoken except for Luke. No one was forced to go. I ate a spoonful of soup.

"This is delicious, Caleb," I said.

Luke's chair scraped on the hardwood floor as he rose. He cleared his throat. "I am thankful for Olivia," he said. "I have finally met my match. I knew from the first time I saw her that we were meant to be together. She is focused and a passionate vintner. I understand this passion. It's in your blood." Luke held up his glass. "To Olivia."

I smiled up at him. My eyes blurred with tears. Then Luke knelt on one knee. What was he doing? He pulled a black velvet pouch out of his pocket and slid out a gold Byzantine band of diamonds. His eyes were infused with unwavering love. "Olivia, will you marry me?"

Five days ago, I thought I'd never see him again, and now he had proposed.

"Say yes," Hailey said, clapping her hands together.

Around the table everyone waited for my response. Was this a movie or reality? I turned back to Luke, kneeling before me, waiting.

"Yes, yes, I will Luke Laroche."

He slipped the ring on my finger and kissed me. Cheers and applause erupted. Lili jumped up and gave me a hug. Violet followed.

I glanced at Dad. He raised his glass, smiling. "To Luke and Olivia."

Mom raised her glass from the end of the table. "Now you can get on with your life."

What did that mean? This was my life.

When things settled down, everyone finished their soup. Cody and Molly cleared the soup bowls. Caleb and Jameson brought in steaming dishes of food and the large platter with the perfectly carved turkey. I held Luke's hand under the table and peered at the ring on my other hand.

I leaned into him. "I love it."

"More than you love me?"

I shook my head, laughing.

Caleb's dishes were delicious. I watched Leroy move the rainbow chard and chanterelles around with his fork and take a wary bite. He immediately took another.

"This is the best dinner I've ever eaten," Hailey said.

"Hey," Violet said. "What about my café?"

"I said dinner. I ate lunch at the café," Hailey said.

"Smart girl," Dad said.

"You know, Olivia," Mom said, "I thought you'd be lonely up here all by yourself. But I see now that's certainly not the case."

Luke squeezed my hand.

"Leroy," Jameson said, "what are you doing at your place? There's so much machinery and cement trucks and noise."

"I have my permits," Leroy said.

"He's drilling a well," Hailey said.

"Why do you need another well?" Cody asked.

"I have plans for my property," Leroy said.

Violet and I exchanged a glance. He was so cagey.

"Water here is scarce, that's for sure," Cody said.

"That's why they need to stop the Chumash Indians from building a huge commercial development," Violet said.

"The property they just bought? I thought they were building tribal housing," Mom said.

"Now they're planning millions of square feet of commercial space," Violet said. "That's not what we want in the valley. Once they get the new parcel designated as tribal land by the feds, the county will have no say in it."

"If it's their land," Leroy said, "they can do what they want."

"And that's exactly what they do," Dad said. "First came the casino, but they weren't going to serve alcohol or build a hotel. Now they serve alcohol on the gaming floor next to a huge hotel."

"So what?" Leroy said. "It's a nice hotel."

"The housing is fine. We all need more housing here," Violet said. "But a commercial center? No. There's no water for that. Send new commercial development up to Santa Maria."

A silence hung in the room. Caleb rose to start clearing plates. I started to help, but Cody and Molly made me stay seated while they cleared.

"So, Olivia," Dad said, "big day tomorrow at the tasting room."

I beamed, thinking about it. "Yes, and I have lots of help." I looked around the table.

"You're going to need it," Violet said. "The weekend after Thanksgiving is one of my busiest. I think all this food makes people hungrier."

"Dessert, anyone?" Caleb asked as he brought in two pies.

Lili groaned, and Jon nodded.

"Count me in," Jameson said.

I glanced at Luke. We had four days left together, and then when would we see each other again?

Chapter Thirty-Five

*F*riday morning, I opened the French doors in the bedroom and gazed down at the valley. A crescent moon hung from the sky, a sliver of light. I fingered my new ring. I should be dancing in the meadow, but my heart was heavy. How was this marriage going to work? I needed to sort out my priorities. Today it was Clos de l'Harmonie. I had set things in motion, and I needed to follow though.

I turned back to Luke. He lay watching me.

"Come here, *ma chérie*."

I lay next to him, and he enveloped me in his arms. I stroked his face, wanting to remember everything about it. His morning shadow of a beard. His brown eyes, matching his hair, which spilled past his ears. Love me. Hold me. I don't want to live without you.

A car horn sounded twice. Cody and Molly were leaving for San Francisco to spend the weekend with their families. I nuzzled closer.

"Let's spend Monday night on the boat before you leave Tuesday," I said.

"I'm not leaving," Luke said.

"Good. I'll pretend that all weekend and not be sad."

At ten o'clock, Luke and I went out to the tasting room to get ready for the reopening. Caleb volunteered to make appetizers to pair with the wine and restock bottles as needed. Luke, Jameson, and I would each manage a tasting bar.

Around eleven, cars started rolling up the driveway and tasters trickled in. Soon the tasting room was full, and we were all hustling. The noise level soared with laughter. Wine tasters always had fun.

Out the window I saw Tom's truck pull up. What did he want? He walked in and sidled up to the counter and surveyed the tasting room.

"You've got quite a crowd here," Tom said. "What are you pouring today?"

I handed him the tasting list. "Ten dollars for a tasting."

He glanced at the list and back to me. "You're not really going to charge me, are you?"

"I've got bills to pay, Tom."

A couple came in and stood next to Tom. The man put twenty dollars on the counter.

"Two tastes, please," the man said.

I handed them the tasting list. "Do you want to start at the top?"

"You bet," the man said.

I poured them the Sauvignon Blanc. "Where are you two from?"

"Los Angeles. We're up for the weekend," the woman said. She put her arm around the man's waist.

Tom took out his wallet and pulled out a ten-dollar bill and set it on the counter. "I'll start with the Grenache Blanc."

I gave him a pour and glanced at Luke. He watched us from his counter. Tom followed my gaze.

"Does Frenchy have a green card?" Tom asked.

I ignored him and described the wine to the Los Angeles couple.

"There's a rumor he might have brought some suitcase vines," Tom said.

"What?" I said.

"What are suitcase vines?" the Los Angeles man asked.

"Vine cuttings smuggled in from abroad," Tom said.

"That's ridiculous. I wouldn't jeopardize the valley vineyards. You need a three-year quarantine on imports," I said.

"I'm just saying…" Tom said.

Luke stood at my side. He nodded to the couple and smiled. "Hello."

The woman smiled back brightly, already enamored after one word.

"What were you saying?" Luke asked Tom.

"Just a rumor," Tom said as he drained his glass. He ran his finger down the list. "I'll try the Syrah. Who did the artwork?"

"Jameson," I said.

Luke went back to his customers.

Tom looked over at Jameson. "Well, well, he's good for something."

I felt heat rise to my face. "He's quite talented. He's designed the labels for our next releases." I walked to the cupboard in the corner and brought back the four labels.

"Wow," the Los Angeles woman said. "Those are captivating. Sort of magnetic and mystical."

"Yeah, it's definitely the twilight zone here," Tom said.

"Are there prints for sale?" the woman asked.

I eyed Jameson, busy pouring wine. "Maybe in the future."

"Well, I'd buy a print," she said. "The detail draws you into the scene."

I poured Tom the Syrah as Caleb came in and refreshed the appetizers. The Los Angeles man filled up a plate and returned to the counter.

"These are tasty," he said, chewing.

A young couple came in and stood at the counter on Tom's other side. "Two to taste," the man said.

People were lingering. Looking at the photographs, eating appetizers. It was not a taste-and-run day.

"You've got an illegal alien serving wine, you're at capacity for the fire code, and you're serving food," Tom said. "Do you have a permit for that?"

"Caleb's kitchen is permitted, and he has a catering license. Try some. He's a professional chef." I was starting to enjoy this.

I watched a couple depart with a full case of wine. We were in business now; wine was flowing out the door, and I wasn't going to let Tom spoil it.

"How did the fermentation go with our grapes?"

"I just added more yeast," Tom said.

"Ah." I put my head in my hands. The grapes' natural properties set off fermentation. He had ruined our grapes, the natural terroir of Harmonie. The wine would finish harsh. I had lovingly tended the grapes, and he had poisoned them.

Chapter Thirty-Six

*L*uke and I sat on the porch off the bedroom drinking coffee. Scents of bay laurel and eucalyptus hung in the air. I leaned back in my chair. The reopening of the tasting room had been a success. There had been a steady stream of visitors all weekend, and I'd sold a lot of wine, critical to financing the vineyard and winery. There were still so many improvements to make.

I glanced at Luke. Deep in thought, he gazed over the still valley. My mood sank. He had to leave tomorrow. I felt my engagement ring, still surprised by his proposal. He'd been such a gentleman, calling Dad from France and asking permission to marry me. But how would this marriage work? I had so much to do here. Barrels to bottle and the biodynamic certification inspection scheduled for January. And then what? I couldn't just walk away from Clos de l'Harmonie. I thought of what my grandparents had told Stan. "She'll know what to do."

Well, in this case I didn't have a clue. I knew two things I wanted to do: make renowned wine and be with Luke.

Luke reached for my hand. "You look so sad."

I tried to smile. We had one more day together, and I wanted it to be memorable.

"Let's leave for Santa Barbara soon. There are some places to explore, and later we can hang out on the boat. I ordered a picnic dinner from Violet."

Luke squeezed my hand. "I'm all yours."

"Before we leave though, I need you to taste a barrel and tell me what you think," I said.

"Do you ever slow down?" Luke stood, pulled me to my feet, and kissed me.

In the barrel room, I picked up my notebook and the pipette and handed Luke a glass. From a barrel near the back of the room, I carefully unscrewed the stopper and inserted the pipette for a sample. I plunged it into Luke's glass. The deep red liquid swirled. "It's seventy-nine percent Merlot, fourteen percent Cabernet Sauvignon, and seven percent Cab Franc."

Luke took a sip, held it in his mouth, and spit it into the bucket. "It needs more time. That's all."

"It's been aging twenty-two months," I said.

"Give it two more. It's a beauty."

Relieved, I screwed the stopper back on the barrel. We walked out into the office area. Jameson was at the desk, sketching.

"What are you cellar rats doing?" he asked.

"Tasting wine," Luke said.

"So early?" Jameson asked, raising an eyebrow.

"You don't swallow. I needed a second opinion," I said.

"Go to Santa Barbara and have fun. You deserve it," Jameson said.

"Tasting wine is always fun," I said.

"Well there's more to life than wine," Jameson said.

Not to Luke and me, I thought.

"Hold down the fort. I'll be back tomorrow afternoon," I said. "I'm having lunch with Mom."

"Better you than me," Jameson said. "I have no answers to her questions other than I'm doing well here, with you."

Jameson stood and held out his hand to Luke. "It was nice to meet you," he said.

Luke shook his hand. "The pleasure was mine."

"So, are you going to move over here?" Jameson asked.

Luke and I exchanged a glance. "We're still figuring things out," I said.

"Take care of Olivia for me and keep an eye on Leroy. Something is off with him," Luke said.

Jameson laughed. "Olivia doesn't need taking care of. I mean, look at this place. It's been transformed by a force of nature. Leroy, now there's another story."

That night, staying over on the boat, Luke held me close. "When will we see each other again?" he asked.

A lump swelled in my throat. I held Luke's chestnut-brown eyes with mine. "Maybe I can come over in February?"

His eyes clouded. "February? That's months away."

"We both have wine to bottle, and I need to be ready for the certification inspection in January."

"We have to make this work, Olivia, now that I have finally found you."

I caressed his perpetual five-o'clock shadow. "We'll make it work. I'll come for a month in February." I had no idea how to pull that off except to hire more workers, which I needed anyway.

"Have you thought about a wedding date?" he asked.

I shook my head. A week ago, I thought I'd lost him to Nicole, and now I was engaged. "You surprised me." I held out my hand and admired the ring.

He kissed me. I closed my eyes and sank into him. I'd do anything for him. We were made for each other. Being with him was effortless, natural. But would I give up Harmonie? I couldn't. My grandparents had trusted me to keep it going.

Chapter Thirty-Seven

*L*uke walked up the steps of the plane parked on the tarmac. At the top step he turned, waved, and blew me a kiss. I returned it, my heart heavy. I waited on the bench outside of the terminal and watched his plane fly south toward Los Angeles, disappearing in the sky. Our future was vast and unknown. Tears wet my cheeks. I sat glum and paralyzed. Love wasn't supposed to feel this bad.

The thought of having lunch with Mom sank my mood lower. I made my way to the car.

Mom, already seated on the patio at the restaurant, waved as I approached. I gave her a kiss on the cheek and slid into the seat across from her. Her gold sparkly sandals complemented her impeccably crisp beige linen suit.

"Thanksgiving was wonderful, darling. And you're engaged! You never cease to astonish me."

"Thanks, Mom. Caleb did most of the work. And I'm as surprised as you about Luke's proposal. I mean, we talked about it in France, but…"

"Your ring is magnificent. And he comes from such a distinguished family. I'm just sad that you're moving to France."

"I'm ah… we don't know what we're doing yet."

"Well you're certainly not going to stay at Harmonie when you could be living on a wine estate in the south of France."

"I love Harmonie."

The waiter appeared, and we each ordered a glass of local Sauvignon Blanc. I needed a drink to calm my words.

"Of course you do. But think of your future."

"My future is to become an extraordinary vintner."

"Oh, I'm sure they'll let you dabble with a batch in France."

Dabble with a batch. The wine gene had definitely skipped a generation with Mom.

Our wine arrived, and I took a sip.

"So, when is the wedding? And just as important, where is the wedding? We need to reserve a venue immediately."

"I don't know. I'm going over in February, and we'll talk about it. Right now, I have so much to do at Harmonie."

"But it will be in Santa Barbara, right?"

"I haven't thought that far ahead, but I can't imagine Luke's aging grandparents making the trip to California."

"Oh. Well, there is so much to think about. Too bad there wasn't time for an engagement party while Luke was here. But I'll get a list of venues for you. Why not have a wedding in France and one in California?"

Mom had zapped my already low energy. I wanted to get back to the valley.

"Mom, I'm running a vineyard and winery now. I don't have time for two weddings."

"We'll see."

I took another sip of wine and closed my eyes for a moment. She only wanted to help. I opened my eyes and picked up the menu.

On the drive home, I felt depleted. Luke and Lili would be boarding the plane in Los Angeles bound for Marseille. Luke and Lili. The thought of them made me smile. Lili had been a surprise. How had her long weekend with Jon gone? I'd have to message her later and say goodbye again.

I pulled into Violet's Café parking lot. I needed to return Violet's picnic basket and containers. Across the street, I noticed a new billboard that read "Protect our water and way of life. Don't frack."

Violet greeted me with a hug. "How did the grand reopening go?"

"Successful. I moved a lot of wine, and Caleb's food pairings were incredible."

"He's going to start a dinner service here three nights a week, Fridays through Sundays," Violet said.

I smiled. "Good for Caleb. What's with the billboard?" I pointed to the sign outside the window.

"The state has been issuing permits to frack for oil and gas."

"That's not right. The fracking fluid is toxic. This is an agricultural community that depends on clean water."

"All we can do is try to shame them," Violet said.

"I have to go. I've been playing around for the past day and half," I said.

"And you deserved it. Did Luke get off okay?"

I nodded as tears welled in my eyes. Stay strong, I willed myself. But the tears spilled anyway.

"I can tell how much Luke cares about you. You're engaged to a hand-some, smart, and sophisticated man. You have a bright future together."

"But that's just it, our future. How can we be together? He's got a vineyard and winery in France, and I can't abandon Clos de l'Harmonie."

"Give it time. Don't rush anything. Keep on with your plans for Har-monie. Everything is going well there, and you're almost certified. Maybe he'll move here. He seemed so comfortable at Harmonie."

"Thanks, Violet."

I thought of Luke's key role at Domaine Laroche. His family was close-knit, and Luke was in charge, even though Bernard was the patriarch. How could he even consider living here?

We hugged goodbye, and I headed for Clos de l'Harmonie.

Chapter Thirty-Eight

*O*n the front porch of the house I was greeted by a huge vase with a dozen red roses. I opened the card. *"Ma chérie, I love you more than ever. Counting the days until we will be together again. Love, Luke"*

I lifted the flowers and carried them into the house and set them on the table in the bedroom. I opened the French doors and sank onto the bed. On the bedpost hung one of Luke's white linen shirts. I slipped it off the post, held it close, and inhaled his scent of musk with a hint of lavender. I hugged the shirt and imagined him there with me.

I woke to the sound of Old Red coming up the gravel driveway. I got up and walked out to the vineyard. Caleb and Jameson were unloading untreated lumber on the far side of the orchard. I walked through a row of vines, in their direction, inspecting the vines as I went. They were healthy despite Tom's rough treatment.

"What are you building?" I asked.

"Vegetable garden boxes," Caleb said. "I am going to set them up at the end of the orchard if that's okay with you."

"Sure," I said, "fine with me. Violet tells me you're going to start dinner service at the café." Jameson continued to unload the wood as we talked.

"Yep. Starting this Friday. But don't worry, it won't interfere with my orchard work and other duties around here."

"I'm not worried in the least. I'm excited for you."

"Thanks. You gave me the idea."

"An idea is just an idea. You're going to make it happen."

I walked through another row of vines on the way to the office. At the desk, I pulled out my notebook and calendar. I noticed new wine label sketches tacked to the wall. Jameson had been busy. He took his job seriously. Did he know how talented he was?

This past week had been so busy with Luke, Thanksgiving, and the reopening of the tasting room, I needed to review the list of things to do for certification. December was less than a week away. That gave me a little over a month to get ready for the inspection.

I reviewed the vineyard documentation notes on the nine biodynamic preparations I had made and used. What was I worried about? Everything had been done according to Demeter Association standards. I needed to organize the notes and type them up and, in the meantime, continue to improve the operation.

I turned to the accounting system on the laptop and pulled up the sales from the opening. If I could consistently sell half the amount of wine every week that I had sold last weekend, I might be able to start paying Cody, Jameson, and Caleb small salaries.

I needed to restart the wine club and revive the marketing plans. I still had the list of previous members. Papa had let the club dissolve. Too much to keep track of, he'd said. Jameson might be good at managing the club. I'd approach him later. He could be charming when he wanted. We would start with the previous members and offer the club to tasting room visitors.

The door swung open, and Hailey bounced in. "They said I'd find you here," she said.

Was school out already? I'd lost track of time and glanced at the clock on my phone. I'd gone two hours without thinking of Luke.

"How does it feel to be engaged? Do you miss him already? When does he come back?"

"Hi Hailey," I said.

"Well?"

"Yes, I miss him, and I'm planning on going to France in February to visit him."

"February! That's so far away. How can you stand to wait so long?"

"I've got wine to bottle, and I need to get the vineyard and winery in shape for the certification inspection. The certification means everything to me right now. We're so close."

"You're so driven. I'd be so excited about marrying Luke I wouldn't be able to think. How can I help?"

"Can you keep taking care of the chickens? That's one less moving part I have to worry about."

"Of course. There are six new chicks, by the way."

Hailey set her backpack on the rough-hewn wooden floor, unzipped it, and waved her cell phone in the air. "I have news. I got into Davis. I got into the University of California at Davis!"

I gave her a hug. "Your father must be proud."

"I haven't told him yet. I just got this yesterday and wanted you to be the first to know."

"Thank you, Hailey. I'm really proud of you. And happy. The world needs more women vintners. When do you start?"

"Fall quarter."

"Wow."

"I know. Olivia, I'm freaked out."

"About what? Davis is a renowned university and town."

"But it's so big, and I've only known the valley. And I won't know anyone."

"I was in the same boat. I didn't know anyone. But I met people. People with the same interests. Like Cody and his girlfriend. We're still the best of friends and helping each other out."

Hailey remained apprehensive as she clasped her hands. Her high school graduating class was small, and Leroy barely let her out of his sight. "I'll tell you what. Once you're done with high school next month I'll take you up to Davis for a few days and show you around the campus and town. I can introduce you to some friends. And Molly is still there until May. She can help you find a place to live."

Hailey's expression brightened. "Thanks, Olivia."

"I need to go weed the yarrow and valerian flower beds. And you, you need to go home and tell your father the good news."

"Well, I'm not sure he'll think it's such good news. He doesn't know I applied. He wanted me to stay close and go to the University of California at Santa Barbara and study business."

"Business?" Hailey did not fit my idea of a business major.

Hailey nodded. "But I made up my mind last summer, talking with your nana. I always feel better on your property, with the vines and flowers and chickens. She was so proud of you wanting to carry on, growing grapes and making wine. And the biodynamic preparations are intriguing."

"My mom thinks I'm wasting my time. But Hailey, my advice is to follow your passion. It's your life. You get to choose. Let me know if I can help with your father."

Chapter Thirty-Nine

On Saturday morning the sunrise radiated a warm rose and apricot glow on the hills. I pulled on Luke's white linen shirt and stepped out through the French doors. The air was cool and fresh.

A movement under the large oak tree by the rock wall caught my eye. A large mountain lion stretched his powerful golden limbs while keeping an eye on me. He had to weigh over one hundred pounds. Such a beautiful animal. Did he sleep there every night? Maybe he watched over me. I smiled as he moved up the hill with a slow, graceful gait.

I shivered in the cool air, breathed deep and exhaled into the sunrise. How beautiful and how lucky I was to be there. Thank you, Nana and Papa.

In the kitchen, I stood waiting for the coffee to brew. Out the window, Cody and Jameson dashed down the road on their morning run.

"And they're off." Now I talked to myself out loud.

I worried Cody would find employment that paid real money. I still needed him in most aspects of the vineyard. He wasn't right for the tasting room. His skills were more those of an operational engineer, like Phillipe at Domaine Laroche. Ah… Phillipe. It had taken him time to trust me, but I think he finally did.

I took my coffee out to the front porch with my notebook and started to organize the next few weeks. I needed to set a date for the bottling when the descending moon stood in warm constellations.

Bottling dates, wine club launch, holiday decorations for the tasting room. My head had been in a fog the past few weeks. And Hailey? I needed to plan a trip to Davis after the certification inspection. Deep into writing notes I hardly noticed Jameson and Cody walk up the steps.

"Got any coffee, boss?" Jameson asked.

"Don't call me boss. Feel free to help yourselves to coffee."

Cody and Jameson returned with mugs of coffee and sank into the porch chairs.

"What's on your list today, Sister?" Jameson said.

"I have a new job for you," I said.

"I'm sure you do. You've been awfully mellow lately," Jameson said. "I've been waiting for your next wild idea."

"I'd like to put you in charge of the wine club. Can you redesign the old form and print some by this afternoon? What better gift for the holidays than a wine club membership? Also, we need to design an email, with some of your artwork, and get it sent out this weekend to our previous club members. They don't even know we've reopened."

"Whoa, what got into you today?" Jameson asked.

"I saw a mountain lion sleeping under the oak tree. He was so graceful. Did you know they are associated with the solar system and solar vibrancy? Some call them sun dancers. And they're guardians."

"Sun dancers? Solar vibrancy? Guardians?" Jameson shook his head.

"I think he's my guardian," I said.

We all took a sip of coffee.

"Cody, I want to decorate the tasting room for the holidays. Can you get us a Christmas tree? A live one so we can plant it afterward. We can decorate it tonight when the tasting room is closed," I said.

"I can get the tree, but I'm not good at decorating," Cody said.

"Thanks. Go to the organic nursery across from the feed store. We have an account there."

"Anything else, Sun Dancer?" Jameson asked.

"Yes, the descending moon is in fruit Monday and Tuesday. Clear your schedules. We're bottling wine."

Jameson finished his coffee and stood. "Mountain lions, solar vibrancy, descending moons? I'm going to go shower before I start my duties as the official wine club manager. By the way, how big was that mountain lion?"

I stretched my arms out to either side. "Big."

Chapter Forty

*I*n the closet of the guest room I found Nana's Christmas ornament boxes. I carried them to the tasting room. Jameson sat at one end of the long desk sketching furiously in his notebook.

"I found the wine club sign-up forms. They do need updating," he said, not looking up from his drawing.

"I'll get you the email and mailing lists of the past members," I said.

"I'm way ahead of you. But there aren't many emails. Mostly mailing addresses, so we'll have to send out postcards. I entered the emails under a new wine club contact group. I also set up an Instagram profile for Harmonie. That's the best way to communicate."

I glanced at Jameson. On the wall above him he had tacked a charcoal drawing of a mountain lion. I walked over to see it better. "You're on a roll."

"That's for you, Sun Dancer. This is for the wine club." He turned his sketchbook to me.

He had drawn a skillful rendering of the vineyard, winery, flower beds, orchard, and the valley beyond including the Clos de l'Harmonie logo. "Wow, perfect," I said. "It's inviting."

"I need you to review the form and update the pricing and any language changes you want. Scribble on it, and I'll make the changes." He handed me a form and started to color in the drawing.

Why had I underestimated him? He took his job seriously. That's what he wanted. His own role at Harmonie. Something he could manage. What else could I put him in charge of? I worked on the language for the club for the next hour, gave my corrections to Jameson, and opened the tasting room.

A wine tour van pulled up, and six young women got out and made their way into the tasting room.

"Girls' day out?" I asked.

"Bachelorette party. And we have a driver," one of them said.

The others laughed.

"A special day," I said. "Have a seat in the center area, and I'll bring the first pour."

Some headed to the seating area and others walked around, viewing the photographs for sale. I tried to guess who the bride to be was as I set up the glasses, bottle of wine, and tasting notes.

"We have six wines to taste today, two whites, a rosé, and three reds. There are others on request. Do you want to start at the top?"

"Yes, yes," said the girl I suspected was the bride to be. She wore an engagement ring.

"This is organic wine. We don't use any chemicals on the farm." I poured the first taste and wandered off to let them talk.

One woman read the tasting notes on the card. "Citrusy with blood orange and lemongrass on the palate. I like the sound of that."

Soon I brought over the next pour, a Grenache Blanc. "We have a wine club, if you want to join. Four shipments a year, or you can pick the wine up. Once you're a member you are welcome to come taste anytime at no charge. Great for holiday gifts."

"I'll get one for my parents," one of the girls said. "That's perfect. I had no idea what to get them."

"I want to join," said the bride to be. "It can be my wedding day gift to my fiancé."

"I'll get our wine club manager."

I went into the office. "I've got some women interested in the wine club. I told them you'd be out to sign them up."

"Already?"

I nodded and went back to the tasting room. Stan and Dolly stood at the counter.

"Hello, Olivia," Stan said.

"We're here to buy wine for the holidays," Dolly said.

"And to discuss a little matter with you," Stan said.

"Oh, is anything wrong?" I asked.

"No, nothing is wrong," Stan said. "But let's start with a tasting."

I set up their glasses and handed them the wine list. "Would you like to start with the Sauvignon Blanc?"

Jameson appeared, nodded to Stan and Dolly, and introduced himself to the group of women.

"Yes, the Sauvignon Blanc, please. It's my favorite. We're having a holiday open house and I want to serve some crisp white wines and your marvelous reds," Dolly said. "You're invited, of course." Dolly surveyed the room. "But I imagine you're quite busy here."

Stan raised his glass to me. "Congratulations on your engagement," he toasted.

"Oh yes," Dolly said. "Congratulations. Your mother is ecstatic."

"You talk to my mom?"

"All the time. We're in the Women's League together and work on the dental care committee for uninsured children," Dolly said. "We've gotten four dentists to volunteer their time."

"Oh. That's a good cause," I said. "Excuse me for a moment." I picked up a bottle of rosé and went to give the women their next taste. They hardly noticed me as they were listening to Jameson explain the wine club choices.

A couple came in the door and peered around hesitantly.

"Welcome. Are you here to taste?" I asked.

They nodded, and I motioned to the other end of the counter, away from Stan and Dolly. I had no idea what Stan wanted to discuss. I got the couple started and went back to Stan and Dolly.

"You're busy," Stan said.

"Yes. And I hope to be busier. Jameson is reviving the wine club. Try this Syrah. I think it would be perfect for your party."

Stan swirled the wine in his glass. The dark purple color foretold hints of berry on the nose. They sipped.

"Yum," Stan said. "Velvety." He read the notes. "Black currant, boysenberry, and plum. This is decadence in a glass."

"It's quite good," Dolly said. "But I want to serve something red in color. To match the decorations."

Now I'd heard everything. Red wine to match the decorations? "I've got a beautiful Bordeaux blend or a Pinot Noir. I'll be right back."

I went off to serve the couple their next pour and tell them about the wine club. Jameson had gotten the women their next wine and was describing the flavors as they listened intently.

I went back and poured Stan and Dolly the Bordeaux blend. A deep cherry red, with vanilla flavors from the Cabernet grapes, plum from the Merlot, and blackberry and smokiness from the Cabernet Franc.

"Olivia, now that you're engaged, don't you think it would be best to sell the vineyard?" Stan asked.

"Pardon me?"

"Don't you think you should sell and move on with your new life?" Stan said.

"This is my life. I love it here. Harmonie will soon be one of the few biodynamic wineries in the valley. I'm not interested in selling."

"But your mother thinks you should simplify your life. She thinks this is too much for you," Dolly said.

"Oh, so she's behind this?" It figured.

"Well, you do have an eager buyer. Tom contacted me again after he heard about your engagement. Aren't you moving to France?" Stan said.

"My fiancé is French, but it doesn't mean we'll live there. This vineyard is my dream. Excuse me."

I went off to pour the couple more wine, eager to get away from the conversation. Mom didn't think I could handle this? Well, I was staying the course to get certified in January. And if we sold more wine, I could pay salaries. I glanced at my engagement ring. What a tangled web I'd gotten into.

Jameson swiped the women's credit cards at the computer. They all left with wine purchases as a foursome entered the tasting room. Saturday had a good flow of tasters. I set the two couples up with a tasting.

Jameson stood talking with Stan and Dolly. We did need two people here on the weekends.

Stan and Dolly departed as renewed members of the wine club after buying three cases of wine for their party. Jameson got the cart and took the wine out to their car and they lingered, talking. At five o'clock, after a steady stream of imbibers, I flipped the sign in the window to Closed. The sun had already set.

I leaned against the counter and surveyed the disarray of glasses and wine bottles.

Jameson came back inside. "Olivia, do you know what you're going to do?"

"Well, no. I… what do you mean?"

"Are you going to sell the vineyard?"

"No! I'm not selling the vineyard. What gave you that idea?"

"I heard you talking."

"That's Mom's plan for me. But I am not selling Harmonie."

Jameson closed his eyes, tilted his head back, breathed deep, and exhaled. "Good. That's good. I like it here. I have my challenges and moods, but I like being part of this ragtag team. Look at all we've done."

"I could use your help here on weekends. We were busy."

"Yeah we were. I can help tomorrow. We have six new wine club memberships."

"Nice job."

"I didn't do much. It's the quality of the wine that motivates people to join."

"I can't wait for next year's crop. We'll make the first wine we can label as bio."

"I've been meaning to ask you, is Luke moving here? And when is this wedding?"

"I have no idea about either of those things. But something will work out."

"Wow, I would have thought you'd have figured out where you were going to live before you said yes to his proposal."

The tasting room door jangled, and Cody stepped in, dragging a hand-cart with a live Christmas tree. "Where do you want her?" he said.

"In front of the window, to the left of the door," I said.

Cody positioned the tree and stood back to admire it.

"Now that's a beautiful tree," I said.

"Let's decorate it," Jameson said.

I brought the two boxes over, set them by the tree, and opened them up. "These ornaments are practically antiques," I said.

Cody left and returned with his speaker and a beer. He sat on the couch and played corny Christmas songs and watched.

Jameson strung the lights while I found a spare extension cord. I spread out the ornaments. They were like old friends from the past. Some were hand painted. Others handmade. Jameson and I had helped decorate Nana and Papa's tree since we were very young. The tree came to life as we hung the ornaments.

"Did you know the French don't have a word for 'winemaker'? They can't conceive that a crafter of wine would be removed from growing the grapes," I said.

"Ha, half of California wine comes from sourced grapes," Cody said. "So, what do they call themselves?"

"Winegrowers."

"Is wine all you think about?" Jameson said.

"No, I think about how to pay the bills, how to start paying you guys, how to keep up with the vineyard schedule, the certification inspection, the bottling we're doing Monday and Tuesday…" And Luke, I thought about Luke. I pulled my phone from my pocket and checked my texts. No response from him. I checked WhatsApp. Nothing.

"I haven't seen Hailey for a week or so. There's a basket of eggs on our porch every morning, but no Hailey," Jameson said.

"I think Leroy has her under lock and key until she graduates next month," I said. "Did you know she got into UC Davis? I should call her and see how that conversation went with Leroy. He had other plans for her."

"Well, she turns eighteen this month, so she can do what she wants. Tell her about the mountain lion," Jameson said.

"Why don't you call her?" I asked.

"I have," Jameson said. "And texted. I think her phone is turned off."

"Maybe Leroy confiscated it. I'll go over there." The thought made me shiver, but I should check in on her. Out the window it was pitch black. "I'll go over in the morning."

Chapter Forty-One

*I*n the bright sunshine, I slipped past the chicken coop and through the gate to the Haywards'. I walked three steps and stopped. In the distance, a new chain-link fence had been erected behind the house. What was he up to now?

I stood frozen. Get this over with. Check on Hailey and leave. I strode to the front door and rang the bell. Just as I was about to pull the rope again the door opened and Leroy appeared in Carhartt jeans and a frayed plaid shirt.

"Now what?" he said.

"I haven't seen Hailey lately and wanted to talk with her."

"About what? Going off to college to become a winemaker? Why did you put that crazy notion into her head? She needs a practical degree."

"It's not crazy, and she made her own decision."

"She did, did she?"

"Leroy, Hailey turns eighteen next week. She can make her own decisions. She can choose her own future. It's her life."

Hailey came into view behind Leroy. She grimaced at me.

"With all this property, you could grow grapes here," I said.

"I have other plans for my property, and they don't involve grapes for God's sake."

"What is the fence for?"

"None of your business."

"Hailey, why aren't you answering your phone?" I asked.

"I'm on restriction," Hailey said.

"That's right. For going behind my back and applying to Davis," Leroy said.

"You should be proud of her and support her," I said.

"And you should leave my property right now." Leroy put his hand on the doorknob.

"Wait, I wanted to tell Hailey there is a mountain lion. I think he's living on my knoll."

"I've seen him," Hailey said. "He's beautiful."

"Well, I'll shoot him if he comes on my property. Cattle and mountain lions don't mix." Leroy slammed the door.

I turned and walked toward the gate. I glanced back. Hailey stood at the far window and watched me. She waved and smiled. If she could get through the next two weeks she'd be free. I waved but couldn't summon a smile.

I took a cup of coffee out to the porch with my notebook and sat gazing at the vineyard. Caleb came around the corner and up the steps.

"Why so gloomy?" he asked.

"Ah, worried about Hailey. Her dad is trying to control her. Help yourself to coffee."

"Thanks. But isn't that what dads do?"

"Not mine. He is supportive. My mom, on the other hand…"

Caleb returned with coffee and sank into a chair.

"How's the restaurant going?"

"The first weekend started slow, but now I recommend reservations. There are only ten tables. When are you coming?"

"Soon. After the holidays. After the certification. By the way, how is Violet? I haven't seen her in weeks."

"Ah…Violet. She's busy with the season. She's an amazing woman. A lovely woman."

"Yes, she is."

"I can't believe how my life has changed since I came to live here. I love this valley, this farm, and Violet, and I'm cooking again."

"I'm glad you and Jameson came here. I have to admit, the first day you guys showed up, I wasn't sure what to expect. Jameson was so edgy, and I was feeling a little guilty for having inherited the vineyard. There is so much to do around here, I knew I didn't have time for the chip on his shoulder."

"That was awkward. Two vagabonds showing up on your doorstep."

"But it all worked out. You've both carved out roles for yourself. I hope to start paying salaries next month."

"I don't need much, but I do need your advice," Caleb said.

"I'm not sure I'm the best person to give advice," I said.

"I want to ask Violet to marry me but... well, I'm afraid. What if she says no? What if it ruins our relationship?"

"If you love her, and you want to marry her, ask her."

"Just ask her?"

I laughed. "You might want to get a ring first." I held out my hand to gaze at my engagement ring and thought of Luke, Domaine Laroche, and the Alep pines inclined in the wind with their exotic scent.

"I guess I do need a ring. My mom offered me my grandmother's ring. I'll get it when I go up at Christmas."

Caleb stood, kissed me on the cheek, and bounded down the stairs. "See you tomorrow morning to bottle wine. Cody signed me up. Oh, and can I use the press for pomegranates? I want to make a glaze and bottle it."

"Of course."

Would Caleb still want to be the orchard manager if he got married? I went inside to type up job descriptions. When I started paying people, they needed a defined role. And I had another idea for Jameson.

Later I went to open the tasting room. Jameson stood behind the counter arranging glasses. A freshly printed stack of wine club forms had been set on the counters. The lights on the tree were lit.

He held up a form. "I'll get these printed in town when I get some time. But these will do for today."

"The artwork is really good. Did you know Luke's mother does their artwork and labels?"

"Well, I'll get to meet her someday if you go through with the wedding. Any mountain lion sightings?"

"Not this morning, but I did see Hailey. Leroy took her phone away. She's grounded for getting into UC Davis."

"What? That guy is a nutjob."

"Hey, read this job description for your position here." I handed him the paper.

"Job description? You're getting formal." Jameson took it and read the headers. "Art director, wine club manager, sales manager—retail and restaurants." He cocked his head. "No manure hauling, cow horn ceremony master, or seaweed director?"

"Well, we all pitch in for some things. But farming skills are not your strong suit."

A car pulled up, and I flipped the sign in the window to Open.

Chapter Forty-Two

I woke to the ring of my phone. I sprang to answer it. "Luke!" Out the French doors the sun had started to rise and under the oak tree lay the mountain lion, watching me, majestic in his pose.

"*Bonjour*, Olivia."

"I've missed hearing your voice. Do you know there is a mountain lion sitting under the oak tree outside my window right now?"

"A mountain lion? The big cat?"

"Yes, and he is big. I think he's my protector. I haven't heard from you lately. Is everything okay?"

"We've been bottling twelve hours a day."

"That's what we're doing today and tomorrow. Dad is coming up to help."

"I miss you, Olivia. I don't think I can wait until February to see you."

I watched the mountain lion get up, stretch, and steal away up the hill. "Luke, we never talked about where we'll live."

"In my house, of course."

I was silent, contemplating this. He was so sure of himself.

"Would you consider moving here?" I asked.

Now he was silent. What did he think I would do with Harmonie? I sat down on the bed and watched the sunrise paint the sky. "Luke?"

"I hadn't thought about living there. I guess I assumed you'd hire someone to manage the vineyard, and we'd live here."

Bring in an outsider to manage Harmonie? Never.

"Is that a no?" I asked.

"No, no. It's not a no. I will consider it. It's just… it would be diffi-cult. This is a big operation. Let's talk about it when you are here. Here in my arms."

"I'll be there in six weeks. How is Pepin?"

"Lonely without you, like me."

All the goings-on at Harmonie I wanted to tell him about seemed trivial now. My joy at hearing his voice slipped away.

"Olivia?"

"Yes?"

"Good luck bottling and give your father my regards. I love you," Luke said.

"I love you too."

We both hung up, and tears moistened my eyes. I needed to snap out of it. There were eight barrels of wine to bottle.

I showered, ate breakfast, and went out to the winery. As I marked the barrels to bottle, Caleb, Cody, and Jameson appeared. Cody had bottled lots of wine before, but Jameson and Caleb waited expectantly. Dad came in the side door with a box of pastries from Violet's Café.

"Caleb and Jameson can bring in the cases of bottles while Dad and I set up the equipment. Cody, you can move the barrels into the fill space."

Dad and I set up the labeling machine at the end of the line on the counter.

"This equipment is ancient. I need to upgrade it at some point," I said. "Who wants to be the bottle washer? I'll fill, Cody can cork, and someone can run the label machine. We need someone to put the bottles into the cases."

"I'll do the labeling. I know that quirky machine," Dad said.

"I'll wash the bottles," Caleb said. "I don't think I can screw that up."

"I'll pack the cases," Jameson said.

Cody put on some music, and the bottling of the Grenache-Syrah began. It took a while, but our workflow found a rhythm.

We talked about the wine I had blended with Papa, a 74 percent Grenache and 26 percent Syrah. Nana's wine label design, a watercolor depicting a flower opening to the natural world, complemented the burgundy-colored background. We fell silent for a while. I thought of Nana and Papa and their legacy at Harmonie.

We stopped as the sun set, leaving four barrels for tomorrow.

"Anyone ready for a glass of wine?" I asked. "You all deserve it."

"I've got to go," Dad said.

"I thought you were staying over," I said.

"Not this time. Your mom has plans for me. Some holiday affair. Believe me, I'd much rather stay here and catch up with you and Jameson."

"Oh, that's too bad," I said. And it was. I'd been looking forward to an evening with Dad. The house felt lonely. I'd rather keep bottling than go back to the empty farmhouse.

Chapter Forty-Three

With the bottling completed and the Demeter certification documentation typed and organized in a binder for the inspection, I focused on the accounting system and job descriptions for Caleb and Cody.

The following week, Cody and I sat in my kitchen drinking coffee at our informal weekly meeting to discuss the vineyard. I handed him his job description.

"Production manager," he read. "I like that."

"Will you stay on? I can start paying salaries in January. I've talked to neighboring wineries and have an idea what they pay their staff."

"So, you're offering me a real job?"

"Yes. Read it over and add anything else you'd like to do. It's a broad role."

"I'm going to have to think this over." He stared at the paper.

My shoulders sagged. We worked together so well. He never complained and was resourceful and innovative. I wouldn't trust anyone else to help manage the vines. Did he have another job lined up? Maybe he'd rather work for a larger winery. One of the big names.

"Well, I've thought it over. And yes, I'll stay on as production manager."

I exhaled. "You had me worried."

"I'll be moving, though, when Molly comes down and sets up her veterinarian clinic."

"Of course. In the meantime, we need to start lining up pruners for next month."

"I've already started asking around. My evenings at the tavern aren't all about playing pool."

"And for the harvest in the fall, what about students at Davis? Some type of working internship? I'm taking Hailey up there next month. I'll talk to Professor Clark."

"Hmm. That might be good for everybody. I wanted to ask you. Is Luke…"

"Don't ask. I don't have an answer. But stop by the tasting room after five today. I'm having an impromptu birthday party for Hailey. I even made a cake last night."

"I wouldn't miss it."

"And Cody, I'm so happy you want to be part of Clos de l'Harmonie."

"You're happy? I'm ecstatic. I'm going to go call Molly. And my parents. They've been wondering where my degree was going to take me in life."

Hailey burst into the tasting room after school. There were three different groups tasting. Laughter filled the room. I went out from behind the counter and gave her a hug. "Happy birthday!"

"I'm eighteen. My life can begin. I accepted the offer at Davis. I'm so excited."

"What about your dad?"

"He'll come around. And if he doesn't, it's his loss."

"Well, stick around. The crew is joining us at five."

"I can wash glasses and restock wine," Hailey said.

I smiled at her. I loved her energy. I hoped Leroy wouldn't stand in her way.

A steady stream of tasters came through. The holidays were good for wine sales. Harmonie was back in business.

Shortly after five o'clock the tasters departed, and Violet and Caleb came through the front door.

"Nice tree," Violet said as she set a small wrapped gift on the counter. She stepped closer to the tree. "It's quaint, sort of whimsical."

Jameson appeared from the office with a watercolor he discreetly hid under the counter, and Cody trailed after him with a book under his arm.

I went into the office and emerged with the chocolate cake, lit with eighteen candles. The pomegranate-and-Syrah-infused frosting seemed to glow red. Caleb began to sing "Happy Birthday" in his deep booming voice, and we all joined in. I set down the cake and took a picture of Hailey, beaming at us.

"Make a wish," Jameson said.

Hailey smiled at him as she blew out the candles.

I poured some Syrah for the group and iced tea for Hailey.

"Happy eighteenth, Hailey," I toasted.

"Happy eighteenth," the group repeated.

I cut the cake and served everyone.

"Start here, on your journey to become a winemaker," Cody said, as he handed Hailey a book titled *Guide to Wine: The ABCs of Wine Tasting and Appreciation*.

"Thank you, Cody. That's really kind of you."

Violet handed her the small wrapped package. Hailey opened it carefully, preserving the wrapping paper. Inside was a bar of Violet's handmade lavender soap. Hailey closed her eyes and inhaled.

"It's heavenly. I bet this is what France smells like," she said.

Jameson handed her his watercolor. An enchanted rendering of the vineyard and winery. "Take this with you when you go off to school. I don't want you to forget us."

"Forget you? Never. You're all I think about… and college of course."

A faint red tint crept up Jameson's face.

"But I will take it with me. I'm sort of nervous about going away."

I handed Hailey an envelope. She opened it and read: "This card is good for an all-expense paid reconnaissance trip to Davis in January." She gave me a hug. "Thank you."

"There are conditions though," I said.

"Ah," Caleb said. "Conditions. She drives a hard bargain."

"It has to be after the certification and after we bottle the next batch of wine. Molly invited us to stay with her."

Hailey nodded, smiling.

"What are you going to do between now and the fall?" Violet asked.

"Get a job in town as soon as school is out."

"I could use your help at the restaurant. Serving and in the kitchen. The bakery business has taken off," Violet said.

"Really? I'd love to work there. This is the best birthday ever."

"Hailey." A call came from outside. "Hailey Hayward." Leroy.

"I better go. He's taking me out to dinner," Hailey said as she gathered her gifts. "Thanks for everything."

"Invite him in for cake," I said.

"No, I don't want to spoil your evening. Plus, he thinks you're corrupting me."

"Voodoo vintner brainwashes girl next door," Jameson said.

Hailey laughed and slipped out the door with her gifts.

Chapter Forty-Four

*L*uke sent WhatsApp messages. At least he communicated, but he was silent on our living situation. Once I got the certification completed, I could think about the future.

Two days before Christmas Caleb and Cody drove up to the Bay Area to visit their parents. I stood on the porch and waved to them as they left, Cody at the wheel, honking twice.

Jameson and I were expected at Mom and Dad's house on Christmas Day, but my heart wasn't in it. What was wrong with me? Things were going well at the tasting room. The next batch of wine was almost ready to bottle. The Demeter certification inspector had confirmed his visit on January 9. Everything on track, except I missed Luke. I sank into a chair, pulled out my phone, and called him.

"Olivia! I was just thinking of you."

"I wanted to hear your voice."

"Are you excited for Christmas?"

"Not really. Are you?"

"In a way. I'm going to Paris tomorrow to spend it with my grandparents."

"You're going to Paris?"

"Yes. It was my mother's idea. She says I'm moping around here. We're going to have Christmas dinner at Nicole's parents' house."

The vision of Luke and Nicole spending Christmas together did not lift my mood.

"What are you going to do?"

"Jameson and I are going to Mom and Dad's."

"You don't sound very happy about it."

"That's why I called you. I'm feeling kind of down. I hoped you'd cheer me up."

"Think of February when we'll see each other again. That's what keeps me going."

I could hear laughter in the background and glasses tinkling.

"Where are you right now?" I asked.

"In the tasting room with Lili. Jon is here, visiting for the holidays. We're trying the new wine we just bottled."

"I'll let you go. Tell everyone hi."

"I'll call you tomorrow night from Paris."

He hung up. A moment later he sent a message. "I love you."

I smiled. That's what I needed to hear. A simple I love you. I responded in kind and went out to the vineyard to inspect the Merlot vines.

On Christmas eve, I opened the tasting room and turned on the lights to the tree. As if on cue, a wine tour van pulled up and three couples spilled out. I wasn't sure how busy I'd be on Christmas eve, but this was a good sign. I hadn't seen Jameson today and wondered what he was doing.

I served the group, and more tasters arrived. What a perfect way to spend Christmas eve, wine tasting. I envisioned Luke in Paris spending Christmas eve with Nicole. His mother sure had a way of pushing them together.

Around three o'clock the tasting room emptied. My phone rang, and Luke's photo appeared.

"Merry Christmas from France."

"Almost merry Christmas from California."

"What are you doing?"

"I'm in the tasting room, but everyone just left."

"You're working on Christmas eve?"

"Yes, we were busy too. How's Paris?"

"Beautiful. There are lights everywhere. It's very festive. Nicole and I went for a walk through the Tuileries."

"Oh? You sound happy."

"Yes, I am. A change in scene is good. You'll love Paris. We'll come here in February. I've got to go. My grandfather is waiting to make a toast."

"Merry Christmas."

"Merry Christmas."

I gathered the glasses and washed them and restocked the bottles I'd sold. I set out more jars of Caleb's pomegranate glaze. It was popular. Was Nicole at Luke's grandparents' house with him right now? I googled the Tuileries. The grand architecture of the palace, the carefully laid out gardens with benches, and the pond with small boats that kids sailed from the side looked idyllic.

I stared out the window. It was idyllic here, too. I flipped the sign to Closed, went to the door and locked it. I walked out through the office door to find Jameson. Old Red was parked under the old carport next to my car. At the bunkhouse, I called his name but no answer. I turned the doorknob and went inside. Empty. No Jameson. I scanned the vineyard rows, the orchard, Caleb's veggie garden, and the chicken coop.

Unconsciously I started up the hill to the old oak knoll. We'd planned to have Christmas eve dinner at the house, just the two of us. I approached the knoll and stopped. Under a large oak Jameson sat cross-legged with his sketchbook. I slowly walked up to the tree.

"Searching for the mountain lion?" I asked.

Jameson nodded. "And peace. Is this the place you come to think?"

"Yes."

"It's nice up here."

I sat down next to him.

"I finally see why you love it here. I never could figure out why you'd rather be here than spending the winter vacation skiing with the family in Lake Tahoe. Tahoe or the valley? We'd sort of joke about it."

"You'd joke about me?"

"Yes. But only the times you wouldn't come with us. But I get it now. I'm glad you inherited the farm. Mom would have sold it."

"At the first offer."

"I don't know what's going to happen if you move to France."

"I don't know what Luke and I are doing, but I'm just taking it one day at a time."

"Ha, that's my mantra."

"Leroy's finished his irrigation pond down there," I said.

"Irrigation? Hailey said it's a trout pond."

"A trout pond? The story keeps changing. At least it will attract wildlife."

"I invited Hailey for dinner tonight, but she had to go to her mom's. She wasn't too happy about it."

"Well, it is Christmas eve." I thought of Luke and Nicole spending Christmas eve and Christmas together with their grandparents, and a wave of jealousy rushed through me.

Chapter Forty-Five

New Year's Day arrived, and Caleb set about cooking a feast for everyone in my kitchen. A celebration of a new year. Hailey read a book on the porch while Jameson sketched. Violet arrived with a berry torte. I carried it into the kitchen and set it out of harm's way. Violet followed me in and kissed Caleb.

"Wait," I said. "Is that what I think it is?"

Violet held up her left hand and smiled. "We're engaged."

"I was terrified, but she said yes," Caleb said.

"And we don't know when," Violet said.

"Join the club," I said and hugged them both. "I'm so happy for you. Let me open a wine. We need to toast this momentous event."

I opened a Bordeaux blend and got out the crystal wineglasses as Cody appeared at the back door.

"Just in time," I said.

"Ah, she said yes, I see," Cody said. "I told you not to worry."

"To Caleb and Violet. To your love and happiness," I toasted.

"Love and happiness," everyone repeated.

"That is good wine," Cody said.

Caleb nodded. "Dark raspberry and forest herbs."

"We're bottling more like this next week," I said. "And… January is pruning time and the certification inspection is thrown in the middle."

"To a glorious month at Harmonie," Cody toasted.

Jameson walked in with Hailey in tow. "What are we celebrating?"

"Hard work," I said. "Oh, and Caleb and Violet's engagement."

"Wow," Hailey said. "Congratulations."

"You're a lucky woman, Violet. A good man is hard to find," Jameson said.

"Oh, I know," Violet said.

I pictured Luke. I had found a good man. He was just so damned far away.

After we bottled the Bordeaux blend, Cody lined up two experienced workers to help with the pruning. They arrived early one morning two days before the biodynamic inspection. We started in the Sauvignon Blanc plot and walked down the rows cane-pruning each vine.

Next door at Leroy's, a steady stream of tanker trucks rumbled in and out of the driveway. Was he filling the pond? I worked between the two men, partly to check their work and to get to know them. We needed to establish relationships for when we needed extra workers.

We talked about different pruning methods for different varietals.

"Which vineyards have you worked in?" I asked.

"Almost all of them at one time or another, either pruning or harvesting," the older man said.

"We worked here last fall, harvesting with Tom," the smaller man added. "But he's not our favorite. He doesn't respect the vines. He's got dollar signs in his eyes, like your neighbor there." He pointed to Leroy's property.

"They don't respect Mother Nature," the older man said.

"Do you think raising longhorn cattle is harmful to the earth?" I asked.

"I'm not talking about the cattle. It's the well," the smaller man said.

"All I know is that he's drilling a water well and building a trout pond," I said.

The two men stopped working and stared at me. Cody continued to prune.

"Is that what he told you?" the older man asked.

"To be honest, he's very elusive. He says it's none of my business."

"Well, I hate to be the one to inform you, but that there is an oil well and that trout pond is a wastewater pit," the smaller man said.

The words hung in the air. "What? What do you mean, an oil well?" I said.

"Leroy's leasing his property to a Texas company for a fracking operation," the smaller man said.

"What about permits and notifying neighboring properties?" I said.

"Oh, they have their permits, and they did notify properties. The Texas company did all that," the older man said.

"Fracking?" Cody said in disbelief.

A wave of nausea billowed through me. I stood paralyzed, watching yet another truck enter the driveway. I remembered the stack of envelopes in Nana's papers from ERG Operating Company, LLC, with a Texas address.

Cody took my arm. "We're going into the office. You guys can continue pruning."

I was light-headed as we walked. In the office, I slumped into a chair. Cody brought me a glass of water, and we stared at each other, incredulous. My mind whirled at the implication.

"We have to stop them," I whispered. "Find Jameson and Caleb."

Cody went out the side door. I sat, stunned. Could I still get Harmonie certified with a fracking operation next door? Did I want to live next to it? I stood and walked to the house. I needed to find the notification to neighboring property owners before I confronted Leroy.

I pulled the miscellaneous paperwork box from the closet and set it on the floor. Inside I found two unopened envelopes secured with a rubber band. The return address listed ERG Operating Company, LLC. I opened the earliest postmarked letter. Enclosed, a copy of the approved well stimulation permit. In the next envelope was a notice that water testing would be provided to all property owners within fifteen hundred feet of the well head if requested.

My head hung forward, and I closed my eyes. I was glad Nana hadn't known. This would ruin the valley. This would ruin Harmonie. The vineyard and farm might be a self-sustaining, living organism, but there would be a toxic wastewater pit ever present next door. I sifted through the paperwork for more correspondence. That is all they had to do? Notify the neighbors after they'd obtained a permit? The box held no other related documents.

I walked back to the office. Jameson and Caleb stood behind Cody reading something on the laptop. They all turned to me. Time stood still.

Finally, Jameson spoke. "Longhorn cattle, my ass."

"I found the regulations," Cody said, shaking his head. "It's pretty unreal. There are no public hearings, no public comment. Only neighboring property notification after the permit is approved."

"I found the permit," I said, holding up the paperwork. "Nana never even opened it. Who would? It was from ERG Operating Company in Texas."

"I'm glad she didn't know. She couldn't have done anything anyway. It would have only upset her," Jameson said.

"Well, I'm going over there to confront him," I said. "I'm not going to let him ruin my dream."

"I'll go with you," Jameson said.

We slipped through the gate by the chicken coop and stood at the chain-link fence. A tanker truck hose connected to the well tower pumped liquid down the well. Three men stood watching nearby. Four trucks idled, waiting their turn.

"Can't you read?" a booming voice said. "This property is posted. No trespassing."

Startled, we turned. Leroy stood behind us.

"Leroy, this is a sacred valley. An agricultural valley. A valley of award-winning wines. I am trying to get my biodynamic winery certified, and you just fucked it up. The entire valley is fucked unless you stop. You alone will kill it. Your father would turn over in his grave if he knew you were fracking on this once pristine property."

"You're fracking?" Hailey appeared from behind us.

"Some people call it that. Others call it well stimulation," Leroy said.

"You lied to me. You said you were drilling a well," Hailey said.

"I didn't lie to you. I did drill a well. An oil well."

"And the trout pond is a wastewater pit," Jameson said.

"Leroy, I need a list of what's in the fluids you're injecting, and I want our well tested," I said.

"There is a number to call on the paperwork sent to your grandmother for water testing. As to the composition of the fluids, well, they are a special cocktail, it's a trade secret, but the permit division knows, they just can't reveal it."

"A trade secret? We have a right to know. I'm growing grapes, vegetables, and fruit next door and selling it to the public."

"The regulations accommodate trade secrets," Leroy said.

Hailey stomped off to the house and slammed the door.

"Olivia, there is oil underground here. The geologists are almost positive. There is an oil reserve under your property. Lots of oil," Leroy said.

"So that's why Tom is so hot to buy my property?"

"And for the grapes."

Hailey reappeared with a suitcase.

"And where do you think you're going?" Leroy asked.

"Anywhere but here."

"Hailey, you're my pride and joy. I'm doing this for you," Leroy said.

"Not anymore. Fracking is your pride and joy. All you can talk about is harnessing the earth's energy. You lied to me. This is a renowned agricultural valley, and you're fracking. I don't want to have anything to do with you."

"What about school? How are you going to pay for school?"

"Loans and part-time jobs. I want nothing to do with fracking money. Olivia's right. Grandpa would be outraged like the rest of us," Hailey said.

I turned and started to walk back. Jameson took Hailey's suitcase, and they followed.

"Hailey," Leroy called. "Wait. I'm doing this for you."

Hailey called back, "The only thing you can do for me is to stop fracking."

Chapter Forty-Six

Cody and Caleb were still reading the Division of Oil, Gas, and Geothermal Resources regulations when we got back. They regarded Hailey and the suitcase Jameson carried.

"So, it didn't go so well, I take it," Caleb said.

"We're doomed," I said.

"I'm sorry," Hailey said.

"It's not your fault," I said. "He deceived all of us for money. If the farm goes under, Tom will be able to buy it cheap. They'll be partners in crime."

"Don't talk like that," Cody said. "The farm is not going under."

"Let's all get back to work," Cody said. "Jameson, you get tasting room duty today and Hailey can help behind the scenes. Olivia, you need to read these regulations to understand your rights, but as far as I can see, there aren't any."

Thankful for his take-charge attitude, I sat down at the laptop to read. But first I would call the number on the notification and schedule the water test. This was a living nightmare, and the Demeter inspector was due the day after tomorrow.

My phone rang, and Mom's photo smiled at me. Not now, please, not now.

"Hi, Mom."

"Olivia, I'm planning your wedding shower. Have you registered anywhere yet? I can help with that, you know."

"We haven't even set a date. I can't deal with that right now, Mom. I have problems in paradise."

"Paradise, where are you?"

"Harmonie."

"That's not paradise."

"It was until this happened. We have to rename it Clos de l'Tragedy."

"What's the matter?"

"Leroy Hayward is fracking next door."

"Fracking? What is fracking?"

"It's injecting a toxic fluid under high pressure into rocks so they fracture and the trapped oil gets pumped out."

"Does he have a permit?"

"Yes. But our well is at risk for contamination, my inspection is two days away, and certification is unlikely now. And who wants wine or fruit from a farm next to a fracker with toxic wastewater pits?"

"Olivia, I really think you're overreacting. To be honest, you need to get your priorities straight. You have a wedding to plan."

"Mom, my dream is going down the drain."

"Even more reason to get on with your life."

"That's all you have to say? I have to go."

"Olivia…"

"Bye, Mom." My God, were we really related?

I called the water testing service and scheduled a test for that afternoon. I read about fracking and the law. It involved a patchwork of state and local regulations and numerous agencies.

I phoned the closest Oil and Gas District office in Orcutt and asked to speak with a supervisor. He pulled the permit and answered my questions. Yes, the well had been inspected. Yes, an inspector had been present when the shutoff was tested. Yes, a twenty-five-thousand-dollar indemnity bond was on file. Yes, the trade secret fracking fluid chemical constituents were on file but not open to the public.

"How do I file a complaint?" I asked.

"What type of damage has occurred?" the supervisor said.

"You mean contamination has to occur first?"

"Well yes, or damage to property."

"I have applied for a biodynamic farm and production certification and now it's at risk for approval."

"I have no knowledge of that term or certification, but if you have been harmed as a business, you need to resolve it in civil court," the supervisor said.

"Civil court? So, he can frack all he wants, ruin businesses and essentially ruin our pristine valley."

"The operator has followed all of the regulations."

"The people in the valley are trying to improve the environment, promote sustainability, produce high-quality products, and promote tourism, and some greedy people in Texas can ruin it. There is something very wrong about that, don't you think?" I said.

"Ma'am, the local landowner signed the contract with the operator. The Texas company is supplying the know-how. They are complying with the permit. Now, is there anything else I can help you with?"

I took Hailey's suitcase into the house and upstairs to the guest room. It would be nice to have someone else in the house, despite the circumstances. I walked outside and through the vineyard to check on the pruning. Not bad. I caught up with Cody and the two hired hands. What had started as a beautiful day, full of promise, had turned into a tragedy for Clos de l'Harmonie. Cody handed me newly sharpened pruning shears and didn't say a word. My expression told him everything. I needed to work with the vines. I needed to think.

Since the operation next door was inspected and permitted, maybe it wouldn't affect the certification. But knowing it was next door made me sick. The chemicals used, the waste pits, the millions of gallons of water wasted. Why didn't he harness the sun and create a solar farm? He could sell electricity. He could lease out his land to a winemaker to grow grapes. But no. He chose to frack, and now he'd lost his daughter. Let him stew on that while he worshiped his oil derrick.

As we finished the row, Caleb, who had been pruning the orchard, walked up. "I've got sandwich fixings if you want to join me at the bunkhouse."

I'd forgotten we offered to feed the workers. "I have to make a phone call. I'll be over soon," I said. "And thanks, Caleb." I walked to my backyard and phoned Luke.

"*Ma Chérie.* I hoped you'd call. Tell me exactly where you are. I want to visualize you."

"I'm lying on the picnic table in my backyard under the big oak tree."

"I wish I was lying there with you."

"Luke, I've had the worst day."

"Is it the pruning or do the vines have a problem? No, let me guess. The workers didn't show up."

"No. It's my neighbor."

"Ah, the deranged cowboy."

"Remember the water well he was drilling and the trout pond?"

"*Oui.*"

"Well, it's an oil well and a wastewater pit."

"Olivia, I know California has the reputation of being a fantasy land, but you must be hallucinating."

"I wish I were. I'm in a nightmare. He's fracking. He has a permit, and there is nothing I can do."

"Fracking? The French Parliament banned fracking years ago."

"It's allowed here and it's happening right next door. My dream is ruined."

"No, Olivia, you still have everything."

"What if I don't get certified because of him?"

"Wait and see. You'll know soon enough."

I closed my eyes and all I could see was the line of tanker trucks pumping water and chemicals into the well.

Chapter Forty-Seven

*E*arly Friday morning, I went out to the office to prepare for the Demeter inspection. I hadn't slept well, nervous about the inspection. Each time I drifted off to sleep, visions of the oil derrick reared up and swept over me like a rogue wave.

Jameson was in the office working on a label design. "I have an appointment this morning with a supermarket chain to stock our wine," he said. "Harmonie will be in the local wine section in two counties."

"That's big. Good job." He took his new role seriously, I was happy to see.

"Turns out, I recognized the distributor's name from college and I called him. He's more than happy to stock a local winery. But you need to tell me which wines you want in the stores."

I turned on the laptop and checked the inventory.

"Are you okay? You look tired," Jameson said.

"To be honest, I haven't slept much the last two nights. I'm worried about the inspection and the consequences of what's going on next door."

"One step at a time."

"Oh, so now it's a step and not a day?" I took out a tasting sheet and checked off four wines. "Let's start with these."

"Okay. I'll be back by eleven to open the tasting room. You've got your hands full."

"Oh, shoot. I forgot about the tasting room. My mind is scrambled. Thanks."

"You forgot something? That's a first. Good luck today." Jameson gave me a hug and left for his meeting.

I watched him leave. Nothing like the person who'd arrived here last year with a chip on his shoulder. He had a purpose now. He knew I counted on him. I picked up the sketch of the new label. I needed to make a wine worthy of this artwork. A special wine. I leaned the sketchbook against the wall. I wanted to see it as I worked.

The Demeter inspector arrived at nine a.m. as scheduled. Relieved, I recognized him as the same inspector who had made the initial farm visit a year ago. I greeted him outside the tasting room.

I took a deep breath and exhaled, trying to keep my nerves in check. "Good morning, John," I said.

"The place is quite different from last year. You've been busy," he said.

"Thank you. I have an admirable team." I clutched the documentation binder to my chest.

"Let's start with the agricultural growing application and move on to the processing application." The inspector attached a checklist to a clipboard. "Let's start with the orchard."

He was all business, which was fine with me.

In the orchard, Caleb stood on a ladder, pruning the apple and pear trees. He stopped work and joined us. I introduced him to John, and he followed us as John asked questions about the preparations used. I opened my binder to the orchard section and reviewed the history and timing with the biodynamic calendar.

"Okay, on to the vineyard," John said.

"That's it?" I said.

"Yes," John said. "I'll inspect the preparation and compost storage areas after we walk the vines."

Caleb winked at me and went back to work.

John and I zigzagged our way through the forty-acre vineyard, stopping to talk about the bio preparation application methods I had used. He made notes alongside his checklist. We inspected the compost piles and checked my documentation for their composition and application dates. He moved on to the preparation storage areas, both in the ground and in the winery. By twelve thirty we had scoured the entire property except for the upper area, left wild for biodiversity, far larger than the 10 percent required.

Cody and the two workers were eating lunch outside the bunkhouse on the hand-hewn picnic table Caleb had built.

"You're welcome to join us," Cody said.

"Sounds good," John said. "I'll get my lunch from the car."

"Help yourself to the refrigerator," Cody said to me.

I returned with a yogurt and two glasses of water. John, Cody, and the two workers were already engaged in a conversation about the soil at Harmonie and the vitality of the vines. I listened and rested up for the afternoon inspection, thankful to Cody for his distraction. Although exhausted, I needed to stay engaged. I'd been waiting for this day.

After lunch, Cody gave John and the two workers a quick tour of the bunkhouse. The workers were impressed.

"I'd stay here anytime," one said.

John and I went into the winery. John switched gears from the farming inspection to the wine-making inspection. In the winery, I showed him the equipment, storage barrels, storage area, bottling method, cleaning agents, and records. When John had finished, we went through the office into the tasting room. Jameson talked with customers as we walked outside.

"You've got a nice operation here, Olivia. A healthy vineyard and orchard. Adherence to the standards. Impeccable record keeping. But I have one concern."

Oh God, here it came. The trouble next door.

He glanced to Leroy's property. "It's what's beyond your fence line."

"Can we sit down for a moment?" I asked.

"Of course."

We sat on the bench in front of the tasting room, and I tried to compose myself. I opened my notebook and took out the well permit. "We've been a certified organic winery for decades. I've converted to a biodynamic farm per the standards. And then my neighbor goes and does this." I handed him the permit, but he didn't take it.

"I've seen the permit. It's available online at the Division of Oil and Gas. We research neighboring properties."

"He's permitted and has been inspected. And there is nothing I can do about it. I only found out what he was doing this past Tuesday, and I've been sick about it ever since."

"It's unprecedented for us. The Evaluation Circle held a conference call before this inspection to discuss the matter. There was some debate. Our standards don't specify what nearby activities are prohibited. I will write up the inspection report tonight and submit it to the Evaluation Circle. They'll review the report and findings and make a recommendation to certify, or not, and provide any additional requirements."

I nodded numbly. I bet there had been a debate within the Evaluation Circle. "Thank you, John. It's been a pleasure having you here. I'm sorry I'm not at my best right now."

"I understand. But please know you've done a good job here. You'll get the Evaluation Circle decision and summary report in about a week."

I stayed on the wooden bench and watched him drive off. That sounded positive. I had to remain positive. The farm, a living organism: self-contained, self-sustaining, following the cycles of nature. And the grapes were expressive. They had a taste of the place. Clos de l'Harmonie terroir.

I walked up the porch steps, sat in the rocker, and put my head back. It was going to be a long week waiting for the report. The sky thickened with clouds, and the air shifted. I watched the curve of the mountain change colors. I thought of Luke and France. I could almost smell the pine and lavender. The distance between us was too great, and I felt we were drifting away from our connection. I imagined living alone here and running Harmonie. I could do it, but my heart felt empty. I closed my eyes and pictured Luke living here. The thought of Luke always made everything better.

I woke to a sound. Jameson, Cody, and Hailey were seated around me.

"Sleeping on the job, I see. How did it go?" Jameson said.

"He liked that we had a mountain lion."

"And?" Cody said.

226

"The farm is healthy; our wine making and processing meet the standards, but… there is an issue beyond the fence line."

"Damn him," Hailey said.

"The committee is discussing it. I'll have their certification recommendation in a week. I'm going to think positive. And stay very busy," I said.

The light faded as a figure approached. Leroy stopped at the bottom of the steps. "Hi, Hailey, I was hoping to find you here."

Everyone was silent.

"How is your job?" Leroy asked.

"I love it. Being in town and talking with the customers. Not being under lock and key."

"I only want to protect you," Leroy said.

"From who? The organic farmers? The vegetarians? The locavores? Winemakers? They are so dangerous."

"Hailey, please come home."

"I won't step foot on that property as long as you're fracking. There are a hundred things you could do there for income, and you chose fracking."

"I don't want to have a rift between us," Leroy said. "You mean everything to me."

"Okay, so do something positive for the valley and stop that operation," Hailey said. "It's not too late."

Leroy turned and strode toward the gate.

Chapter Forty-Eight

*T*he restaurant was noisy and warm. Candles flickered on white linen tablecloths. A more elegant atmosphere than the café at breakfast and lunch service. Caleb had insisted we all come on Saturday night. Violet joined us. It felt good to get out. Most days I never left the farm. I needed to get away from Harmonie and the pending certification recommendation.

Caleb seated us. He glowed in his element. A waiter brought menus and two bottles of wine. I recognized him. My grandfather occasionally hired him during the harvest or for odd jobs. One had to be versatile to live here.

"Best wine in the valley," the waiter said.

I smiled at the Clos de l'Harmonie labels. Caleb brought Hailey an iced drink with sprigs of mint and lavender. "Fresh lemonade with a lavender infusion."

Menus were passed around. Jameson's colorful artwork created a border, and the menu of the day was inserted under tabs.

"Oh, the hibiscus citrus papaya salad is to die for," Hailey said. "And you have to try the lime tartlets with orange blossom cream for dessert."

I glanced her way. Five months ago, she didn't have a clue what half of the menu items were. Now she knew her way around the kitchen.

"You've had them before?" Cody asked.

"When Caleb perfected his recipes, Violet and I were the tasters," Hailey said.

I smiled at her. A confident foodie. I took a sip of the Pinot Noir. It had aromas of earthy cedar, and supple berry, and it had a fresh edge and a silky-smooth finish. I silently gave a nod to Papa. We had created this wine together. And it was good. Around the table, our group, once a ragtag team, was now truly seamless, willing to do anything to get the job at hand done. I lifted my glass, "Life is good."

"Life is good," Violet and the others toasted. Caleb raised a water glass to me from the window of the kitchen.

We ordered and soon the first course arrived, grilled shrimp with a basil lemon pistou. The conversation quieted to murmurs as we concentrated on our first taste.

"This is yummy," Hailey said.

"I'm going to start a blog," Jameson said. "We'll highlight what we're doing on the farm. The magical potions, the best celestial days to drink wine…"

"Every day is a good day to drink wine," Cody said.

"According to the lunar calendar, fruit days are the most favorable days to drink wine," I said.

A couple at a neighboring table got up. I recognized them. They owned a winery about a mile down the road from Harmonie. They stopped at our table as they were leaving, and we exchanged greetings.

"We want to stop by and see what you've done," the woman said. "We hear the tasting room is getting a lot of traffic."

"Yes, please do," I said.

"I hope the oil well doesn't hurt your business," the man said.

I nodded, unable to speak. My chest tightened, and my throat closed. Violet squeezed my hand as they went out the door. I felt like a fool. Was I the last to know what Leroy had been up to? But he had been secretive. He'd deceived Hailey, and she lived there.

"Don't listen to them. The wine speaks for itself. And with what Jameson is doing now with marketing, business will be booming," Violet said.

The waiter served the main course, sea bass with lemon fennel butter.

"The oil derrick looming next door is a curse on the farm," I said.

"Come on now," Violet said. "We got you out to take your mind off things."

Hailey stared at her lap. I'd made her feel bad, the last thing I wanted to do.

"Hailey, as soon as I get the certification recommendation we'll set a date for our trip to Davis this month."

"I'd like that," she said.

And in February, I'd be in France, with Luke. I warmed at the thought of him yet felt conflicted about time away from Harmonie with so much to do. Did I really say I'd stay a month? But we probably needed a month to figure things out.

Chapter Forty-Nine

On Sunday, I went into the office to plan the vineyard activities for the upcoming season based on the biodynamic calendar. Fortunately, except for continuing to prune, February was a quiet month for applications. Jameson came in with a cup of coffee.

"What's on the schedule for this week?" he asked.

"We're bottling another batch of the Bordeaux blend Monday and Tuesday. Dad's back at work, so Violet and Hailey are going to help."

Jameson flipped through his sketchbook. "Here." He held out a page. "T-shirt design?"

An intricate yet whimsical design of the tasting room and vineyard. "I like it," I said.

"Here's the one I'm working on for Violet. She wants her staff to wear matching T-shirts." He flipped to another page and held it up. "On a pale violet shirt, of course."

I laughed. "That's perfect for the café." He did have talent but didn't want any praise, so I withheld my admiration. I could manage a stick figure drawing but that was about all. He had inherited Nana's talent, and I hoped I'd inherited Papa's wine-making skills. We'd see. The wine about to be bottled was mine alone.

"The grocery store distributer is picking up their wine tomorrow morning. I'm going to pull the cases and set them inside the loading dock. See you in the tasting room later."

"Aren't you going for a jog?"

"No, Sunday is a day of rest."

"I'm going to get my workout raking the pruned vine canes with Cody and stacking them for a new compost pile."

"Better you than me." Jameson picked up some paperwork and went to the storage area. I heard the small forklift engine whine.

I met Cody in the Sauvignon Blanc plot. He had already raked part of a row and loaded the cart hooked to the quad. Jack Johnson wafted from his speaker. Cody always had music.

"Morning," I said.

"It's a good morning," he said.

I put on my gloves and began to rake. He pulled away with a full container to empty it on the other side of the barn, near the compost windrows.

The music faded with him. I continued to rake. It was quiet next door, but granted, it was Sunday morning. The constant whine of the trucks driving in and out delivering the fracking fluid had become part of the landscape noise.

Cody returned and so did the music. "Cody, what if we start an internship program here for students at Davis to work and learn about biodynamic practices? We could take on two or three at a time, certain times of the year. They would get course credit and we would get some labor and promote biodynamic practices."

"Are you trying to create more work?"

"No, think about it. They would work alongside us and we explain what we're doing, contrast it to typical farming methods. They can read the Demeter principles and standards. Remember how hard it was for me to find an internship on a certified vineyard?"

I thought of Luke and Domaine Laroche. I would be there in three weeks. I smiled and kept raking.

"Well, students need real opportunities, not just the test plots we managed. But don't you think you're getting ahead of yourself?"

"What do you mean?"

"You're not certified yet."

"I'm thinking positive, but that is on my mind day and night. Did you notice there are no trucks next door today?"

"It's Sunday."

"They were there last weekend."

"Well, maybe the fracking part is over, and the oil is ready to pump."

The hedgerow blocked the view of Leroy's property. Would they build an oil storage tank? How big would it be?

Chapter Fifty

Early Wednesday morning, I updated the tasting notes and website, adding the Bordeaux blend we finished bottling the night before. We'd bottled for the past two days and we'd had fun. Loud music blared as the bottles whirred down the line. And best of all, it had gone smoothly. Jameson had mastered the labeling machine, and Violet had brought us food in the evening and helped box the finished bottles.

I checked my email for the tenth time to see if the certification recommendation had been sent. Nothing from Demeter, but it hadn't been a week yet. There was a WhatsApp message from Lili.

Olivia,

Everyone is excited to see you in February. We're planning a little celebration for your engagement. It's supposed to be a surprise, but I wanted to let you know. If you're like me, you don't like surprises. Also, Mom wants to take photos of you and Luke for a press release.

See you soon.

Kisses,

Lili

Thank you, Lili, for the heads-up. Photos for a press release? A celebration? I had nothing to wear. When would I have time to go shopping? There were not many shops with dresses in the valley. I'd have to go to

Santa Barbara. I'd call Mom and invite her to come with me. She certainly knew all the shops. And Hailey. I'd invite her too. She could use a day out.

I went outside and walked through the vineyard and up to the oak grove. I could see the goings-on of Harmonie. Two figures jogged up the driveway, Jameson and Cody. I had a bird's-eye view of Leroy's place. It was so quiet there. The oil derrick stood out like a sore thumb, incongruous with the longhorn cattle grazing on the slope. The tanker trucks were gone, and the ERG Company's white work truck was parked by the unsightly chain-link fence. Two figures stood talking. I recognized Leroy in his tan Carhartt jeans, his fracking uniform. They were probably plotting where to build a storage tank.

I walked back down, keeping an eye out for the mountain lion. Did he live on the knoll? I hoped so.

Back in the winery, I cleaned the bottling area. We'd been too tired the night before to bother with it. The cleaning brought me satisfaction. We'd bottled 230 cases of a very unique wine. I would take a few bottles to France and ask Bernard and Phillipe for their opinion. No year and no harvest were ever the same. It was never boring. I hurried into the house to shower and get ready to open the tasting room.

Thursday afternoon I picked Hailey up from her job at Violet's Café. Jameson had agreed to take the tasting room duties for the afternoon. Hailey jumped into the car, smiling from ear to ear.

"Girls' trip," I said, as we set off for Santa Barbara to meet Mom downtown.

"I've never been on a girls' trip," Hailey said. "But I'm excited."

"You'll have to put up with my mom."

"I like your mom. She's sophisticated."

In the first store, Mom had called ahead, and the salesclerk had five dresses picked out. They liked to cater to Mom, a regular in the shop.

"This should be easy," I said.

"You're so thin," Mom said. "Are you eating enough? Or is it prewedding jitters?"

"Mom, we haven't even set a date. I've just been working hard."

"Why don't you let the boys do the manual labor? You should stay in the tasting room," Mom said.

"It doesn't work like that. It's all about the vines, the grapes, the soil, the compost, the preparations, the wine in progress."

She held out the first dress. A sleeveless white cotton shift. "Oh, try this one."

"It's nice, but it's winter there," I said.

"Try it on. Summer is almost here."

Hailey wandered around the store picking out more dresses.

"Okay," I said. "I'll try them all. Can you find a wrap or something warm to wear with it?" I went into the dressing room.

"I want to see them on you," Mom said.

I shook my head. This was going to be a trying day. I slipped on each dress and consulted Mom. None of them seemed to work. Hailey held up a few other dresses, but they weren't right either. They didn't feel like me.

"I think we need to move on to another store. Something for the younger crowd," I said.

Hailey agreed. Mom, resigned and disappointed, followed us down the street. Three stores later I found the perfect dress, pale blue, above the knee, with long diaphanous sleeves and delicate beading. I felt comfortable but elegant.

"It's a little bohemian, isn't it?" Mom asked.

"Yes, I love it," I said and twirled around, the material flowing with me.

"It's you." Hailey handed me a pair of shoes. "These are perfect with the dress."

I slipped them on and tied the delicate ribbon around my ankles.

"Well, I have to say, you do clean up well when we get you out of jeans and a T-shirt," Mom said.

Hailey smiled back at me in the mirror. Success.

Mom found a hair clip the same color as the dress. "Always accessorize," she said.

I bought the dress, shoes, and clip. "Let's find an outfit for you, Hailey, then we can go eat dinner."

In another shop, we found Hailey a sweater with a Native American pattern and skinny jeans.

"My treat," I said.

"No, I have a bank account now that I'm working," Hailey said.

The outfit would clearly wipe out her bank account.

"No, this is payment for helping us bottle wine. I insist. You'll need your savings for school."

She hesitated but agreed.

We were seated in a booth at Mom's favorite restaurant on State Street. Pictures of old Santa Barbara hung on the walls, and the starched white tablecloths and napkins gave the restaurant an intimate atmosphere. I relaxed. I had found a dress and envisioned how surprised Luke would be when he saw me in it.

Mom and I each ordered a glass of Pinot Grigio and Hailey iced tea.

"How is Jameson?" Mom asked. "Is he doing okay?"

"He's doing well. He's now the sales and marketing manager and bringing in some business. I'm proud of him."

"He never comes down to visit."

"You are always welcome to come up. He's quite busy with his art, T-shirt designs, the tasting room, the wine club, and marketing. Oh, and he's starting a blog."

"A blog? And what, pray tell, is he going to blog about?" Mom said.

Hailey giggled.

"Clos de l'Harmonie, the valley, whatever strikes him as interesting."

"Believe me, nothing of interest happens in the valley. Tell me about your trip. Are you going to set a wedding date?"

I knew this was coming. "Maybe."

"And as important, where are you going to settle? France?"

"You wouldn't move away, would you?" Hailey said.

"One thing is sure. Harmonie isn't going anywhere. Luke and I are going to figure it out next month," I said.

"I think you should sell Harmonie and simplify your life," Mom said.

"Yes, I know that's what you think. You've made it crystal clear. But Nana and Papa wanted me to keep Harmonie and nurture it as a vineyard and winery. I can't let them down."

When Hailey and I arrived back at the house, we'd no sooner turned on the lights when Jameson came through the back door.

"Hailey, Leroy stopped by the tasting room this afternoon asking for you," Jameson said.

"Okay, thanks. I'll call him tomorrow after work."

"He seemed edgy. Like it was urgent."

Hailey and I exchanged a glance.

"I'll call him in the morning. I don't want to ruin my day," Hailey said.

Chapter Fifty-One

*F*riday morning, Cody and I corralled the sheep and led them to the Cabernet Sauvignon plot to graze on the cover crop. The fava bean plants were waist high and the sheep all but disappeared in the flowers.

"Eat up so we can get in here and prune," I said to them.

"Any news from Demeter?" Cody asked.

"Any day now I hope."

We walked over to the Syrah plot and began pruning. The two workers were a row over from us. They'd agreed to work all month pruning. They were skilled and worked fast. Cody turned on music from his phone, and we worked silently, alone in our thoughts.

Just before eleven, I left to change clothes and open the tasting room. On my way to the house I saw Leroy standing in the driveway.

"Can I help you?" I asked.

"I need to talk with Hailey," Leroy said.

"She's at work. Jameson told her you wanted to talk and she's going to phone you."

"I need to talk in person. When does she get back?"

"Usually about four."

He said nothing but turned and walked toward his property. Jameson was right. I should put a lock on the gate and post a No Trespassing sign. The man creeped me out.

Hailey found me in the tasting room as I was trying to close. A small group had ordered a bottle of wine and sat on the couch and chairs in the middle. I didn't mind if they lingered. Their laughter warmed the room. It had been a busy day, and I needed to restock for tomorrow.

"I can wash the glasses," Hailey said.

"I'm sure you've had enough dishes for one day at the café. You can help me restock though."

We went about our tasks talking. The group finally stood and came up to the counter. They raved about the new Bordeaux blend and bought half a case. I couldn't wait for Luke's family to taste it. Soon, very soon. After they left, I turned the sign to Closed and went into the storeroom and filled the mop bucket with hot water.

Hailey sat on the couch and flipped through a biodynamic guide. "I don't get how it works," she said.

"How what works?"

"Preparation 500, the cow horn manure. This says you need one quarter cup mixed with three to five gallons of water for one acre. A quarter cup seems like a miniscule amount for an acre."

"Well, you apply it three times a year."

"So what does it do?"

"500 makes the soil more permeable. It stimulates microorganisms and allows the soil and vines to receive the planetary influences."

A loud knock on the door jarred me.

"Hailey, are you in there?"

"Oh shoot. I forgot to call my dad." Hailey went to the door and opened it. "Hi, Dad."

"I'd like to talk to you," Leroy said.

"Come on in," Hailey said, opening the door wide.

Leroy shook his head. "No, let's talk out here."

Hailey glanced back at me and motioned with her head to join her. I put the mop down and followed Hailey out the door. We stood under the porch light.

"Hailey, I've given lots of thought to what you told me. I don't want to lose you. I canceled my contract with the Texas company. They stopped work earlier this week. We had to finalize the paperwork."

Did I hear him right? He canceled the contract? I stared at him, speechless.

"You stopped it?" Hailey said.

"You told me it's not too late. You mean more to me than anything," Leroy said.

I stared at Leroy over Hailey's shoulder. Could this be true? Could we trust him? "What about all the equipment and the wastewater?" I said.

"There is a close-up procedure they'll follow," he said. "The wastewater will be taken to a treatment plant. So, Hailey, you can come home now."

Hailey looked back at me. There was a long pause. She turned back to Leroy. "No, I like it here. I'm going to stay here until I go to college. But I'll bring you eggs."

His face fell. She was eighteen.

Leroy turned to leave. "You did the right thing, Dad," Hailey said. She slowly approached him and gave him a hug.

I finished mopping the floor and locked up. Hailey and I went back to the bunkhouse to tell the others the good news.

Hailey blurted out the news.

"Just like that? He canceled the contract?" Jameson said.

"Somewhere, deep down, he does have a heart," I said.

"This calls for a celebration," Cody said. "Let's go to the tavern."

"I don't do taverns anymore. After my gallant effort to save that girl and ending up in jail, I'm done with taverns," Jameson said. "But you two should go."

"Come on, Olivia, you need to get out, and it is Friday," Cody said.

"All right, I do need to get groceries. There is nothing to eat at the house. But only one beer," I said. I still had paperwork to do.

Cody drove. I was still incredulous about the news. I'd call the Demeter inspector in the morning to let him know. They were probably still debating the recommendation.

In the tavern, we sat at the bar and ordered two draft local beers. We toasted our glasses and I couldn't stop grinning. The nightmare was over. Cody nodded to his acquaintances. I recognized a few of the customers.

The tavern door jingled, and the two workers we'd hired to prune walked in and came up next to us at the bar. They ordered beers and lifted them in a toast to us.

"You look happy," the shorter one said.

"Ecstatic. Leroy canceled the fracking contract," I said.

The older man choked on his beer. "Is that what he told you?"

I nodded. An uneasy feeling crept up my spine.

"Ha," the older man said. "This afternoon we heard there wasn't enough oil down there. The geologists had it all wrong."

"The oil company is the party canceling the contract," the shorter man said.

"The oil company canceled?" I said. My mind swirled with Leroy's deception. He'd lied to Hailey. He'd lied to me. He would have kept fracking for the money, I was sure of it.

"Well, in any case, he's done with his get-rich fantasy," Cody said.

"I can tell a lot about people, and I could never trust Leroy. Now his father, on the other hand, was an honor to work for," the shorter man said.

"His father was a good man," I said.

Leroy's dream was dashed, yet he had the nerve to try and get Hailey back in his good graces with a lie.

The two men turned to their own conversation. I shook my head. "Leroy has a lot of nerve, misleading Hailey. But I don't think she has to know who canceled the contract. She's been hurt enough."

"That's unlike you to not play it straight," Cody said.

"I know. But it's just valley gossip in the tavern. Besides, I have a motive. Maybe something good can come of this. He really does love her. If she doesn't become estranged from him, he'll help her with college expenses. And who knows, at some point, she could start her own vineyard there. The land is perfectly suited for a vineyard. And as for Leroy, it's never too late to change."

Chapter Fifty-Two

Saturday morning, I waved at Hailey as she left for work in my car. I set my coffee cup down on the porch rail and phoned Luke with the good news.

"So, you'll get certified?" Luke said.

"Yes, well, I hope so. I have to call Demeter and tell them the news."

"And then what?"

"What do you mean?" I said.

"After you're certified. How is this all going to work?"

Luke was in a mood I'd never heard before, terse and distant. Was he mad at me?

"I thought you'd be happy about it."

"Fracking should be banned."

"I agree, but it's not banned here. I'm so relieved he's stopped."

There was silence on Luke's end.

"Are you okay? Is this a bad time to talk?"

"I'm fine. I'm just tense. I don't have a clear picture of our future."

"Well, that's what we're going to figure out next month when I come to France." More silence. "Luke? Do you not want me to come?"

"Of course I want you to come. I miss you. I only know I don't want to have a long-distance relationship, and right now I can't see our future clearly."

"Well, it is complicated, but I do know I love you."

We said goodbye, and I sat there. What was I trying to prove here? I stared at the softly rounded hills in the distance. I could see Caleb on a ladder in the orchard. A gust of wind blew, and the cover crop grasses rippled. It seemed the earth was alive. I couldn't abandon Harmonie. I needed to stay focused. One step at a time. Get certified.

I called John, the Demeter inspector.

"Hi John, sorry to bother you on a Saturday."

"Hello, Olivia, it's not a problem," John said.

"I have some new information for you."

"Oh?" John said.

"They've stopped fracking next door and are closing the operation. Apparently, there wasn't enough oil down there to make it profitable."

"That's good news. I'll pass it along to the Evaluation Circle. They have had quite the discussion over your application, but you'll have your recommendation by Tuesday."

"Thank you. I look forward to hearing from you. Have a good weekend."

"You too."

I hung up. Right. More like I was dying to hear from you. All nerves, I unrolled my yoga mat on the porch and tried to focus on a vinyasa yoga flow. Yoga always put me in a good place. Let it flow, let it flow, let it flow.

Sometime later, as I rolled up the yoga mat, Caleb bounded up the steps two at a time.

"Read this," he said, and handed me a magazine with the pages folded back.

The headline read "Fine Dining in the Valley." A color photo showed Caleb inside the restaurant surrounded by diners. The lighting was soft and inviting and drew you into the picture. The article raved about the flavorful food, seasonal selections, and the quality.

"Wow, congratulations. This is a major endorsement. You have to send it to your parents. They'll be proud of you."

"Ah, maybe. They never understood my passion to be a chef."

"I know how that feels. My mom doesn't understand me wanting to be a winemaker."

"She makes that clear. She'd rather envision you as a countess, living on a hill in France."

"Well, Domaine Laroche is on a hill, but Luke is not a count, and they work very hard."

"I want to thank you for everything," Caleb said.

"You already have. I need you more than you need me. The orchard has never been healthier."

"Biodynamic farming. You're responsible for that."

"I need to run into town before I open the tasting room. We need some owl boxes to encourage owls. The gophers are chomping on the roots. Need anything?"

"Yeah. I need to see you smile. You're too serious."

"I know. I feel pressure. The certification, Leroy's mess over there, and the wedding? How is this going to work? Luke won't live here, and I'm not giving up Harmonie. I just don't see a clear path."

"If you love him, you'll find a way to be with him."

I closed my eyes and pictured myself in the ocean, between the continents, arms out, being pulled in each direction.

Chapter Fifty-Three

I worked in the winery office on Tuesday updating the accounting and inventory system and checking my email every twenty minutes for the Demeter inspector's report. I called Professor Clark and finalized our meeting at UC Davis for later that week.

"Why don't you take a break? You're so wound up you're making me nervous," Jameson said, as he worked nearby.

"Once we're certified, you'll have to get Demeter to preapprove the text before printing labels or marketing materials," I said.

Jameson nodded. "I know. I've read everything about it and talked with the other bio winery in the valley. It seems straightforward."

Of course he was on top of it. I didn't have to nag. I checked my email again and saw the subject line "Demeter Inspection Report and Findings." I exhaled. "It's here."

Jameson stood behind me as I opened the attachment.

Evaluation Circle Decision: Certification Approved.

I jumped up, hugged Jameson, and danced around the room. "Yes, yes, yes!" My relief was immediate. My emotions spilled as I wiped tears from my eyes.

"Congratulations," Jameson said. "You did it. You achieved your goal. Nana and Papa will be dancing in heaven."

"Thank you, Brother." I looked upward. "I'm sure they are."

"There's more here," Jameson said. "A list of suggested actions and requirements. And it says you have to acknowledge the Evaluation

Circle Decision and Summary Report and sign off on the acceptance of requirements."

We read through the short list of suggested actions. No problem. We already operated that way. I just needed to document it. My cheeks hurt from smiling. I dialed Mom's cell phone. I wanted to share my success.

"Hi, Olivia, is anything wrong? You never call me in the daytime."

"Everything is wonderful. I got the report from Demeter. Harmonie is now a certified biodynamic vineyard, winery, and farm."

Jameson gave me a wry smile.

"And?" Mom said.

"And? It's a distinction that the farm is a living organism: self-contained, self-sustaining, following the cycles of nature and the astronomical calendar. I can't wait for this year's harvest."

"Honestly, Olivia, I doubt cow manure fermented in a buried cow horn and the odd herbal preparations you add to the compost will change much other than you'll be singled out as sorceress. Is that what you really want?"

I held my cell phone out and shook my head.

"Okay, Mom. I wanted to share the news. I have to go. A delivery truck just pulled up. Bye." I hung up and slumped in the chair.

"What did she say?" Jameson asked.

"I'm a sorceress."

Jameson laughed. "Well, it is true, but in a positive way. Look, she's not happy with my life either. But I am. I'm painting, I like my job here, and we're carrying on our grandparents' legacy. And I like the valley now. You should be happy with your life too. You've accomplished a lot."

"I wish I could do something she's proud of."

"You know, I have finally learned, you have to follow your own dream and not live your life doing what other people want you to do. You've accomplished one of your dreams. Be happy."

I nodded. He was right. I preached that but inside I wanted to do something she was proud of. Had I ever? She did like the tasting room decor. I guess that was something.

"Here, sign this." Jameson handed me a printed copy of the Demeter acceptance of requirements. "I'll mail this at the post office before I make deliveries in the valley."

"More deliveries?" I asked.

"Clos de l'Harmonie wine is in demand."

Smiling, I took the document and signed it with a flourish. I was officially certified. "Thanks, Jameson." Tears of happiness again welled in my eyes. I couldn't wait to call Luke. I didn't have any answers for him, but I did have good news.

Chapter Fifty-Four

At five o'clock Wednesday, I closed the tasting room and locked the door. I was updating the inventory when I heard a car pull into the gravel parking area. I figured I could open for one last group. All I had to do tonight was paperwork and pack for Davis. Hailey and I were leaving in the morning for two nights.

A knock sounded. I opened the door. Dad stood there with a large bouquet of exotic flowers. "Congratulations," he said and held out the bouquet. "You did it."

I took the flowers, set them down, and hugged him. "This is a surprise. Thank you. And thank you for the flowers."

"This calls for a drink, don't you agree?" he said.

I laughed. "Yes, it certainly does." I moved the flowers to the table in the center of the sitting area. "I have the perfect wine for you to try. We just bottled it. Where's Mom?"

"Oh, she has an evening appointment with a client, finalizing details of an interior makeover."

I popped the cork and poured two glasses. "Keep dreaming big," he said, clinking my glass.

Headlights from another car streamed into the room. Violet and Caleb walked in with trays of food and a growler of lavender-infused lemonade. Jameson, Cody, and Hailey soon followed.

I glanced at Jameson. "Did you have something to do with this?"

"You know what Papa used to say… all work and no play makes for a very dull boy—or was it day? Well, something like that."

Caleb cleared his throat and lifted his glass. "Congratulations, Olivia! You're our angel that flies close to the ground."

"To Harmonie and celestial rhythms," Jameson said, raising his glass.

"We did it," I said. "Thanks for all of your hard work and for believing in me." I took a sip of the magical Boudreaux blend. How could I ever leave Harmonie and this dedicated family? If only Luke were here, celebrating with us, his strong arms around my waist.

Dad pointed to his glass and nodded. Talk drifted to stories of our challenges that now seemed humorous. No one mentioned fracking. Still too close to home. I shuddered at the thought of the whole mess next door.

Hailey and I drove back from Davis in a rainstorm. The car engulfed in torrents of water. But it was good. We needed the rain. Hailey chatted away, excited about college. The trip had gone well. We had toured the campus and met with Professor Clark. He agreed to try four interns in the fall for the harvest season for course credit, if anyone signed up. I assured him they would. What enology or viticulture student wouldn't jump at the chance to be involved in a harvest and the crush?

We had stayed with Molly and her roommate. Her roommate needed a replacement for Molly next fall and invited Hailey to live there. Hailey jumped at the chance. I was relieved she'd have a mentor there. Davis was quite a change from the valley.

As Hailey talked, I daydreamed about my reunion with Luke in less than two weeks, and soon we pulled up the drive to Harmonie. It was late Saturday afternoon. The sight of the farmhouse and tasting room filled me with peace. It always calmed me.

Hailey, still excited with all the information, wanted to tell her dad she had a place to live and all about the trip. She practically skipped to the gate. I laughed out loud. That's how I'd felt going off to college.

I put my bag in the house and walked over to the tasting room. A few cars were in the parking lot. Jameson poured wine for a group of four, and Cody was behind the counter packing a mixed case for a couple. I felt guilty about being away when we got so busy. I needed to hire someone to help in February. Cody did fine, but the tasting room wasn't his thing. He'd much rather be out with the vines or keeping the equipment in working order.

"You're back," Jameson said. "Can you relieve Cody? He needs a break. It's been nonstop."

"I can cover now," I said to Cody.

Cody gave me a grateful smile. "Here's Olivia, the winemaker. She'll finish your selection."

I exchanged pleasantries with the couple as Cody slipped me a note. I glanced down and read:

We're holding a meeting here after the tasting room closes.

I raised my eyebrows at him and nodded. A meeting? Why a meeting on a Saturday evening? Had he received a job offer while I was away? I couldn't do without Cody. Molly had told me he was happy here in the valley. It must be about the vines. No, he would have called me immediately about the vines.

Unsettled about the meeting, I greeted customers and poured wine. After closing, Jameson washed glasses, and I updated the inventory.

"What is the meeting about?" I asked. I couldn't wait any longer.

"You'll see. How was your trip?" Jameson asked.

"Hailey is on top of the world. She's going to live with Molly's roommate next fall."

He smiled. "That's good. She'll have someone to show her the ropes."

Cody came in the side door with a notebook and a stack of papers. He plopped down on the couch. Jameson and I stopped working and sat across from him in the armchairs. They really were comfortable. No wonder our patrons lingered. I sat expectantly.

"You're killing me, Cody, what's up?" I said.

"We've had a series of meetings and have come up with a plan for Harmonie," Cody said. Jameson exchanged a glance with Cody.

A plan for Harmonie. "Who is we? And a series of meetings?"

"Caleb, Jameson, and me," Cody said.

"But... I was only gone for two days."

"Don't say anything until we've outlined the plan. And think about it. Think about it on your trip," Jameson said.

"We can make any adjustments you'd like, and you can fine tune it to the biodynamic calendar," Cody said.

"So, you're not leaving?" I asked Cody.

"Leaving? Not unless I get fired. Let me get you a glass of wine, and I'll walk you through it," Cody said. "What makes you think I want to leave?"

"You seem so serious, and a meeting on a Saturday evening? That's not like you."

He handed me a glass of Malbec, its inky-purple color hinting at its complexity and velvet tannins. I took a sip and closed my eyes, tasting the blackberry and violet flavors. "Okay, I'm ready." I put my glass down next to the huge bouquet of exotic Australian flowers Dad had brought the other evening.

Cody handed Jameson and me a multipage typed document, neatly stapled in the corner. I sat back and listened as Cody walked me through the "Plan for Harmonie."

Chapter Fifty-Five

I tried to read a book on the plane to Marseille, but my thoughts, and questions, and self- doubt made it impossible. I reread the "Plan for Harmonie," as Cody had titled it. It would never work. Or would it? I put in my earbuds and listened to music and thought of Luke. He seemed to have grown distant and impatient, yet he remained fiercely protective. Our physical attraction was undeniable but being apart frustrated him. Would our meeting be awkward?

And how would I be received by Marguerite now that we were engaged? When I left in August, she had been relieved, and now I was returning with an engagement ring, soon to be married to her only son. We had to work all that out. And we had a whole month.

A whole month away from Harmonie. Jameson and I had hired two part-time workers for the tasting room, and I'd trained them on the inventory and sales system. Jameson was confident everything would run smoothly. February was quiet on the farm. Cody and Caleb said they could handle it. Last night I had worked until one in the morning, paying bills and calculating payroll. At dawn Jameson had driven me to the Santa Barbara airport. Tired, I closed my eyes and leaned my head on the window. I fingered Luke's leather bracelet and tried to sleep. There was nothing I could do now, thirty-five thousand feet in the air.

After getting through customs, I scanned the waiting crowd for Luke. I immediately picked out his tall, lean frame. He waved, and his smile warmed me. I'm in France, Luke is real, and I can forget about my Harmonie worries. At least for now.

I wheeled my suitcase through the crowd toward Luke. My legs were unsteady, and I was nervous. It was probably jet lag. Luke scooped me up in his arms and hugged me tight. I laughed and couldn't resist running my fingers through his long hair.

"You're here. Finally. I was beginning to think I dreamed you up," Luke said, putting me down.

He took my suitcase and my hand and led me out of the chaotic arrival hall. We stepped into the brisk February afternoon. I shivered and slipped on my coat.

"Are you hungry?" he asked.

"No, but if you are we can get something."

"No, let's go home. I'm cooking you a quiet dinner at my house tonight."

"Your house? What about your parents' house?"

"They're in Paris visiting my other grandparents for a week. So, us kids are doing our own things, taking a break from the family dinners."

In a way I was relieved I wouldn't be the center of attention tonight when I was so jet lagged, but had his mom planned it this way so she wouldn't have to greet to me? Was this meant as a signal to me that I wasn't their first choice?

"You look sad. What's the matter?"

"Oh, I had envisioned one of the family meals, and I haven't seen everyone since we got engaged."

"Don't worry. Mom is planning something for when they get back. This is better. We get a quiet week alone without all the formality. They go to Paris the first week of February every year. It's our quiet time here. I told them to keep their plans."

He opened the passenger door of the van, and I slipped in. He was such a gentleman, protective, attentive, and old-fashioned, yet spontaneous and playful. He drove with one hand on the steering wheel and the other tightly holding my hand, filling me in on the news of Domaine Laroche. This was much better than our phone conversations. He really did not like to talk long on the phone. I started to relax. I couldn't wait to see Lili and Angelica. They were both allies.

Luke drove into the hills above Bandol. Gnarled canes stood bare in the rocky soil, row after row, like soldiers. The white flowers of the cover crop blossomed between the vines. Gray clouds blocked the sun, but patches of brilliant blue opened in the sky. The occasional mimosa tree bloomed with brilliant yellow flowers that cheered the February starkness.

Luke turned into the open iron gate at Domaine Laroche. I gripped his hand. Why was I nervous?

"Lili will want to see you, and then you can rest," Luke said. "We'll stop at the tasting room."

Pepin ran down the long driveway at the sound of Luke's van.

"Pepin!" A wave of happiness surged through me.

"Wait till she sees who I've brought," Luke said as he parked the van. Pepin waited expectantly outside his door, her tail wagging. Luke got out, patted her head, and came around to open my door.

"Pepin," I called.

She tore around me in circles, barking. I bent over for a nuzzle, and she pounced on me. I hugged her and smiled up at Luke. His smile and the sparkle in his eyes made me laugh. I needed to laugh more. Be happy and laugh more.

"You know she's not going to let you leave this time."

Luke offered his hand, and we walked toward the tasting room, Pepin close by my side. Luke held the door open, and I entered with Pepin.

"Olivia!" Lili ran toward me, high heels chattered on the tile, her tight skirt restricting her movement. She gave me three kisses on both cheeks.

"I've missed you," I said.

The customers in the tasting room stared at us, but I didn't care. I was so happy to be there.

"This calls for a toast," Lili said.

She poured a taste of red wine into three glasses. "To Luke and Olivia."

We raised our glasses and took a sip. Ah, Mourvèdre. I wanted to plant Mourvèdre vines at Harmonie. A few vintners had small plots in the valley to use in their blends, but they were further north.

We caught up briefly with Lili until Luke led me away. We drove up the hill, Pepin running ahead of the van. Luke parked at his house and took my suitcase. I followed him in. A huge vase filled with mimosa flowers emitted an intoxicating scent. I leaned in and breathed deeply.

"You're staying with me this week, but when my parents return, you'll have to pretend you're sleeping in your old guesthouse. They're old-fashioned that way."

I laughed and nodded. After I showered and changed Luke pulled me into his arms and kissed me, long and hard. I leaned into him and closed my eyes. This is what I'd missed and wanted. He pulled me toward the bedroom, and we made love, tenderly. Afterward, he held me, and we talked about what we'd do that month. Paris for sure. I drifted off to sleep, secure in his arms.

I awoke to muffled sounds. I tried to discern where I was. Dark, antique furniture stood out in the half light. Pepin lay at the side of the bed on a small rug. I smiled and reached down to pet her. I was so far from Harmonie.

I found Luke in the kitchen surrounded by an array of pots on the stove. The aroma of herbs and spices wafted through the air. He wrapped his arms around me. "I can't get enough of you now that you're finally here."

I hoped he wouldn't press me on our plans at least for a day or two. I stroked his hair back and lightly caressed his cheekbones. "It's good to be here." Filled with a strange joy, I stood on my tiptoes and kissed him.

Chapter Fifty-Six

Phillipe and Angelica found us the next morning sitting on Luke's patio drinking coffee and looking at the sea in the distance. It was cool, but we had our coats on and the sun shone. Pepin rested her head on my leg. Angelica handed me a small wrapped gift.

"Congratulations," she said. "This is from Phillipe, Lili, and me. We're all very happy for you both."

I hugged her. "Thank you. That means a lot to me." And it did. To have both of his sisters' approval meant we could have a close relationship. I only hoped his parents approved as well. "Wait, I have something for you too." I went inside to my suitcase and found the gift for the baby. I handed it to Angelica. "Congratulations on your baby."

Angelica and Phillipe smiled proudly. Phillipe put his hand on her stomach. "It won't be long now," he said.

They sat, and we opened our gifts. I gasped when I opened the small gift-wrapped box. Inside was a necklace. The delicate gold chain held a small gold pendant with the Domaine Laroche seal. "I love it," I said. "Thank you."

"All the Domaine Laroche women have one," Phillipe said.

"Luke, help her put it on. My fingers are too swollen to do it," Angelica said.

Luke slipped it around my neck and grappled with the clasp. "There," he said.

I fingered the delicate medallion as Angelica opened her gift. She held out the finely woven baby blanket and rubbed it against her cheek. "It's beautiful and so soft. Feel it." She held it out to Phillipe.

"It's hand spun and hand dyed by a weaver who lives near me. And the best thing is you can wash it over and over and it gets softer. I have one."

"*Merci*," she said, running her hand back and forth over the blanket.

"You have a baby blanket?" Luke asked, his eyebrows arched.

"A full-size blanket," I said.

"I want one," Phillipe said.

Everyone laughed at the image of rugged Phillipe with a softer than soft blanket.

"I'll get you one," I said.

Phillipe nodded, smiling.

Lili walked up the drive with a large wicker basket. She set it down and sank into a chair.

"Thank you," I said, holding out my necklace.

"It looks good on you," Lili said.

Pepin set her head back on my knee.

"That dog," Lili said. "She moped around here for months waiting for your return. Luke too."

Luke smiled sheepishly. "It's true," he said.

A van pulled in below and parked by the wine cellar. Phillipe stood. "I have to get to work, but I want to hear about your certification and who is running the farm while you're here."

I nodded. "I brought pictures to show everyone. And I brought wines to try."

"*Très bon*," Philippe said as he kissed Angelica and went down the hill.

"Lili loved your tasting room design," Angelica said as she stood.

"I used ideas from here," I said.

Angelica picked up the empty wicker basket. "I'll cut the flowers today."

"Thanks," Lili said. "I'm lazy this week without the parents around. It's our winter respite."

"The calm before the storm. Mom will be back in full force getting ready for the engagement party next week," Luke said.

I glanced at Angelica and Lili. "What is she planning?" I asked.

"About one hundred of our closest friends, a photographer, the mayor, and the priest," Lili said.

"The priest?" I said.

"Oh, he loves a good party," Luke said.

Angelica laughed and went off to cut flowers.

I swallowed the lump in my throat. One hundred people? The mayor? Luke reached for my hand. "Don't worry. I won't leave your side all night."

I panicked. We needed to figure out our plan for our life, we needed answers before the party. And for his parents. Or did we? At least I had bought a new dress to wear thanks to Lili's heads-up about the event.

Chapter Fifty-Seven

The week unfolded with Domaine duties. Luke made time for lunches in Cassis and Bandol. We hiked the coastal trail that hovered above inlets of crystal-clear turquoise water. I began to truly relax and enjoy the countryside, the dramatic ocean vistas, the idyllic grounds of Domaine Laroche, and Luke's affection.

I felt marvelously alive and realized Luke was so important in my life. I began to think about the plan for Harmonie that Cody and Jameson had sent me off with. It could work if I kept an open mind and let go. But could I let go? Not completely.

On the eve of Luke's parents' return we sat on the couch in his living room. Luke had lit a fire in the fireplace, and a hint of pine filled the air. He wrapped his arm around my shoulder, and I leaned into him, warm and content.

"What are you thinking?" Luke asked.

"I'm wondering what it would be like to live here."

He smiled, leaned in, and kissed me. "It is my dream for you to live here."

We sat silent for a moment. "We could get a house in town if you don't want to be so close to all the family," Luke said. "Or we could buy a house on a hillside near here if you want land around you. Anywhere you'll be happy. I want to make you happy."

I tried to envision us living in town or on a separate property. But I felt warm and protected here on the hillside with the view of the sea and

Domaine Laroche below with its majestic grandeur. We would have our privacy in Luke's house above it all, and I liked being around his sisters.

"I like it here."

At Harmonie, without Luke, I was restless and not entirely happy. Something was missing. I realized now I wasn't my true self. Here I felt calm and happy and in love.

Luke poured us a glass of Mourvèdre. "But what about Harmonie?"

I got up and pulled the "Plan for Harmonie" out of my bag. "Let me show you something. It needs changes, but it might work."

I went over the plan for Harmonie. I would be the winemaker and bio-dynamic manager, traveling to Harmonie six times a year for the harvest, fermentation, and bottling and most of the bio applications. Cody would continue as the production manager in charge of the vines and seasonal help. Caleb would oversee the bio preparations with my assistance and the orchard maintenance and sales. Jameson would continue as the sales and marketing director, tasting room manager and wine label designer.

I went on. "Cody and Molly will take over the farmhouse. Caleb is moving in with Violet in town, and Jameson wants to stay in the bunk-house to be near his art studio in the office off the tasting room."

Luke seemed stunned. "You would do this for me?"

"I think so."

"You've had this with you all week?"

I nodded.

"Do you know how nervous I've been about you not wanting to live here? I can hardly sleep."

"I've had it, but it is only now that I think I can do it. Just today. I knew we had to decide. And I realize I can do both. Harmonie is in capable hands, and I can oversee the accounting and other work from here and still be the winemaker."

Luke leaned in and kissed me. He tasted of dried herbs and hints of violet from the wine.

"Olivia, you're a better person than me. I tried to think about leaving here and moving to California, but the pull is strong here. It's my heritage, this place. And I'm the only son to continue wine making."

"I understand. I struggled too, but this feels right. There is one thing though."

"Anything you want."

"I want to make a Mourvèdre blend. I really love that grape."

Luke laughed. "Of course. Once you marry into the Laroche family, you are part of the team."

"And everyone will be fine with it?"

"My father and I are the winemakers, and he's taking a back seat more and more. He will be fine with it."

He raised his glass to me. "To my beautiful and courageous soon-to-be wife."

We clinked glasses. "Where do you want to get married?" I asked.

"I'll leave that up to you."

"My mother has a fantasy of a French wedding," I said.

"My mother would like that. Here at Domaine Laroche."

"But she'll want a reception in California too."

"As long as it is what you want."

I nodded and could finally envision our wedding. The solution to our living situation was freeing. Luke wrapped his arm around me and pulled me close. I hoped his parents' return tomorrow would go well. I felt for my new necklace and fingered the raised gold seal.

Chapter Fifty-Eight

*L*uke carried my suitcase as we walked to the guest cottage in the morning. Pepin trotted ahead. She seemed to know where we were going. A bouquet of fresh mimosa blooms had been set on the table. Who had brought them, Angelica or Lili? Their scent filled the room, and I breathed deep. Luke set the suitcase down and moved a lock of my hair aside and kissed me.

"I'll see you soon," he said. "I have to get to work."

Lili had asked me to help her in the tasting room. Phillipe and Angelica had left earlier for the markets in Marseille and to pick up Bernard and Marguerite at the train station.

I unpacked my small bag and hung up my new dress. My nerves tingled as I thought about the large engagement party. But they wouldn't be holding a party if they didn't approve, would they? My self-doubt crept back. I thought of Jameson's motto, one day at a time. That's what I'd have to do. Move forward and figure this out one day at a time. I wanted to call Jameson, but it was too early in California. I wanted to tell him my decision.

I had a few hours free as I didn't have to be at the tasting room until eleven a.m. I pulled out my laptop, the "Plan for Harmonie," and studied the biodynamic calendar. After an hour, I had a schedule in place of when I would be at Harmonie for bio preparations and applications, harvest and fermentation and bottling. And of course, visits to my parents.

I found Lili in the tasting room when I arrived thirty minutes early. Music blared. She sang along as she polished the counters in a black-and-white polka dot dress that shouted Paris. I waved and fell into work behind her, setting out glasses and the day's tasting notes. Lili turned the sign in the window to Open and turned down the music as a wine tour van pulled into the parking lot.

"Who will we meet today?" Lili asked, her eyes sparkling.

She loved her job, that was clear.

Late afternoon, Angelica, Bernard, and Marguerite emerged from the private door to the house. I was pouring wine for a couple from Cassis, and I looked up to see them staring at me. I excused myself from the customers and went over to greet them. I lightly brushed Marguerite's cheeks with one kiss and repeated with Bernard. They seemed solemn. I glanced at Angelica, who feigned a smile.

Bernard took hold of both of my shoulders. "Welcome to the family. We are happy for you and Luke."

A smile finally formed on his mouth, although his voice was serious. Marriage was serious.

"Thank you. I am honored to be part of your family."

Marguerite stared at my necklace and reached out and touched it. "Where did you get this?"

Angelica swiftly jumped in. "Lili, Phillipe, and I had it made for her. It's an engagement gift."

Marguerite nodded and attempted a weak smile. "Well yes, welcome to the family. I need to go unpack and start dinner. We'll see you later." She turned and pulled Bernard with her.

A slight chill ran down my spine, and a lump formed in my throat. I wasn't sure I could ever gain her respect as I wasn't her choice.

"It was the same for Phillipe," Angelica said. "But through his hard work and dedication to the vines, it passed in time. You have the same dedication. She knows Luke has made up his mind. She'll get over it."

"Even if I'm not French?"

She laughed. "It will just take longer."

At least she was honest.

264

At dinner, I brought out two bottles of my Boudreaux blend to try. Luke opened one and poured as we waited for Marguerite to set the last dish on the table. When she sat down between Bernard and Angelica, Luke made a toast.

"To Olivia and Clos de l'Harmonie," he raised his glass.

Bernard followed with "*Santé.*"

I watched him swirl his glass, sniff, and take a sip. Phillipe did the same.

He took another sip. I glanced at Phillipe. He did the same. What was I trying to prove with this long-established wine family? I sat up straight. I was trying to prove I could make good wine.

"It's delicious," Bernard said. "Silky, harmonious, and vibrant."

"*Très bon,*" Phillipe said.

"I can taste the California sun," Lili said.

Marguerite took another sip and nodded and began to pass the platters. Angelica smiled at me as Luke took my hand and squeezed it.

We got through dinner with small talk about their trip to Paris and the grandparents. After dinner, I helped clear the table and stack the dishes.

We sat around the table idly chatting. No one seemed to want to leave. Luke opened my other bottle.

"Can we see the pictures of your vineyard and tasting room?" Angelica asked. "I'm curious about this barn."

"Yes," I said, pleased. I wanted the family to see what I was so proud of. Especially Marguerite. Perhaps she would appreciate my efforts, as they were lost on my mom. I reached in my bag, pulled out my laptop, and opened the Harmonie photo file. Phillipe stood over Angelica's shoulder to see. Bernard and Marguerite leaned in for a view as Angelica flipped through the photos.

"Oh, the tasting room is so elegant. Not what I expected. It's so inviting," Angelica said.

Angelica came to pictures of some of the new labels I'd photographed. Marguerite leaned in closer. "Who did the artwork?" she asked.

"My brother, Jameson. He's the sales and marketing director, runs the tasting room, and does the artwork. And much more."

Marguerite sat back. "Your brother, the, the…"

"Yes, the one who was in prison. He's out now and doing really well with anything he touches."

"I loved him," Lili said. "And his artwork is very good. It's magical. He captures the smallest details."

When she got to the barrel room photos, Phillipe leaned in to inspect. He glanced my way. "I wouldn't change a thing. It's efficient."

I smiled. Coming from an engineer, that was a compliment. My grandfather would have been proud. Bernard seemed mesmerized as they scrolled through the photos of the vineyard, the picture of my grandparents' house. My house now, charming with its fresh paint. The last photo was one I had taken of the mountain lion.

"I'd like to go there someday," Bernard said. "I want to see the California vineyards. I want to see your vineyard. And I especially want to see this mountain lion."

My legs were unsteady as I dressed for the engagement party. I didn't like being the center of attention. Of course, tonight, Luke would hold the spotlight as these were his family's friends. But I'd be by his side. I slipped on my pale blue dress, threading my arms through the long gossamer sleeves. I ran my hand over the darker blue beading. Brushing out my hair, I attached the small blue clip Mom had found. I laughed when I heard her voice in my head saying "accessorize." I slid on my new shoes and tied the silk ribbon around my ankles. There was a light knock on the back door.

Luke entered wearing a dark blue suit and pale blue shirt and paused inside the doorway. He was cleanly shaven, but I knew his five-o'clock shadow would return before the evening was over. His long hair framed his face, and he tucked the right side behind his ear, a gesture I'd come to love. I was filled with an unusual joy that frequently came over me lately.

"My enchantress," he whispered.

Made in the USA
Columbia, SC
07 June 2019